To my lovely wife, Leona.

THE AWFUL TRUTH
ABOUT THE SUSHING PRIZE

THE AWFUL TRUTH
ABOUT THE SUSHING PRIZE

MARCO OCRAM

A Tiny Fox Press Book

Tiny Fox Press LLC
North Port, FL

PRAISE FOR *THE AWFUL TRUTH ABOUT THE SUSHING PRIZE*

'True literature is created only by madmen.'
—Yevgeny Zamyatin

'Always write the first thing that comes into your head.'
—Herbert Quarry

ABOUT THE AUTHOR

Little is known of Marco Ocram's earliest years. He was adopted at age nine, having been found abandoned in a Detroit shopping mall—a note, taped to his anorak, said the boy was threatening the sanity of his parents. Re-abandoned in the same mall a year later, with a similar note from his foster parents, he was homed with his current Bronx mom—a woman with no sanity left to threaten.

Ocram first gained public attention through his bold theories about a new fundamental particle—the Tao Muon—which he popularized in a best-selling book—*The Tao Muon*. He was introduced to the controversial literary theorist, Herbert Quarry, who coached Ocram in a radical new approach to fiction, in which the author must write without thinking—a technique to which Ocram was naturally suited. His crime memoir, *The Awful Truth about the Herbert Quarry Affair*, became the fastest selling book of all time, and made him a household name. It was translated into every known language—and at least three unknown ones—and made into an Oscar-winning film, a Pulitzer-winning play, a Tony-winning musical, and a Golden Joystick-winning computer game.

Ocram excelled at countless sports until a middle-ear problem permanently impaired his balance. He has yet to win a Nobel Prize, but his agent, Barney, has been placing strategic back-handers—announcements from Stockholm are expected imminently (and it might not just be physics and litera-ture). Unmarried, in spite of his Bronx mom's tireless efforts, he still lives near his foster parents in New York.

CHAPTER ONE

In which Marco revives a character from his last book,
offends France, and starts the story after a minor digression.

I WAS TWEETING UPON #POSTMODERNISM, and wondering why nobody else was, when Doris Day sang *Que Sera Sera* in the pocket of my anorak.

"Publishing legend Marco Ocram speaking. How can I help you?"

"Writer, it's me."

The words were like a cattle-prod up the jacksie. Only one person calls me Writer—Como Galahad, the giant black detective from the Clarkesville County Police Department.

"Como!" I typed an exclamation mark to denote surprise, even though all my books start with a call from Como on the first page. "What gives?"

"I need you down here. Right now. Drop everything."

A paragraph later I was racing down the N66 to Clarkesville, taking a fictitious route to miss the traffic. At the helm of my black Range Rover with tinted windows, I tried to invent a convincing reason for Como's call. For helping me solve the Herbert Quarry affair—the most sensational criminal case in the history of publishing—I had promoted him to Police Chief. A proud and capable investigator, he would need a special reason to ask for my urgent help—I would have to invent something big, something really big.

With only a mile to go, I still couldn't think of a convincing reason for my breakneck dash to Clarkesville from my home in a stylish quarter of New York. (If there isn't a stylish quarter of New York, pretend I said somewhere else.) I decided to copy a plot twist I'd just read in a French bestseller, about someone's new TV; it was absurdly lame, but I couldn't think of anything better. So . . .

At the Clarkesville County Police Headquarters, the officer at reception recognised me immediately. In minutes, I was mobbed by her colleagues, who thronged ecstatically to welcome me back and quiz me about tau muons—the fundamental particles I had famously postulated before I'd broken into fiction. Embarrassed by their adulation, I asked where their Chief was, explaining that I'd raced from New York at his urgent request.

"Oh, the Chief's at home. He's got the day off. There's a big game on TV, so he's staying in to watch it."

Odd, I thought.

Back in my black Range Rover with tinted windows, I punched Como's address into the sat-nav. In a few minutes I reached a nice, ordinary, suburban area where nice, ordinary people led nice, ordinary lives—the kind of area where I too had lived a nice, ordinary life before *The Awful Truth about the*

2

Herbert Quarry Affair had become the world's fastest-selling book and made me a literary mega-star.

'Pull over at the Police Chief's place,' said the sat-nav.

I did as she said, then walked the few steps to Como's house. His door opened to my excited knock, and there was the heroic detective to whom I was tied by immutable bonds of comradeship and mutual respect.

After a man-hug, I grilled him about his sensational new case.

"Spill it, Como. What's the big news?"

"You're looking at it, Writer." He nodded at a seventy-two-inch TV newly affixed to the far wall of his living-room. "Sure is a beauty, ain't it?"

There was a strained moment while I absorbed the big news.

"A new TV? A new TV? You got me racing all the way down here to see *a new Tee Vee*?"

I wagged my head in disbelief at the corniness of the French plot twist. How could anyone write such tripe and hope to get away with it?

"Hey, it might just be a TV to you, money bags, but it's a home entertainment focus centre to me. You might have a cinema in your basement, but let me tell you this, Mister Fancy Pants Writer—when a police chief in a town like Clarkesville gets a seventy-two-inch home entertainment focus centre he gets his friends round. And do you know what?"

My sullen silence showed that I didn't know what.

"They're pleased for him. They say well done. They tell him it's the best TV they've seen. They make him feel good. Because that's what friendship is."

"Como, I'm sorry. It's the best TV I've seen," I lied, not wishing to upset him. "But it's just that . . . I . . . I thought you'd got me here to solve another sensational case. You and me, working together. Just like the old times." I punched him on the arm in a comradely way, hoping comradely was a real word and not one I'd just made up.

Como stared at me. "You? Work with *you*? On another case like the last one?"

He fell back on his couch in some kind of fit, eyes rolling, mouth gasping, limbs flailing, like an upturned giant turtle having a dream about killer whales.

"Como. Como!" I knelt and patted his face to snap him out of whatever I'd snapped him into by mentioning our last case. "Como. C'mon Como."

He blinked four big blinks.

"You OK?" I asked.

"Yeah. Gimme that."

He snatched the remote for his TV, and looked at me coldly.

"You want me to work with you on another case like the last one?" He shook his head. "Firstly, no way. Secondly, no way. Thirdly, no way. Fourthly, no way. And you wanna know what fifthly is?"

I didn't but he told me anyway.

"Fifthly, no way. And you're talking about Clarkesville, don't forget. What's the chance there'd be another mega-sensational crime in sleepy little Clarkesville straight after the last one? Even a crap writer like you couldn't make up trash like that."

I wasn't so sure about the last point, but I could appreciate his drift. I flopped dejectedly beside him on the settee. I'd counted on Como having a sensational case to crack, a case even more thrilling than the Herbert Quarry affair, a case that would provide the plot for my next book—and here we were, looking at his new TV. It was hardly material for a bestseller—unless we moved to France.

I stared at the blank screen of the giant TV. If I was hoping he might spot my dejection and make some encouraging concession, I was hoping in vain.

"You're the writer, Writer. If you want an amazing new case in Clarkesville you're gonna have to invent it yourself. I've got a game to watch." He blipped the TV to life and grabbed a handful of nuts from a side table.

He was write, sorry, right, of course. As the writer, I carried the burden of the plot; I couldn't offload it to one of my characters. I stared at his uncaring profile as he munched nuts in anticipation of the game. OK buster—have it your way. But if I have to invent the plot all by myself don't blame me for what happens.

Following the priceless literary advice of my mentor, Herbert Quarry, I wrote the next thing that came into my head.

"Shit," said Como, lowering the tone of the chapter disgracefully. His police chief mobile was chirping in his pocket. He fumbled it to his ear. I watched as he took the news from the caller, the phone like a toy in his massive hand. After a few 'uh-huh's, 'okay's, and 'you sure?'s, he killed the call and faced me with confounded eyes.

"What?" I asked, as if I didn't know.

"A body. Down at the container port. We need to go right now." He moodily zapped off the TV. "So much for watching the game."

CHAPTER TWO

In which Marco writes himself into an uncomfortable experience with an attractive minor character.

WE DROVE TO THE PORT in Como's police chief Range Rover, which was a bit like mine but without a picture of my Bronx mom embroidered in the roof-lining. It even had tinted windows.

Como drove aggressively, as if annoyed by his thoughts. He threw an angry glance at me.

"Did you know anything about this? If I find it's you that's made me miss the game I'll . . ."

His words petered out as if he were struggling to imagine a fitting reprisal for someone who made him miss the game on his brand new seventy-two-inch TV.

"Honest, Como, I swear, on my Bronx mom's life."

I wished I hadn't written that—my Bronx mom would kill me when she read it.

In ten minutes we reached the container port, a vast complex blighting three miles of coastline south of the town. Having stopped at the gate for directions, we made our way through the sprawling site to where emergency vehicles were clustered around a fire-ladder propped against a towering stack of containers.

"Hi Chief," said one of the policemen near the foot, or, if you prefer, feet, of the ladder.

"What have we got?" said Como.

"White male, forties, no ID."

"Okay. Let's take a look. C'mon, Writer."

Como heaved himself up the ladder. I let him get so far then followed. It was as I stepped off at the top that I wished I'd set the scene somewhere safer. The roof of the container upon which we stood seemed about a mile high, a huge trip-hazard of corrugations and reinforcing struts, with nothing to stop me tumbling off the edge. In a panic I grabbed the hem of Como's coat, and we stepped our way carefully over the various obstacles to where something was being examined by police officers wearing jackets the spell-checker said were Hi-Viz.

When I saw what the something was I threw up on Como's sleeve.

What had once been a person had been squashed into the corrugations of the container, presumably by another container stacked on top of it.

Como shook off the thick of my sick and dabbed at the rest with a handkerchief, giving me a look while his officers grinned.

"Okay, Mister Smarty-Pants Writer, if you're through showing us your lunch, tell us what you make of the body."

I inched cautiously towards the squashed remains, typing my observations as they formed in my mind. It had been a man—there was stubble on the flattened face. Dark brown hair, some greying, no evidence of glasses, nondescript clothes and shoes. Surprisingly little smell. The body had been there for days—the stuff that had been squeezed out of it had solidified like . . . like nothing I could imagine without thinking for much longer and holding us all up.

"Likely cause of death?" said Como.

"Squashing?" I ventured.

"Congratulations, Sherlock. Did you work that out all by yourself?" He turned to one of the officers kneeling by the squashed corpse. "When's Flora due?"

"Any minute now, Chief."

Flora! I'd forgotten all about her. Flora Moran was the Clarkesville County Chief Pathologist. I kept thinking her name was Flora Moron, even though she's quite clever, especially compared with me. Flora and Como had been having an affair when I put them in my last book, so I wondered if there was still something between them. I was about to find out. Como was staring over my shoulder. I turned, and there was Flora Moran stepping off the ladder, lugging her case of specialist tools.

Como went to help the beautiful pathologist over the trip-hazards, but remembered his arm was covered in sick and changed his mind. Flora made it unaided and was surprised and delighted to find me at Como's side.

"Marco Ocram! What an incredible pleasure and honour to see you. Your book about the Herbert Quarry affair was the most brilliant I have ever read. I was so impressed by . . ."

To my and her annoyance, before Flora could list the hundreds of things that had impressed her about my last book, Como butted-in rudely: "Ok, you can do all that in your own time. The PD's paying for this, so can we please get down to business."

Flora edged past him coldly, then began her examination of the flattened body.

I knew Flora's work would take at least an hour, so I wrote an excuse to get down from the scary stack of containers.

"I'll leave you here to consult Doctor Moran," I told Como's back. "When you've finished you'll find me at the Harbour Master's office."

In a medium-to-high panic I stepped unsteadily across the trip-hazards to the ladder. Getting on it was even scarier than getting off, and I closed my eyes and thought of my Bronx mom until I reached the bottom. Phew!

Now was my chance to give the plot a boost without Como's interference. I beckoned one of the nearby patrolmen.

"Patrolman, have you ascertained who is in charge here?"

"Sure, Mister Ocram. It's Chief Galahad."

I tutted with impatience at his fat-headed reply, which was a bit unfair given that I'd written it.

"No, I mean who's in charge of the container port?"

"That's Harbour Master McBeany. You just missed her. She's gone back to her office."

"Take me there, would you."

The kindly patrolman drove me to the administrative hub of the container port, stopping now and then to avoid the tall machines—each like a cross between a crane and a spider—that were carrying containers around the site. I was shown to McBeany's office, where she came beaming from her desk as I entered.

"Mister Ocram, I cannot tell you what an honour it is."

"Call me Marco, please," I wrote, anxious to avoid any awkward fawning on her part.

"If there is anything we can do to help you shed light on the cause of the tragic squashing . . ." she said, initiating a dialogue of unsurpassed clumsiness.

"I'm sure there is. To begin with, I assume the movement of containers within the complex is controlled by software?"

"Yes. All of the movements are scheduled automatically, and instructions are radioed to screens in the cabs of the straddles."

"Straddles?"

"Yes— the tall machines, like a cross between a crane and a spider, that carry containers around the site."

So that's what they're called.

"I see. And how was the squashed body discovered?"

"It was noticed by one of the straddle drivers. She lifted a container from the top of a stack, and as she went back for another she saw the body and raised the alarm."

"I see. And what visibility does the driver have when stacking containers?"

"You can see for yourself. The straddle cabs are quite spacious, so I can take you for a spin if you like."

She made her offer with a smile I was powerless to resist, and in five minutes I found myself confronted by one of the giant machines. It had eight wheels, each as tall as Como. Up in the clouds were its cab and the bits that grabbed containers.

McBeany started up a ladder welded to one of the thing's legs. "Not scared of heights, I hope."

I smiled a sickly smile at her idea of a joke, then followed up the ladder with a grip that left finger-marks in the rungs. To my immense relief, the walkway from the top of the ladder to the cab was enclosed by mesh, which kept my inner-lemming in check. By the time we'd climbed into the relative safety of our seats, the demeaning look of terror had faded from my noble authorly countenance.

The view from the cab was stupendous, in a horrific sort of way, with unrestricted visibility forward. A Perspex panel in the floor let the driver see whatever was directly below—currently a drop that made my guts squirm.

McBeany started the engines, the vibrations from which set us swaying like a boat on a swell. Marvellous. As if the vertigo weren't enough, I was now to be sea-sick. I wagged my head and cursed myself silently, as I thought of all the other directions in which I could have taken the plot. Why hadn't the body been squashed between the hulls of two yachts of the most luxurious design, berthed in the world's most exclusive harbour? I could have been quaffing cocktails on an immaculate teak quarterdeck as my beautiful suspect—in the skimpiest of bikinis—attempted to lure me with both her body and her murdered husband's billion-dollar will. I could be . . .

McBeany interrupted my morbid reflections.

"The instructions to the driver are relayed here," she said, pointing at a screen. "The blah blah blah blah blah . . ."

Too sick to listen, I let McBeany believe I was following her explanation, nodding as she spoke. She put the thing into gear, and it shied like a giant shopping trolley. Before my horrified brain had figured out where we were heading, we were already going somewhere else. I shut my eyes.

"Ok, so we'll take the top container here," said McBeany.

I opened a cautious eye to see McBeany leaning forward as she coaxed her straddle over a stack of containers. We stopped. Some whines and clanks showed she had activated the hoisting mechanism.

"It's all automated from here. The lights on this panel show when the container's attached. There we go . . ."

Through the glass floor—or did I say it was Perspex?—I saw the top of a container rising to meet us, thankfully blocking the view of the drop. There was a buzz of a buzzer and we were off. The straddle was steadier carrying weight, so I risked opening my other eye before putting a question to McBeany.

"Can you drop this container onto another stack for me?"

"Sure. Take your pick."

"That one will do." I waved vaguely at the nearest.

"Ok. This is the complicated bit."

McBeany explained the nuances of aligning the straddle with the target stack. I didn't need to listen. I'd already seen what I wanted to see. There were no blind spots. The driver of a straddle had a clear view of the top of any stack they approached. The body couldn't have been squashed by accident. I'd written a murder.

"D'you want me to move another one?" said McBeany.

CHAPTER THREE

In which Marco wastes no time introducing another twist.

B ACK ON SOLID GROUND, I had some important questions to ask.

The first was why I hadn't thought of getting the crime-scene container lowered to the ground so that the investigation could have been carried out in safety, sparing me a horrific climb? Technically two horrific climbs—one up and one down.

The second question was who had dropped the container on the body, and when had they done it? Really they were the second and third questions, but I hoped my readers would be too excited to notice. I put the question, or, rather, questions, to McBeany.

"Harbour Master McBeany—since all the container movements are computerised, I suppose you can tell from your records who placed the container that squashed the body, and when they did it?"

"Of course, but I . . ."

"But what?"

"I was just wondering why nobody had thought of doing that already."

It was a good point, but too late to be worrying about that now. If you had to do a re-write every time you found a flaw in a plot, you'd never get a book finished.

"That's the difference between true crime and fiction. In true crime, people make mistakes. Now can we please look-up those records?"

"Of course."

We went back to McBeany's office, where she motioned me to take a chair next to hers.

"This won't take a minute. I just need to pull up the schedules . . . here . . . yes . . . it was . . . no . . . wait . . . that can't be possible . . . I . . ."

McBeany started paging through columns of data in an increasingly frantic and desperate manner. I was feeling increasingly frantic and desperate myself at what might be coming. She confirmed my worst fears.

"It . . . it can't be true. Someone's erased the movement records for that container."

CHAPTER FOUR

In which Marco introduces a suspect, and Como misbehaves.

I SLUMPED FORWARD AND PROPPED my head in my hands, trying to rally from the double whammy of a corny plot twist and an absurdly short chapter. I had no idea what to do. I remembered Herbert's advice and wrote the next thing that came into my head.

"Who has access to erase movement schedules on the IT system?"

"Nobody."

I tutted mentally. The movement schedule hadn't been erased by the movement schedule fairy, so someone must have done it. I explained my faultless logic to McBeany.

"That movement schedule wasn't erased by the movement schedule fairy, so someone must have had access."

"Yes, I'm sorry. What I meant was that nobody was meant to have access."

Against all my kindly instincts, my face set into an iron mask of disapproval. Sloppy IT-security was my bête noir. "Let's have your head of IT here on the double."

"I'm afraid that's impossible," said McBeany, a tremor of fear in her voice.

"Nothing's impossible when I'm investigating a murder, McBeany. Get him here now." I thumped the desk to underline my impatience.

"No, I mean it's really impossible. He died last week."

Cripes. I couldn't believe what I had just typed. I stared around the room, totally at a loss. Only four chapters in, and already the case was out of control. I would have to get a grip. Think, Marco. Think. Someone must have erased those schedules. But who? And why? And when? And how? And . . . And . . .

I ran out of questions.

I had an idea. I called Como.

"Chief Galahad speaking."

"Como, it's me."

"Let me guess—you've uncovered a startling new development in my case."

"Wrong. I've uncovered two startling new developments in your case."

I told Como about the erased movement schedule and the suspicious recent death of the Head of IT. I caught what sounded like muffled oaths before Como came back on line.

"Where are you?"

"Where I said I'd be—in the Harbour Master's office."

"Don't move. I'll be right over."

Five minutes later, Como burst into McBeany's office. In language that did no credit to the Clarkesville County Police Department, he began by asking what did I think I was doing by muscling in on his case, and from there he went on to criticise my lack of note keeping, my failure to notify witnesses of the importance of telling the truth, and various other shortcomings in my performance, which to his narrow and blinkered mind seemed to amount to an utter lack of respect for proper police procedure.

All fair enough, but it was he who had dragged me all the way from New York under false pretences, so I returned as good as I'd got. I pointed out his failure to examine the movement schedules, the lack of health and safety barriers around the precipitous edge of the crime scene, the overlooked opportunity to lower the crime scene to the ground, and sundry other schoolboy errors in his handling of the case.

Just as I'd folded my arms magisterially to signify the end of the discussion, Como went and twisted it all round in a nasty way, saying that I was the writer, and if anyone was responsible for . . .

I'd had enough. I put my foot down. This wasn't getting the baby a new frock.

"Can I get either of you a coffee?" I made McBeany ask, in a timely and well-meaning intervention.

I said I'd like a soya latte with organic chocolate, and Como went for an espresso with an extra shot and melon syrup. Como asked if he could have a muffin too, so I asked for one as well. McBeany went to get our refreshments.

"Okay, Como, you're right. I'm sorry. I shouldn't have gone behind your back. But now that I have, let's make the most of it. What have you found about the likely time of death?"

Como tetchily explained that Flora Moran had developed a new technique that allowed the time of death to be pinpointed through an analysis of the breakdown of certain blood plasmas on exposure to air and sunlight. According to Flora's new technique, which I had cleverly invented as I typed it, the body on the container roof had been squashed thirteen days ago.

"OK. So here's what we'll do," I said. "We'll get McBeany's IT people to trace who erased the computer records. In the meantime, we'll get every straddle driver who was on duty thirteen days ago and grill 'em."

"We can't just 'grill 'em.' We'd have to get subpoenas from the court, and the court's not going to give us subpoenas unless we've got compelling grounds."

I wasn't sure that we needed subpoenas to question people, but I'd always wanted to write the word since I'd heard it in Hawaii Five-O, so I pretended we did.

"You mean you can't just take these guys down to the precinct and bust a few asses until they spill the beans?"

"Are you kidding? We'd be up to our necks in complaints. We'd have human-rights lawyers crawling over the PD like ticks on a moose."

I sighed and looked through the window at the vast container port. No wonder most crime thrillers were full of unbelievable crap—if you wrote realistically about police procedure you'd bore your readers to death.

"Ok, Como—you're the Police Chief. What do you recommend?"

"We'll do some background research on each of the drivers first. See if we can spot one with a motive. We'll get McBeany to take us through the list."

Conveniently on cue, McBeany returned with the coffee and muffins. We explained what we wanted. She went to her desk and extracted some folders.

"These are the employment records for the straddle drivers," she said. "I can remember who was on duty thirteen nights ago because one of them called in sick and I had to get a replacement from the straddle driver agency."

Como and I raised eyebrows at each other.

"These are they," she said.

McBeany selected five folders and laid them on the table for us to inspect. Three female drivers and two male. All with solid respectable employment histories, references and family backgrounds. A series of phone calls confirmed that none of them had any criminal records, financial problems or unexpected bank deposits. Not a shred of a whiff of a hint, in fact, of anything suspicious whatsoever.

Which left the agency driver—just as I'd suspected when I made him up.

"What about the agency driver?" I asked.

"He was a new guy. We hadn't used him before. A Bulgarian. Timo Tsatarin."

McBeany fished a page out of a folder headed 'Agency Drivers for the Straddles' and slid it across her desk for us to see. Stapled in the top right corner was a photo of a swarthy, dangerous-looking individual with dark brown hair. Como and I did the eyebrow thing again.

"Can we get a copy?" asked Como.

"Sure. Give me two minutes."

While McBeany went to make a copy, Como and I confirmed we'd correctly read each other's thoughts. Thanks to disgraceful racial stereotyping, we had no trouble agreeing the swarthy Bulgarian agency driver looked a more likely villain than the five permanent staff with solid respectable backgrounds.

When McBeany returned, we thanked her for her time, coffee and muffins, impressed upon her the importance of auditing the IT system, shook her hand, and left.

Our first call was the employment agency—a seedy-looking organisation in a seedy-looking office in a seedy part of town. The blonde receptionist asked in a strong east-European accent how she could help.

Como flashed his badge and asked to see the boss. Two minutes later, the boss appeared. He could have been Timo Tsatarin's brother—his meaner, swarthier one.

"How can I help?" he asked, just like the blonde, but with less cleavage.

"We're here on official police business," said Como, flashing the badge again. "We believe you supply straddle drivers to the container port—is that correct?"

"We supply many drivers to many places. Maybe one is the container port."

"Definitely one is," said Como. "And this is a driver you provided thirteen days ago."

The man took the photocopy Como had proffered and pretended to study it. "Maybe."

"We need his address," said Como.

"We have rule in business," said the boss, omitting to say 'a' before the word 'rule', in what I hoped would suggest a convincing east-European accent. "All is private for our workers. We cannot be giving personal details and addresses. Is the law."

"Wrong, buster. I'm the law." Como grabbed the man's greasy lapels in one big fist, marched him backwards into the rear office, and threw him against some filing cabinets, while I thanked my lucky stars there was no-one else to witness the brutal tactics I'd just written.

"Now you get me this man's address now, or you're gonna find that offices are dangerous places where accidents happen." Como took a stapler from the boss man's desk, and before I could stop myself—click, click, click, click, click—he'd stamped five staples into random parts of the boss man's hand.

The boss man stood holding his stapled hand as far away from him as possible, as if that made it easier to bear, and he screamed and screamed and screamed what I took to be east-European profanities, which seemed reasonable in the circumstances. I, meanwhile, was crapping myself at typing this sudden extreme violence in what was meant to be a light spoof.

"The address, NOW," shouted Como, "or do you want the next five in your fingernails?"

Whimpering and still holding his right hand at arm's length, the boss man fiddled in his pocket with his left hand, extracted a bunch of keys and threw them at the filing cabinets. "Take it, take it you mad crazy bastard. Take it."

I rushed for the keys he'd thrown. They included eight of the same pattern, obviously for the row of eight filing cabinets against the wall of his office, but there was no way of knowing which key was for which cabinet, nor, for that matter, which cabinet held Timo Tsatarin's address. Taking one of the keys at random, I slotted it into the nearest filing cabinet and unlocked the drawers. The first folder in the first drawer was labelled "Straddle Drivers' Addresses (Container Port)."

Yes, I know—that was completely and utterly unbelievable, but did we really want to get into a long, boring hunt through eight filing cabinets? That's no way to write a bestseller.

A quick glance in the folder confirmed that Tsatarin's was one of the names on the list. I nodded to Como, and we started backing out of the office.

"My hand. My hand," wailed the boss man. "You crazy bastards."

"If you don't like it, complain to the Police Chief," advised Como. "Police Chief Como Galahad. Haw haw haw."

THE AWFUL TRUTH ABOUT THE SUSHING PRIZE

Como was still laughing as I said goodbye to the bewildered receptionist and signed her copy of my book on tau muons.

CHAPTER FIVE

In which Marco meets a kindly lady and invents a clue.

AS WE DROVE THROUGH THE lazy Clarkesville traffic to Timo Tsatarin's address, I ruminated on the disturbing trend of the last chapter. Como's high-handed and brutal treatment of the boss man, and his subsequent demented laughter, worried me. Had power gone to his head? Had I been wrong to make him Police Chief? Was the responsibility of the job getting to him, or was he just on some kind of sick power trip? Should I get him busted down to patrolman for his wanton breach of police ethics, or should I just accept that in a world in which red-tape and political correctness had tipped the field in favour of the bad guys, it sometimes needed a maverick like Como to restore the balance and mete out some rough and simple justice?

I couldn't decide.

The other thing that worried me was my description of the boss man holding his stapled hand at arm's length. Would the readers appreciate its subtle humorous irony, or would they assume it was the tautologous gaffe of an incompetent writer? Would . . .

"What was that address again?" Como broke in on my thoughts.

I repeated the address from the file. Apartment 1007, Block D, Hacienda Apartments, Clarkesville. I was just enunciating the zip code, when Como said:

"That'll do. It's that block over there."

The Hacienda Apartments were five identical blocks of cheaply built condos which had benefited little from the care of house-proud tenants. They were a filthy hole, or five filthy holes, depending on how you looked at it, or them. The street was strewn with litter and with dismantled cars waiting to be remantled. The communal stairwells stank. There were discarded needles and condoms on the landings. I couldn't believe people could sink so low—shameless addicts knitting in copulo.

"A rough part of town," commented Como, unnecessarily.

All of Clarkesville seemed a rough part of town to me, but I said nothing and followed Como to Apartment 1007. He buzzed the bell. There was no answer, and no sound from inside. Como put his big thumb on the buzzer and left it there for almost a minute. Again there was no answer from inside, but a neighbour popped her head out.

"No use ringing that bell, mister. Ain't been nobody home for a couple of weeks."

Como walked over to the woman and showed his badge. She had to lift her specs to see what it was.

"Police, huh," she said. "He in trouble?"

"What d'you know about him?" asked Como, ignoring her question.

She shifted uneasily in the doorway, unsure of what to say.

"Como, let me handle this," I said, nervously getting between him and the woman. For all I knew, there might be a stapler on her hall table. I held a fifty where she could see it but Como couldn't. "It would be a great help, ma'am, if you could tell us anything about your neighbour's whereabouts, behaviour, and associates."

She snatched the fifty, raised her specs to examine it, then raised them again to examine me. "Hey, aren't you that Marco Ocram, the famous writer and particle physicist? You can come in, but he's staying outside."

I shot an apologetic glance at Como as I was yanked into the apartment and the door was slammed in his face.

Inside, the apartment was just like my Bronx mom's, except that it wasn't completely filled by signs of obsessive baking. I was able, therefore, to take a seat on her settee without first having to move a tray of kichel or a catering tub of hundreds and thousands. The neighbour introduced herself as Mrs Petersen, following which I quickly learned that she shared one of my Bronx mom's special interests, namely that of marrying me to any of her friends' daughters.

"I read in the National Enquirer that you're not married, and such a nice young man."

She sat down beside me, shuffled the waistband on her skirt to relieve pressure on some part of her abdomen, and leant to pull a photo album from between some magazines under a coffee table. She flicked through the photos, stopping at one that showed a collection of similar ladies seated on the very same settee we were now occupying. Old school-friends of Mrs Petersen, it seemed.

"These are *the girls*. We get together every Tuesday for tea and cakes. This is Ivy. Her Herby passed away last year—perforated bowel."

Mrs Petersen made a facial expression conveying the view that the less said about Herby's perforated bowel the better—a sentiment I shared wholeheartedly.

"He left her with three daughters, Mister Ocram, and hardly a dollar, but three nicer daughters you could never meet. I've got pictures of them somewhere. Lordy, you must think me very rude, Mister Ocram, talking to you like this without offering any refreshments. You just sit there while I fetch some tea."

While Mrs P fetched some tea, I hunted among the icons on my iPad and found a foto-fit app I'd dreamt up to get myself out of a plot-jam in *The Awful Truth about the Herbert Quarry Affair*. I clicked it to life and selected a few parameters—gender, age, ethnicity—to get a stock facial image that Mrs Petersen might refine into lifelike representations of Timo Tsatarin and his associates. As I configured the app, I was distracted by bizarre squeaks and monkey-noises from Mrs Petersen's kitchen, as if she housed a small menagerie of exotic and vociferous pets there. However, before I could make sense of the ludicrous sentence I'd just typed, Mrs P returned with a tray.

"I hope you like treacle cookies, Mister Ocram. They're not the freshest—I think I made them yesterday—but the girls always say they taste wonderful."

I bit into one of the cookies, then wrestled to detach it from my teeth. It seemed to be made of rancid oats steeped in superglue and baked a month ago. Its upper surface was sprinkled with some strange decorations, which even the compendious baking knowledge of my Bronx mom might have failed to identity— various sizes of squidgy grey-brown cylinders, pale whitish flakes, and oddly shaped splats of grey icing, collectively presenting a most unusual appearance and flavour.

"Delicious."

I waved the cookie at Mrs Petersen, wondering how I could avoid eating the rest of it.

"I'm so glad you like them. There are plenty more. Do have some tea."

As Mrs P poured the tea, I asked about Timo Tsatarin.

"He's a nice, quiet gentleman, very respectful. He always calls me Mrs Petersen. Never makes any noise. But those friends of his . . ."

I asked about his friends.

"Three of them. Real shifty types. I wouldn't have them in the house. Always speaking some foreign language. Never a nice word from any of them."

I showed Mrs P the stock image I'd set up on my iPad.

"Did they look anything like this?"

Twenty minutes and three revolting cookies later, I closed the foto-fit app, having saved the four pictures that Mrs P and I had created of Timo and his associates.

"That's very kind of you, Mrs Peterson. These foto-fits could be of immense importance in our investigations. But now I really must be going. I fear that I have already taken too much of your time."

"But there are still some cookies in the kitchen. Let me make you a little doggie bag."

I helped put the tea things on the tray and gallantly offered to carry it to the kitchen. There, two mysteries were revealed.

The first was the source of the strange animal noises—a huge parrot, like an iridescent eagle, was swinging on a wooden bar suspended from the ceiling, clutching its perch with impressive talons, and chattering dementedly to itself.

The second was the explanation for the strange cake decorations. Mrs P's cache of cookies was in an uncovered plastic box directly below the parrot's perch.

"You might as well take the rest."

She shook the contents of the box—cookies and various types of parrot waste—into a clear plastic bag, while I watched with growing nausea.

"That's very kind."

I took the bag and held it as far away from me as I decently could.

"I'm baking them all the time. Let me have your address, Mister Ocram, and I can send you a regular supply. It's no trouble, honestly."

I explained that I was surfeited with cookies and other baked items, thanks to the devotions of my Bronx mom.

"She sounds a lovely lady," said Mrs P, as she showed me to the door.

"As lovely as your cookies," I agreed diplomatically.

I backed out of the apartment, waving my thanks with one hand, and dangling the cookie bag between the fingertips of the other. Como was waiting with his arms folded and a glum look.

"Don't blame me," I said, getting my defence in first as Mrs Petersen's door closed behind me.

"Don't blame you? Who'm I meant to blame? One of us has just been impeding an official police investigation, and it wasn't me. I could get you banged-up for that. Now that I think about it, I should get you banged-up for that."

"Be reasonable—what else could I have done? She practically dragged me in there. I can't help it if she didn't like the look of you."

"You can't help it? You're the Writer, and you can't help it?"

"Christ, Como, you don't think any of this shit's deliberate? You think I wanna be stuck in the dumpiest part of Clarkesville? I'm sick of telling you—I can't control what I write, it just sort of comes out. Anyway, I got the dope."

"You got the dope, huh. How'm I meant to know that it's the right dope? How'm I meant to know you got it through proper police procedure, and didn't just make it up?"

It was a fair question, given the circumstances, but I ducked it, not wishing to encourage Como's train of thought, as who knew where that might lead.

"Tsatarin's lived there about a year. Keeps himself to himself mainly. However, he's had regular visits from three guys whom Mrs Petersen described as disreputable, which is rich in a neighbourhood like this. He—"

"She say what they looked like?" interrupted Como.

I gave him the kind of look that said what did he take me for, and pulled my iPad out of my satchel.

"'Did she say what they looked like?' he says," I said, in a voice that sounded disturbingly like my Bronx mom's. "What d'you think I was doing in there all that time?"

"Eating cookies, by the looks of it." Como nodded at the bag.

"Mrs Petersen gave me these specially for you." I handed him the bag, hoping the gift would put him a better mood—or hospital. Either way, it would stop his carping.

I held my iPad where he could see it and brought up the foto-fits of Tsatarin's disreputable visitors. The faces were all swarthy with heavy features. One had a distinctive crew-cut with a pattern cut into it, and another had AS tattooed on the left cheek.

"AS," wondered Como. "What can that mean?"

"Athletischka Sofia," I answered. "It's a Bulgarian football team. The pattern in the other guy's hair-cut is their logo."

Como said nothing to my startling revelation, but eyed me in a manner suggesting he still suspected me of making it all up, which was reasonable enough.

"Anyway," I said, putting the iPad back in my satchel. "He's not been home for two weeks. His car's missing too. It's a black Lancia Monte Carlo. She didn't know the number, but it had foreign plates and the last three characters were 148, which she remembered because that's her IQ."

Como whistled, presumably at the thought of an IQ so much higher than both of ours added together. "Shouldn't be too difficult to trace a black Monte Carlo with foreign plates ending in 148. We'll get this guy and clear this little mystery up in no time." He started rooting in the plastic bag for the pick of the cookies. "Might as well try one of these, since they're a special gift. You want one?"

CHAPTER SIX

In which Marco's clue-finding prowess proves too fruitful.

OUTSIDE APARTMENT 1007 COMO CALLED the office for a check on the black Monte Carlo—the type of car that always belongs to the baddies in my books. They would call him back.

"May as well look round since we're here," said Como, following which he heaved his giant shoulder against Tsatarin's flimsy front door and burst into the apartment.

Como pulled out his gun, and I my iPad, and we walked warily in.

"Don't touch anything," said Como, having another dig at my complete lack of police training. I said nothing, in a cold way connoting hurt and reproof.

We walked down the grubby hall and checked each of the adjoining rooms. The apartment was deserted. Como holstered his gun and pulled some disposable plastic gloves from his pocket. He threw a pair to me and put on his own. On my sensitive writer's hands, Como's massive gloves dangled like long johns. I was almost tripping over the fingertips.

"Let's have a look round," said Como. "But if you pick anything up put it back where you found it."

"Ok."

"I'll start in here. You do in there."

"Ok."

'In there' turned out to be a spare bedroom that Tsatarin used as a cross between a storage cupboard and an office. There were some weight-lifter's weights on the dusty carpet, a broken exercise-machine, discarded clothes, and a small, cheap desk littered with letters. I flicked clumsily through the documents on the desk, cursing the oversize gloves I'd written. Tsatarin clearly subscribed to the random school of filing, because there was no order whatsoever to the jumble of correspondence.

"Hmm," I said to myself to pad out a few extra words. Some of the papers were bank statements, and Mr Tsatarin had a hefty balance indeed for a temporary straddle driver—over $500k.

"Como," I shouted. "Come and look at this."

Como came and looked. "Nice work, Writer. Get a picture, then see if you can find some more."

I took a picture of the bank statement with my iPad, making sure it was against a nice, tasteful background, then worked through all the other letters. By the time Como came back from searching the rest of the rooms, I had dreamt up the following clues: eight more bank statements; a bill for dental work, which might get us a source of dental records if by some spooky coincidence a subsequent plot twist uncovered a Tsatarin-like corpse; a telecoms bill, which would allow us to trace Tsatarin's mobile phone; and a covering letter that had accompanied a membership card for a Clarkesville gym. I had no idea why I'd invented the gym membership, but I trusted my instincts and left it in.

I took pictures of what I'd got and showed them to Como.

"Good," he said. "But this is even better."

He was holding a black sports bag which he opened before my inquisitive gaze.

"Wow!" The ejaculation burst from my lips at the sight of the contents. There must have been fifty thick wads of currency nestling under a smelly towel.

On the strength of our haul, Como called the office and ordered a full forensic team down to the apartment.

While we waited for the full forensic team, Como's phone chirruped again. It was about the black Monte Carlo. The car was registered to a Philip Wrath at 1007 Hacienda Apartments.

Philip Wrath. The name sounded vaguely familiar, but neither Como nor I could place it, so he obviously wasn't a big author or a pillar of the Clarkesville community. We decided to treat it as a cover name for Tsatarin until we found evidence to the contrary.

We heard the slapping of feet and the opening of doors. The forensic squad filed in. Como issued terse instructions about the priorities for the search, then we headed back to HQ.

In the car, Como got Flora Moran on the hands-free to ask what progress had been made with the examination of the squashed body.

"It's Como. Whatcha got?"

"Not much. No sign of any stab wounds, cuts, blows, or bullets. Victim was probably alive when he was crushed, but maybe unconscious. We've recovered a mobile phone from his clothing, but it's smashed and full of congealed blood, so could take a while to investigate. I've asked to have a look at the underside of the container that crushed him, just to see if there's anything stuck there that will add to the evidence."

I turned my mouth down as a sign that I was impressed by Flora Moran's initiative. I wouldn't have thought of looking at the bottom of the other container. I wondered how she'd actually manage it, and whether they'd have to turn the thing over or let her examine it from underneath while it was held in the air by a straddle. You wouldn't catch me under one of those things.

"Ok," said Como. "Call me when you get anything else."

"What now?" I asked.

"What now is that we try to trace Timo Tsatarin," said Como alliteratively.

"And how do we do that, Chief?"

"We'll start with the phone records."

He called out another number to his phone and was connected with another female voice.

"Fovantski," said the voice.

"Fovantski, it's Como. Can you get me a phone look up?"

"You want a legit one or a quick check?"

"Quick check."

I took it from Como's collusive tones that a quick check meant one conducted without all the usual approvals insisted upon by the naïve politically-correct do-gooders who hamper our law enforcement agencies at every step and have turned our country into a paradise for every type of criminal underclass scum; do-gooders who stand-up for rapists and murderers and vicious robbers; do-gooders who think it better for a hundred innocent people to suffer rather than one hardened criminal be jailed by mistake; do-gooders who should consider themselves personally responsible every time an innocent child dies from . . .

34

Como interrupted my enlightened reflections.

"Have you got that number?"

"What number?"

"What number do you think? Tsatarin's mobile number from the phone bill you photo'd."

"Just a min."

I fired up my iPad to look for the picture of the phone bill. The iPad showed my pictures in chronological order, starting with those I'd taken three years ago outside the shop where I bought it. There were the ones from the party my Bronx mom had thrown with all her friends from the salon, and then the ones of Keith and Mick with the hot actresses at Mick's party in Mustique where I'd done the 'Smoke on the Water' riff on one of Keith's guitars and nearly got it right on the tenth go. Then there were the ones from the day when my new black Range Rover with tinted windows had been delivered with a bow on it, and I got my mom to stand with me in front of it. And there were the ones . . .

"For fuck's sake, Writer," said Como with a touch of impatience. "The number. The number. We're nearly back at police HQ."

"Ah, yes, sorry Como, I was just checking there were no new emails from Interpol or the FBI or anyone like that." I made up the excuse because I didn't want him to know that I'd been distracted by my photos, otherwise he'd think that I lacked the ruthless determination to track down baddies.

"The FBI? Are you shitting me?"

"No. Here we are . . ."

I called out the number of Tsatarin's phone, and Fovantski read it back to check she'd got it right. She told us to hold on while she logged a search, then let us know that Tsatarin's phone had last been used at 8.47pm thirteen days ago, for an outbound call. Como asked her to trace the number Tsatarin had called. He also asked her if there was 'any GPS,' which I took to mean a record of where Tsatarin's mobile phone had been when it was last used.

There was a wait of another few minutes, after which Fovantski's voice came back on the line.

"GPS says the phone was somewhere in the Clarkesville Container Port when the last call was made and stayed there for about another two hours until there was a hard abort."

"What's a hard abort?" asked Como, beating me to the same question.

"Means the phone went off air all of a sudden, probably from a flat battery."

"Thanks," said Como. "Call me as soon as you trace that last call."

Fovantski said she would, and Como killed the call. Traffic was heavy, and Como seemed content to mooch along with it rather than clearing a way with his lights and siren. I reflected on how much he had changed since we worked together to find the awful truth about the Herbert Quarry affair—in those days we never went anywhere without sirens and burning rubber.

Como's phone rang.

"Como," said Como.

"Fovantski. I've got that number. The call was made to an address in Clarkesville Southside. 1007 Hacienda Apartments. Registered to Timo Tsatarin."

Cripes. We'd turned a complete circle. Timo's last known call from his mobile was to his own landline. So much for Como's clearing the case quickly up.

CHAPTER SEVEN

In which pride precedes an unforeseen fall.

WE WERE STILL THREE MILES from police HQ, and the
traffic was as sluggish as my thoughts. I tried to think of a
way forward, as we'd got precisely nowhere. Timo Tsatarin—our
main suspect—had been missing since the murder, and the last
known trace of him was back at the container port where we'd
first sniffed his scent.

We stopped at lights. I looked out of my tinted window.
Como looked out of his. I was losing the will to write. I looked at
the neon signs on the various ugly buildings along my side of the
street, making them up as I typed. A nail bar. A self-storage
facility. A burger joint. A gym . . .

A gym!

I quickly checked the gym membership renewal letter I had
photo'd with my iPad. Yes, it was Timo Tsatarin's gym.

"Como, pull over."

Como looked in his mirror and pulled over.

"OK, what is it now, Writer?"

He had loaded his 'now' to insinuate that somehow all of the tiresome unexpected twists in the case were my fault. Call me over-sensitive, but I was hurt by it.

"Como," I said, drawing myself up to my full sitting-down height, "I don't wish to offend, but you are sounding more and more as if you resent my helpful interventions in your police work. I can always return to New York if you find my presence unbearable."

Como leant across me and opened my door.

"Give my love to New York," he said.

"Come on, Como. Stop being so negative. Look, that gym over there. Timo Tsatarin's a member. Let's go take a look. Come on. What could go wrong? We might learn something, and we're practically parked in its lobby anyway . . ."

I paused to let my silken words take effect.

"OK. We'll do it your way. Maybe they'll be showing a replay of the game on their TVs."

We moseyed over to the gym. I'd put up the hood of my anorak to minimise the chance of being recognised as the famous author and particle physicist. I didn't want to waste a page signing copies of *The Awful Truth about The Herbert Quarry Affair* and answering questions about tau muons.

Inside, the gym looked like an annex of the Clarkesville County Correctional Facility. And I mean the Maximum Security Wing thereof. To my indescribable disappointment, there were no female gym-goers in skimpy leotards. The clientele was limited exclusively to thuggish criminal-types, sporting the widest range of tattoos, scars and body piercings it had been my privilege to observe since the last party with my Bronx mom's friends. The sudden presence of a huge police chief and his sensitive, delicate sidekick caused an understandable murmur of interest.

The wary receptionist was all crew cut and muscles.

"Yeah?" she said, following her customer-welcome script.

"We're looking for this guy." Como held out the photocopy of Timo Tsatarin's picture.

"Never seen him before."

"His name's Timo Tsatarin."

"Never heard of him."

"Well, can I just say," I butted in, "that you must have heard of him, because he's a member. So there."

Ha. That would put an end to her impertinent dissembling.

"Alright. I'll tell you everything," she crumbled. "But not here. Please step into the back office."

Wondering who would be the more astonished—Como or the readers—at the receptionist's miraculous capitulation, I inflated my chest in a self-satisfied manner. People were going to learn that for all my inexperience with proper police procedure, I had an innate animal cunning for dealing with the criminal underclass.

She beckoned us toward a door behind her desk. As I stomped purposefully through it, something hit me hard on the back of the neck and everything went dark.

CHAPTER EIGHT

In which Marco and Como deal with baddies.

WHEN I WAS ABOUT EIGHT or nine, there stirred a rebellion at the school I then attended in which an unruly gang of pupils decided they would no longer comply with the rules requiring all to wash their hands after play-time. The unbending authoritarian teachers organised a harsh clamp-down. All children, they said, before returning to classes would line up in the yard and display their hands for inspection. Any found with less than immaculate mitts would be referred to the Principal.

An angelic pupil, I had assiduously scrubbed my hands after play-time and was just awaiting inspection when I heard a voice say 'Here, Ocram, catch!'

I looked and one of the older rebels threw towards me a football so slathered in mud that it might have been freshly dredged from the Mississippi for the purpose. I reacted exactly as the young thug had expected and caught the ball before I realised what I was doing. The inevitable followed. When ordered to present my hands for inspection, I watched in tears as the brown gunge oozed off them and dripped onto the teacher's shoes. I will not recount the details of the subsequent injustices, which are still too painful to recall, but I will merely say that my emotions at the time were an intense blend of bitterness at the unfairness of it all, and fear about the impending consequences.

I mention this because I felt the same blend of emotions as I came round groggily from the slugging. I was hogtied on the floor of a brightly lit office. Como was next to me, still under. We had not been gagged, and I was too groggy to work out that the lack of gags meant that those holding us captive were not in the least concerned about us shouting for help. So I shouted bravely for help.

"HELP! HELP! HELP! SOMEONE. PLEASE. HELP! HELP! HELP! FOR GOD'S SAKE HELP! HELP!"

No-one came to help, but my shouts did rouse Como, who groaned next to me.

"'What could go wrong?'" he mimicked my voice. "Fuck you, Writer."

"Fuck me? You're the big-shot Police Chief. You're the one who says he knows everything about proper police procedure. And yet you let me type us straight into a clichéd trap. How does that work?"

Como was too pissed off to argue. He lurched his body more upright and looked round the room, analysing our predicament. I didn't want him gaining the initiative, so I did a bit of predicament analysing of my own. It seemed that the office was a flimsily partitioned corner of a warehouse, presumably one abutting the gym, since I didn't see how we could have been transported any distance without waking en route. The door from the office was open, so I shuffled across the floor to it and looked out.

It was definitely a warehouse. There were row after row of industrial steel shelves filled with boxed merchandise. In the dim light, I could just make out that the cartons nearest to me were labelled in a strange language, presumably Bulgarian. I cursed my stupidity at making it a language I didn't understand. I shuffled back to Como.

"I don't suppose you speak Bulgarian?"

He glowered and said nothing.

"Only asking," I said. I was getting cold on the floor, and I was starting to want to pee. It struck me that protagonists in books never seemed to pee. I wondered if I was breaking new ground by mentioning it, or committing some enormous literary gaffe. Either way, I was going to wet myself if something didn't happen.

Luckily, something did. Lights came on in the warehouse, then we heard feet walking our way. Three thugs came in. One looked down at us and said, "Get them up," conveniently speaking in English. The other two hoisted me to my feet, then did the same with Como, which was a miracle given his weight.

The leader looked at us for a moment. "I'm going to free your feet so you can walk, but don't try any tricks or you'll be dead men." He nodded at his underlings. One bent to cut the bonds around my ankles while the other cut Como's. "Get them in the car."

The two henchmen motioned to us to move.

"No, no, wait," I said.

Everyone looked at me. The chief baddie jerked up his chin as a sign that I should explain my interjection. I tried desperately to think. Como's hands were tied behind his back, so he couldn't use his arms. I wondered if I could get him to overpower the Bulgarians in some way, thus providing a perfect opportunity for a pun about 'unarmed' combat. I just couldn't quite see how to word it. Damn!

Sensing that I was stalling, the chief repeated his order to his men.

"Get them out of here," he said, sneering contemptuously at my lack of verbal dexterity in a tight spot.

We were led out of the warehouse and bundled into the back of an anonymous grey Chevy, with no consideration whatsoever for my toilet needs. There was an impromptu consultation in Bulgarian, then the two junior baddies got in the front and we set off.

We pulled round the side of the gym, then nosed into the traffic. I wondered what they would do with Como's police chief Range Rover, which stood out in front of the gym like a vibrator on a nun's mantelpiece. Surely they'd have to hide it. Had they taken Como's keys? With my tied hands I patted the pocket of my anorak—it felt like my keys were still there, and my phone too. Our kidnappers were either very lax or very confident, and I wondered which way to evolve the plot.

We were soon on the N66 running south past the container port, with the Barton Hills exit coming up fast—the only exit that ever appears in my books. We took the exit, then immediately took another left onto a narrower road.

I exchanged looks with Como.

We both knew this road.

This was the road that climbed out of Clarkesville to a viewing point high above the ocean, a viewing point that might not be visited for weeks at this time of year.

This was the road that skirted the very edge of precipitous cliffs, at the bottom of which wild waves pounded the ancient rocks.

This was the road with nothing but a rotting safety rail between the tarmac and the precipitous drop.

This was the road from which baddies in my books always sent people plunging to their deaths!

On a hunch, I twisted in my seat and glanced back. Yes, Como's police chief Range Rover had just taken the turn onto the road about a quarter of a mile behind us, presumably with the chief baddie at the wheel. I nudged Como's thigh with my knee, then twitched my head sideways to tell him to look behind us. I felt him shifting round to look then settle back in his seat. We didn't need to talk. We both knew what was in the minds of our evil kidnappers. We both knew that our little convoy would soon pull up where the road met the cliffs. That we would be moved at gunpoint into the police chief Range Rover—the police chief Range Rover that by then would have been manoeuvred to the edge of the short steep apron of grass that separated the road from the drop. That the police chief Range Rover would have been left in neutral with its parking brake off. That as soon as we were in our seats, our hands still tied behind us, the three ruffians would put their shoulders to our vehicle and launch us over the edge, then drive home in the anonymous grey Chevy uttering crude east-European jests at our stupidity.

I squirmed with fear—and the need to pee. Unless I could think up a credible plot twist, I faced a death that combined my two worst nightmares—great heights and the destruction of a Range Rover with tinted windows. An ineffable poignancy settled over me like a mildewed duvet. I thought of my Bronx mom, about her friends, and how none of their daughters would ever settle down with me with six kids in an apartment in the Bronx. I thought of . . .

But before I could think of what I was thinking of next, the world turned upside down. Or, rather, the anonymous grey Chevy did. Como had leant back against the door, lifted his feet and smashed them into the head of the driver, almost decapitating him. My adrenal glands popped like firecrackers as the car hit a rock at the side of the road and spun over, sparks flying from its anonymous grey roof as it scraped to a stop along the road, its un-tinted windows horribly smashed.

All four of us—me, Como, the semi-decapitated driver's sidekick and the semi-decapitated driver—were in a heap on the inside of the car's roof, which was now its floor, liberally sprinkled with a million crystals of shattered glass, a few of which were dancing on my chest to the hammering of my heart.

I twisted painfully onto my back and looked up at the upside-down seats and controls and the folds of the dangling airbags, wondering how I was going to write my way out of this. None of the others moved. Through the glass-fringed hole that had been the back window I could see the lower portions of Como's police chief Range Rover pull up about twenty yards away, its tinted windows hidden from my view. Then I saw the bottom edge of its driver's door open, and two feet step out and walk hesitantly towards us. The feet walked round to the side of the upturned car, halting by the smashed window near my own feet. I held my breath, my eyes shifting repeatedly between my own nice feet just inside the broken window and the evil baddie feet just outside. Then I heard a sound I recognised from watching *Wallander*—a gun being cocked. The verminous coward was going to shoot us as we lay defenseless in the upturned wreck!

I felt a sudden blaze of indignant disgust, liberally dosed with naked terror. Of all the ways to go—snuffed out in only my eighth chapter. Not even in double figures. I was incensed. The would-be assassin bent down to spot his targets, peering through the broken window right by my feet. Abandoning all authorial control, I copied Como and stamped out with all my might at the would-be assassin's upside-down face.

CHAPTER NINE

In which Marco and Como recover from their ordeal.

HAVING NEVER INFLICTED SIGNIFICANT PHYSICAL violence on anybody before, I didn't know what the effect of my enraged kick would be. But now I was looking at it. The distorted head of the gun-toting baddie lay sideways on the tarmac just beyond the smashed window, with blood oozing from various outlets, some of them new. The eyes looked vacantly at mine. They weren't the eyes of someone about to spring to life.

I squirmed through the back window, somehow got to my knees, then stood unsteadily.

Wow! The trail of our barrel-roll was spectacular—a hundred-yard smear of paint-scrapings and glass, with the car at the end like the dot of a giant exclamation mark. I couldn't believe I'd written something so dramatic after all the boring guff beforehand. I staggered to the unconscious would-be assassin. With my tied hands I couldn't pick up his gun, so I kicked it along the road and under some grass. I was pretty pleased with the way I'd got us out of the tight spot. It had been implausible, but much better than the tsunami/earthquake/volcano scenarios that I'd almost been panicked into writing by the sound of the cocking gun.

What I needed to do next was get my hands loose. The first idea that came into my head was to get Como out of the car so we could stand back-to-back and untie each other's bonds. I walked round the upturned car, peering through its smashed windows to survey and assess its contents. There were four problems:

Problem One. Como was still unconscious.

Problem Two. Como was entangled with the other bodies inside the wrecked car.

Problem Three. Huge weight of Como relative to puny strength of self.

Problem Four. Difficulty of pulling grossly-corpulent police chief out of car with hands tied behind back.

And for all I knew the door might have been jammed, too.

I went back to the trunk or boot, depending on whether I'm meant to be American or English, and managed to work the button to open it, hoping to find something inside I could use to free my hands.

As an aside, I learned from this experience a painful health-and-safety lesson. The lid of a boot or trunk is heavier than you might think, because springs take most of its weight when you open it in what one might term its conventional attitude. When you open an upside-down lid, not only do you contend with its full weight, but the springs are now assisting rather than resisting gravity, and the thing is freighted with the contents of the boot or trunk which have all fallen onto it. In short, the lid opened with such force that it nearly took off my hand, while my legs were nastily buffeted by the assortment of objects that fell out onto the road. I kicked through them, looking for something to cut my bonds.

I was in luck. There was a knife, a hacksaw blade, a sharp shard of glass, a cut-throat razor, a pair of wire-snippers, a battery-powered saw, sheep-shearing shears, hedge clippers, an old regimental sword presented to Captain Hugh Beard of the Seventh Cavalry, three pairs of scissors and a blow-torch. I wondered why I'd included a blow-torch, until I remembered the scene in *Moonraker* where James Bond had used one to burn through his bonds, gritting his teeth against the searing heat. I smiled at the thought of the melodramatic nonsense that had once been so popular. You'd never get away with it now.

I lowered myself awkwardly to sit on the road, grasped behind my back for the wire-snippers, and cut myself free at the ninth clumsy attempt. I nursed my chafed wrists. Someone was going to pay for this. A groan from the smashed car interrupted my thoughts of reprisals. It was Como disentangling himself from our ex-kidnappers. Wishing to aid his exit, I yanked open the door he had his back to. He fell out backwards and cracked his head on the tarmac.

"For fuck's sake, Writer."

He glared at me so aggressively I was glad his hands were tied. I helped him up and he leant against the car while I bent and tried to undo the congealed knot of the plastic rope that the baddies had used to tie him up. It was too tight, so I used the snippers, just managing to resist the blow-torch.

"Ok," said Como, rubbing his wrists, "let's get organised."

He stomped back to his police chief Range Rover, and I followed, wondering what he would do next. There was probably some standard police procedure for dealing with the aftermath of a failed kidnapping-cum-murder-attempt where the failed kidnappers-cum-attempted-murderers were themselves dead or close to death, but I had no idea what it was. I was relying totally on Como's expertise. I watched and listened closely, therefore, as he picked up the radio handset and clicked the PTT button, which I subsequently learned stood for 'push to talk.'

"Chief Galahad here," said Chief Galahad in his best police-chief voice. "I want all available units to the warehouse behind the gym on West 24th Street, and I want two ambulances, a scene-of-crime detail and a wrecker truck to my current GPS location. Units to proceed to warehouse with all caution. Possible armed felons in area. Units to secure or contain warehouse and occupants. Over."

There was some technical dialogue between Como and the dispatcher which I'm not qualified to invent so I'll let you imagine it. He put the handset back in its holster, got another couple of pairs of gargantuan evidence gloves from a box behind the driver's seat, and threw a pair to me.

"Let's go see what we've got."

We went back to the wrecked car to see what we'd got. Como felt the neck of the baddie I'd kicked in the face and said there was a pulse. He then squirmed into the car and felt the neck of the baddie he'd kicked in the face and said there was no pulse. Then he felt the neck of the baddie neither of us had kicked in the face and said there was a pulse. I began to see a pattern.

By the time we had frisked all the baddies for weapons, ID and other incriminating evidence, our back-up had arrived. Como issued a string of orders, and his competent underlings set about their work. Relieved of the immediate responsibility for action, Como and I rested for a moment in the comfortable seats of his police chief Range Rover, each of us staring blankly through the tinted windscreen at the automotive carnage before us. Como was first to break the exhausted silence.

"What now?"

It was a good question. In truth I was feeling rather spent after the creative climax that had facilitated our narrow escape from a clichéd death. I decided it was time to get back to formulaic police procedure, which was less taxing to write. I replayed my mental list of outstanding leads and picked one that would be easy to develop.

"We ought to get back to Flora Moran and see what progress she's made with the forensic examination of the squidged remains, and then we'd better try to invent, sorry, find, a motive for our kidnapping."

"OK," said Como. "But no more crazy plot twists. They're doing my head in."

I knew how he felt.

CHAPTER TEN

In which Flora Moron—sorry, Moran—dashes
Marco's hopes of a breakthrough.

A S WE POOTLED BACK TO town in Como's police chief
Range Rover, I stared through my tinted window and
brooded on the path I had taken as a writer. Como's crack about
crazy plot twists was fair enough, but writing the first thing that
comes into your head isn't easy. Well, it is easy, actually. What I
meant was that living with the consequences of writing the first
thing that came into your head wasn't always easy. If he thought
our narrow escape from death had been tough, what about me?
Two thousand words ago I'd written that I was desperate for a
pee, so heaven knows what I must be feeling like now.

We got to the Clarkesville County Pathology Lab without
any crazy plot twists and found Flora bent over the squidged
remains with an instrument in her hand that was too specialised

for me to describe. At the sound of our entry, she turned and removed her mask. Her face fell when she saw us.

"What's happened to you?"

Como and I looked at each other. We presented, indeed, a disturbing sight, each bearing the signs of blood, bruising, and broken safety-glass. Como waved his hand in a manner signifying that our ordeal had been too trivial to warrant description. I, on the other hand, gave vent to my attention-seeking inclinations.

"We've suffered indescribable hardships and narrowly escaped a dreadful death in the pursuit of justice."

Actually, I should have said two dreadful deaths, but she didn't argue.

"Oh you poor things," she said, her maternal instincts blossoming. She came and fussed around Como, totally ignoring me. I stared dejectedly at the ceiling while she mothered him.

"Don't mind me," I said.

She didn't.

After a few 'Oh Como's' and the like, I decided enough was enough.

"What have you found about the remains?" I said.

"Soreeeee. What did you say?"

"I said what have you found about the remains?"

Flora composed herself and was once more the icily professional pathologist I'd intended her to be. She snapped out her latest findings.

"Analysis of the blood plasma suggests the victim had been administered Rohypnol at thirty micrograms per kilogram of body weight."

I nodded silently. It was just as I had expected—the textbook knock-out dose, copied straight from Wikipedia. I articulated the implication of her announcement.

"So the victim was unconscious at the point of death."

"Correct," she confirmed, helpfully nudging up the word-count a tad.

"Can you say how long before the point of death the narcotic had been administered?"

"No," she said, confirming my worst fear. "There is no way to determine the time lapse. The products of the metabolic breakdown of the drug are indistinguishable from those of a thousand other comestibles. We can't say whether he had a larger injection of the drug a long time before his death, or a smaller injection shortly beforehand that was preceded by a burger and fries, since the breakdown products in the two scenarios are interchangeable."

Oooh, burger and fries. I was almost fainting with hunger. I fought the temptation to shift the action to a fast-food outlet and redoubled my focus on the case.

"And what about the phone that was found with the body?"

"They managed to trace it. The email's here some-where..." She paged through her voluminous in-box. "Yes, they traced it to a Timo Tsatarin, Apartment 1007, Block D, Hacie—"

"... Hacienda Apartments." I finished the address, causing her to look at me with astonishment.

"How did you know?" she asked, predictably.

"We have our methods," I replied, in the time-honoured manner of unimaginative crime fiction. I was too tired to write anything more original. I sat on the edge of one of the stainless-steel dissection tables and stared at the floor, which made a change from staring at the ceiling. Reluctantly, I acknowledged the dispiriting conclusion that the squidged body was most likely that of Timo Tsatarin—the person who had been, up to now, our most promising suspect for its murder. There was one way to be sure—I booted my iPad and showed Flora the dental bill I'd invented in Tsatarin's apartment.

"This dentist is likely to hold records for Timo Tsatarin. I suggest you implement whatever legal process is required to compare those records with the teeth of the squashed corpse. Como and I will retire elsewhere for a case conference and expect your feedback at . . .," I consulted my bespoke Rolex with the face of my Bronx mom picked out in gems on the dial, ". . . shall we say twenty-one hundred hours O'clock?"

Just as I finished, the swing doors of the lab swung open and two paramedics wheeled in the body of the Bulgarian baddie whom Como had half decapitated.

"If Timo Tsatarin's dental records don't match the squidged body," said Flora Moran looking over the newly arrived corpse, "should I compare them to this one too?"

"What might be the point of that?" I asked.

"I just thought it might give you a hook to return to if you run out of plot twists."

I told her not to bother. I had a spooky feeling we weren't going to run out of plot twists.

CHAPTER ELEVEN

In which Marco survives an existential crisis,
and invents a major development concerning books.

I DECIDED THE BEST PLACE for a case conference with Como was a burger bar next door to Flora's lab, as I was desperate for food. It had plenty of vacant tables, so we were unlikely to be overheard. Even if we were, I didn't suppose anyone would make sense of our discussion—I certainly couldn't.

I replayed the key facts for Como's benefit.

"So, we have a body—possibly that of Timo Tsatarin, a Bulgarian of unknown background—which was squashed in the container port two weeks ago."

Como nodded to signify agreement, his mouth too full of fries for speech. I went on . . .

"Only a trained straddle driver could have squashed the body, since the controls of a straddle are complex, unconventional, and even counter-intuitive. An opportunistic murderer attempting to drive the machine without experience would end up doing something stupid, like driving over the edge of the dock backwards with the horn blowing."

I paused to digest the implications of my words. Surely that meant we could find suspects by looking up all the trained straddle drivers within a given radius of Clarkesville. I hoped Como wouldn't work that out for himself, or we might end up finding the killer when we're not even a quarter of the way through the book. I said nothing about my concerns, therefore, and continued my summary.

"The victim was probably unconscious at the time of death, which raises two immediate questions: where was the Rohypnol administered, and how was the unconscious body moved to the top of the container?"

I thought about it a bit more . . .

"Also, why was the Rohypnol administered, and why was the body moved to the top of the container, given that it would have been just as easy to squash it by dropping a container onto it on the ground, or even just driving the straddle over it? In fact, why crush it at all? Why not just throw the body into the water? In fact, why not administer a lethal dose of Rohypnol?"

I had typed myself to a halt, my thinking in a hopeless muddle. I wondered why Como hadn't chipped in, until I saw he was looking at a TV showing a football game, quite possibly the one he'd wanted to watch before the whole squashed-body thing started. I snatched moodily at some of his fries, wondering why I'd picked crime as a genre. It seemed to me that the crime writer was burdened with achieving an extra level of authenticity in the construction of a plot. In a romance, say, one could write any old rubbish and it could be believed, but in crime there had to be an internal logic.

Hmmmmmmm . . .

For a few minutes I munched reflectively on Como's fries and speculated on the possibility of morphing the story into a romance between Como and Flora, a pivot that would conveniently eliminate the tedious requirement to come up with an internally consistent plot. No, I concluded, it wouldn't work. A romance between two other people would be fundamentally incompatible with the reflexive tone of voice I'd established for my own character.

That said, what about a romance between *me* and Flora?

It was a tense existential moment. I felt the course of my writing career, and indeed my very existence as a complex meta-fictional character, was at a multi-dimensional equilibrium point, capable of tipping in any of several mutually exclusive directions.

There were some straightforward considerations that might help me decide my fate. The most important was whether I fancied Flora enough to spend another sixty thousand or so words in her company. I decided it was too risky. Her character was under-developed. She might turn out to be my eternal soul-mate, but she might equally turn out to be entirely incompatible in philosophical outlook, objectives, taste, sexual deviances, toilet habits, and so on. On balance, it would probably be easier to engineer a tolerably plausible crime plot from the hopeless muddle I'd got into than build a lasting relationship with a strange woman who cut up dead bodies for a living.

I finished the last three of Como's fries and wiped my hands on a napkin to signify the end of my introspective deliberations. It was time to get back to breath-taking plot twists and break-neck narrative pace. I nudged Como heavily in the ribs to distract him from the game.

"Time to go."

In fact it took a bit longer to get back to break-neck narrative pace than I'd hoped, as Como started arguing about his share of the bill.

"You're expecting me to pay half the tab? I hardly had a fry. You ate them all."

"I didn't eat *all* of them!" I said, outraged by his blatant hyperbole.

To prove the point, I took him back eleven paragraphs to where his own mouth had been too full of fries for speech. While the embarrassed and impatient waitress tapped her pen on her tray, Como looked hard at me and leant sideways to ease a wad of notes from his hip pocket. He peeled a ten from the wad, threw it among our discarded cutlery and stomped off, leaving me to tip the waitress and sign her copy of *The Awful Truth about The Herbert Quarry Affair*.

Back in his police chief Range Rover with tinted windows, Como sullenly waited for me to decide what to do next. I was ashamed of his petulance—a police chief carrying on like a school kid. Words of the most severe admonishment had half-formed in my mind when I remembered we were meant to be back in high-octane action mode. I hit the switch for the lights and sirens.

"The warehouse, and make it quick."

Como slammed his foot to the floor, and we burned as much rubber as a diesel police chief Range Rover constrained by US emission laws was able to burn. Which wasn't very much, but symbolically it put us back in the action groove, and seemed to boost Como's mojo. He radioed HQ and issued a stream of terse and decisive commands to ensure that all was ready for our inspection when we arrived at the warehouse. The dispatcher confirmed each of them in turn, then said he'd pass them to the senior officer at the crime scene.

THE AWFUL TRUTH ABOUT THE SUSHING PRIZE

It was as we were pulling up at the warehouse that I thought to ask Como the name of the senior officer at the crime scene.

"Lieutenant Steve McGee," said Como, yanking on the parking brake heavy-handedly.

"McGee???!"

"That's what I said, Writer. What's your problem?"

"McGee???!" I gaped at him. "McGee???!"

How couldn't he guess what my problem was? Como's predecessor in my last book had been Chief McGee, the corrupt official who had framed Herbert Quarry for the gruesome murder of Lola Kellog, and had come within seconds of killing both me and Como after I exposed him at the Clarkesville Island Hotel. By weight around 68% of McGee's accomplices had been other members of the McGee clan. I had never encountered a family so extensively tainted with socially unacceptable traits. And now Como calmly tells me another McGee is in charge of our crime scene.

"Tell me he's not related to Chief McGee," I said, slumped in my seat.

"What's the point of telling you that? He *is* related to Chief McGee. He's his nephew."

"But . . ."

"But nothing. Just because a person's related to someone doesn't mean they're the same as them. I'd trust Steve McGee with my life—in fact, I have trusted Steve McGee with my life. Besides, half the people in Clarkesville are related to Chief McGee one way or another, so we'd have no-one to run the PD if we ruled them out. Come on."

With which, he climbed out of his police chief Range Rover with tinted windows. It was easy for him to say I shouldn't be worried by the appearance of another McGee, but I wasn't so sure. I was even less sure when Como introduced me to him.

Steve McGee was virtually the double of the dead relative who'd tried to kill me. He was tall and heavily built—not quite in the Como class, but big enough to be scary. He gave me the kind of friendly look you'd expect him to give to someone responsible for the death of his uncle and for trashing the reputation of his clan.

"Pleased to meet you, Ocram," he said, the insincerity of his words exposed by his sadistic handshake.

I muttered something back, and retrieved my mangled hand, flexing my fingers. Miraculously nothing was broken. I was still able to type . . .

"Ok, what have we got?" asked Como.

"Beats me, Chief. I've never seen anything like it. It's just books."

"Books?" said Como and I in unison.

"Yeah, millions of them. All the same. Warehouse is full of them."

I gave Como the kind of look that said, why don't we go and see for ourselves.

"Let's go see for ourselves," said Como.

Como stepped over, and I stooped under, the police crime scene tape that had been used to tape off the warehouse. Inside were row upon row of heavy-duty shelving, and virtually every shelf was filled with identical cartons about two-feet on edge. The cartons were stacked on pallets, so they could be moved with a fork-lift. Here and there cartons had been opened by the forensic team, showing they contained new paper-backs. I went over to one of the opened boxes and pulled out one of the books.

It was *Dragon's Claw*, by an author I'd never heard of, and seemed to be a thriller. Como pulled out a copy too and started to look at it. I gave him the kind of look Ollie gave Stan when Stan was doing something even more stupid than usual.

"What?" he said.

"Which of us, Como, is the publishing legend?"

"If you mean which of us is the fancy pants writer who's up his own ass, then it's you."

"Exactly, so if an examination of the book is going to yield new information to shed light on our case, which of us is more likely to find it? Do you understand the deconstructive analysis techniques of post-structuralism as first articulated by Derrida and others?"

"Maybe not," he said, evasively.

I wasn't sure I did either, but Como wasn't to know, so I snatched his copy out of his hands.

"Leave the reading to me. I will subject the book to a penetrating analysis later. In the meantime, what else have we got?"

I directed the question to McGee, who nodded at us to follow him to the little office in the corner where Como and I had been held captive only a few hours earlier. I was amazed by how ordinary and innocuous it seemed. I had imagined it was my death cell when I was hog-tied on its floor.

McGee picked up a sheaf of transparent plastic evidence pouches, each containing paperwork found in the office. He went through them one by one, explaining their significance as he did so.

"Warehouse is rented to a Panamanian company— Invenmeste EDS—which doesn't appear on any of our databases. The lease is for a year and was taken three months ago. The legal documentation has the stamp of a US law firm, so we can probably find out more from them. There are also leases for four other warehouses around Clarkesville. I've got plain-clothes officers monitoring each of them. The books in the warehouse were shipped from Europe by container in the last three weeks. There are shipping notices from Rotterdam, but some of the documentation's in a language we don't understand and haven't yet identified. Otherwise, it's clean as a whistle—no evidence of any other goods having been stored at the warehouse since the lease was taken up."

"Nice work, McGee," said Como.

I wasn't so sure. It had been a long paragraph without a single joke, and there was at least one pleonasm. Besides, I had a feeling McGee was holding something back. However, when you write tripe like this for a living, your disbelief has to be in permanent suspense, so I went along with things for the sake of the story.

"I think we should take a look at the other warehouses," said Como, beating me to the same suggestion by about half a second.

CHAPTER TWELVE

In which Marco loses control of his character, Como.

THE FIRST OF THE OTHER warehouses was so close we could have walked there, but I couldn't resist a ride in the police chief Range Rover so I could mention its tinted windows. Besides, if anything happened, we would have looked foolish to have left our transport behind. I was startled to find that I was thinking like a real policeman.

Como recognised the unmarked car with two plain-clothes officers watching the warehouse. We sidled over. Como leant down on the roof of the car to speak with the senior detective inside.

"What have we got, Dinh?"

Dinh was a Vietnamese woman in a brightly patterned dress showing bare shoulders and a very delicate bone-structure. Her wrists were about as thick as Como's thumbs. I wondered how she coped with the more physical side of police life, which sometimes called for plenty of muscle. In another example of disgraceful racial stereotyping, I wondered if she might be a martial arts expert. I made a note to return to the possibility if she ever appeared in a subsequent scene.

"Absolutely nothing, Chief. No-one's been in or out."

"Let's take a look," said Como.

The warehouse was a giant steel shed with half-a-dozen loading bays with roller-shutter doors, all currently closed. It looked as if it had been built a decade ago, which was a shame, because if it had been older I could have padded out a page with moodily atmospheric descriptions of its patinated dilapidations. The loading bays faced a huge tarmac apron upon which sat several trailers, and no one was less surprised than me to see they were the type used to haul containers.

The front door was locked. We looked through the glass but couldn't see through to the warehouse proper. The door was just an ordinary door with an ordinary lock. There were no CCTV cameras, and luckily no sophisticated security gizmos that I didn't understand enough to write about.

"Let's try round the back," said Como, thoughtlessly curtailing my opportunity to write further descriptions of the front.

Round the back was a fire door and a shelter with a sand bucket full of cigarette stubs—clearly the place where members of staff had their nicotine fixes, but I typed the explanation anyway to pad out a few words. Como did something to the fire door that I couldn't quite follow, and it opened outwards.

"It's an old police trick," said Como in response to my surprised look. "Let's look inside, but don't touch anything."

We went inside. The lights were off, but enough light filtered from the skylights for us to find our way around. The warehouse was full of shelving, and the shelving was full of cartons. Como opened one with a pocket-knife—it was full of new copies of *Dragon's Claw*. I roughly estimated how many books were in the carton, how many cartons were on each pallet, how many pallets were on each shelf, and how many shelves were in the warehouse. It gave me around two million books. If there were the same number in each of the other warehouses, there'd be about ten million books.

Ten million books.

I stood there staring into space. I had absolutely no idea where this was heading. And neither, clearly, did Como.

"Ok, smarty pants Writer, where do we go from here?"

It was a good question.

I mulled over the possibilities. I'd said that there were five warehouses, and we'd investigated two of them. I wasn't sure I could face the tedium of writing three more scenes where Como and I broke into three more warehouses to find three more lots of two million books. I was waiting for the next thing to come into my head when the chirruping of Como's police chief mobile interrupted my introspections. His face became increasingly grave as he spoke with the caller.

"What?" I said, when he'd finished the call.

"It's bad news, Writer. That guy you kicked in the face . . ."

"What about him?"

"Hospital's just reported that he died . . ." Como checked his watch ". . . seventeen minutes ago."

"Shit. One less witness."

"It's worse than that, Writer."

"What d'you mean?" I asked, beginning to dread what might be coming next.

Como grabbed my left wrist in his massive hand and snapped a cuff over it. "Marco Ocram, I am arresting you in connection with the death of Olmev Kamogin."

"What?"

"You have the right to remain silent."

"Are you kidding?"

"Anything you do say may be used against you in court."

"Como!"

"You have a right to have an attorney present during any questioning."

"Como it's me!"

"If you cannot afford an attorney you have a right to ask for representation at the expense of the relevant public authorities."

Although I've written the conversation above as if Como and I were talking in turn, actually he talked without a break and I said things while he was talking, but a limitation of prose is that there isn't an accepted standard convention for conveying simultaneous speech by two or more people. At least, there isn't one yet—I might be working on it.

Como grabbed my other wrist, spun me round, and cuffed my arms behind my back, while I stared at him with unconcealed disappointment, or would have done had I been facing the other way.

"Como, am I or am I not the Writer?"

"You're the Writer, Writer."

"And have I or have I not been working tirelessly at your side to track down and imprison the felons responsible for the heinous crime at the docks?"

"If that's what you call getting in my way, yes."

"So how can it possibly be right for you to be arresting me?"

"I can't start making special favours, Writer, not for anyone. Justice is justice. If I'm gonna be the dumbass policeman at least I'm gonna be the dumbass policeman with principles, and not someone who drops them whenever it suits you to fix a hole in your stupid books."

My stupid books? That was rich. He was quick enough to call them our stupid books when there was a chance to get credit for them.

"Como, if this is your idea of a joke, let me tell you now that it's not a joke I find funny. Call me a sourpuss if you like but . . ."

Before I could tell Como the things that would remain true if he called me a sourpuss, he pressed a button on his police chief radio and spoke words to the effect that the suspect Marco Ocram had been detained and would be brought into Clarkesville County Police HQ for questioning.

"Sir, I have to ask you to follow me to the police vehicle you can see parked just along the road there."

Enough was enough. There was no way in the world that I was going to suffer even one more word of this totally unacceptable plot twist, even if I had rather carelessly written myself into it.

"Como, no. N, O, no. I have changed my mind. I am not doing it."

I sank to the floor, passively resistant and Gandhi-like in my aloof majesty, wondering how long it would take Como to realise it was in his best interest to stop this foolishness before it got out of hand.

What Como actually did was to apply what I believe is technically termed a 'come-along hold.' He grabbed my arm above my elbow and jabbed his thumb into a nerve in a way that sent an electric shock up into my shoulder, so that I virtually sprinted towards his police chief Range Rover, forgetting to mention its tinted windows in my anxiety to escape the pain. He bundled me onto the back seat and shut the door behind me. Then he got into the front and started the engine.

I was overcome by a sudden surge of impotent fury. I slipped sideways on the seat, and raised my feet and drummed a tattoo with my heels on the wire screen that separated my half of the car from Como's. It wasn't a long tattoo because I slid off the seat and ended up wedged painfully in the rear foot-well.

"Como, for fuck's sake."

"You're the writer, Writer," came Como's voice from the front of the moving car. "You kicked that Bulgarian guy in the face and now he's dead. If you wanna go back and change everything that's up to you, but as things stand he's died from what you did to him so . . . you know . . . we've got to go through the proper police procedure."

I stared at the lining of the roof and thought about what he'd said.

"But what about the one you killed? How come you haven't arrested yourself?"

"That's because I'm a licenced law enforcement official, and I killed a felon in the line of duty for self-defence, and you witnessed that it was done in self-defence."

"But I kicked the other guy in self-defence too!" I shouted. "He was looking in the car to see where I was so he could shoot me!" I shouted even more loudly.

"That may be true, but there ain't no witnesses to confirm it, and we have to go through a due process."

"What d'you mean no witnesses? You were in the fucking car with me!"

"Yeah but I was unconscious and didn't see it."

"Como! That's a technicality." And if the tone of my voice implied bitterness, then it was a justified bitterness. "You know as well as I do that it was in self-defence."

"It may be a technicality to you, Writer, but it's police procedure to me. If we start bending the rules for our friends then that's the start of an awfully long and awfully slippery slope."

"You fucking hypocrite. What about all the rules you've bent? What about breaking into the warehouse? And breaking into Tsatarin's flat? And . . . and . . ." I mentally replayed the book thus far to remember what other rules he'd broken . . . "and smashing the agency guy into the filing cabinets, and stapling his fingers. Christ, Como, you staple some poor bastard's fingers and then you've got the nerve to talk to me about rules."

I continued to rant in a frenzy of self-righteous indignation until Como put on the sirens to drown me out.

CHAPTER THIRTEEN

*In which Marco spoofs a court scene from a legal potboiler,
and thereby introduces a key character.*

THE POLICE CHIEF RANGE ROVER with tinted windows
stopped, the sirens stopped, and the engine stopped, in that
order. I heard Como climb out of his seat and slam his door
behind him. The rear door I was facing opened, revealing
Como's smug mug.

"Sir, if you can please step out of the vehicle."

"Don't be an asshole, Como."

"Sir, there's no need for offensive language. Please step out
of the vehicle."

"I can't 'step out of the vehicle'," I said, imitating Como's
stupid voice. "I'm wedged in."

I couldn't have got up if the car had been on fire.

Como's face disappeared, and I heard him shouting orders
to underlings. The door propping-up the back of my head was

opened and I was hauled out of the car backwards by two officers grabbing the shoulders of my anorak. They spun me round, and that's when I saw about a thousand people with microphones and cameras mobbing behind a barrier to get at me. Someone had leaked news of my arrest to the media, and I readily imagined the someone might be a seven-foot-tall police chief harbouring a grudge for missing a game on his new TV. I had a moment of regretful melancholic introspection about why I'd saddled myself with such disloyal characters, then steeled myself to face the barrage of shouted questions from the intrusive news-hungry reporters.

"Mister Ocram, why have you been arrested?"

"Mister Ocram, is it true you've killed a man?"

"Mister Ocram, why are you in Clarkesville?"

"Mister Ocram, are you investigating a new mega-sensational case?"

"Mister Ocram, is it true that you have ghost-written all of Salman Rushdie's books?"

I said 'no comment' to all but the last question, and was about to startle the world with the truth about Rushdie when Como nodded at his two officers and they frog-marched me into the Clarkesville County Police HQ.

Inside I was taken through the degrading steps by which a once-upstanding member of the community is gradually converted into a contemptible worthless piece of scum—the steps, to Como's amusement, including an entirely unnecessary rectal search, which was as unpleasant for me as for the poor officer conducting it.

After resuming my stylish Terylene boxers and corduroys, I was left in a cell with sundry other hoodlums awaiting assessment. They recognised me immediately, and I spent an hour satisfying their burning questions about tau muons, and telling them what it was like to be a mega-selling author who mixed with the other rich and famous people. Three of them were just showing me their *Awful Truth* tattoos—one of which was very imaginatively placed—when the door opened and the name Marco Joel Ocram was called.

I rose and left the cell, high-fiving my new friends as I went. The door was locked behind me, cuffs were re-fastened to my wrists, and I was led first to the reception desk—where some obscure police formality was completed—and then to a waiting car, which to my unspeakable disappointment was not a Range Rover with tinted windows but an everyday prowler, into the unsanitary rear of which I was bundled.

After a short drive, I was released from the squalid confines of the prowler, and found myself at the steps of the only example of classical architecture in Clarkesville—an imposing building fronted by thick stone columns. It was City Hall—I'd been there to look up birth records in my last book.

I was led up the broad steps and through the handsome double doors into the ornate interior, richly gleaming with old polished woods and exquisite stone work. Past a security barrier and along a corridor, we reached an old wooden door with 'Court Number One' on a brass plaque.

Time froze in my fizzing mind as I stared at the words on the plaque. I had never been inside the courtroom, but I knew every inch of it. Clarkesville County Court Number One had been the scene of the world's most infamous literary battle—the libel action between my mentor, Herbert Quarry, and the billionaire polymath Professor Sushing. In *The Awful Truth about the Herbert Quarry Affair*, I had invented my legendary hypnotic powers to regress Como to the astonishing climax of the case, in which it was proved that the Professor had a psychotic hatred of Herbert, one rooted in unconscious feelings of inferiority which Herbert's literary success had stoked in the Professor's twisted mind. And now my latest book had brought me to the very same courtroom. Might it be fate, or just the laziness of a writer who couldn't be bothered to invent new locations? There was only one way to find out.

We went inside.

"Mister Ocram, what an immense pleasure to meet you."

It was the judge, hastening towards me with an outstretched hand. I tried to reach out with my own hand from where it was cuffed to its partner behind my back. The judge stopped dead with a puzzled look that quickly morphed into one of outraged astonishment.

"Un-cuff this man! Who is responsible for this barbaric treatment of a distinguished visitor to our fortunate town?"

"Chief Galahad, Your Honour," croaked one of the patrolmen, nervously fumbling for his key to release my cuffs.

"Chief Galahad! I knew that bonehead should never have been promoted. I'll get him busted down to patrolman if there's any more of this disgraceful indecorum in my courtroom."

I couldn't have put it better myself. I waggled my arms to restore my circulation, then proffered my hand to the judge, who shook it warmly.

"Your work on the tau muon, Mister Ocram, does credit to our proud nation. And your role in clearing Herbert Quarry from a supreme injustice is an example to all our law enforcement agencies. Although whether they will learn from your example is another matter. Frankly, incompetence is so deeply rooted in the ranks of our police that I am sometimes surprised that any felon is brought to justice in these courts. Would you mind stepping into the dock for a moment? Please consider it a quaint formality, rather than an indication of the court's intentions. I'm sure you will not be there for long."

She saw to it that I was comfortably installed in the dock, then climbed to her lofty position at the top of the bench.

"Who is prosecuting this case?" she barked to no one in particular.

One of two men sitting at a table near the front of the court rose hesitantly.

"I am, Your Honour."

I had no idea who he was, but I rewound my memory of a legal pot-boiler I'd read by Scott Grisham. I think it was *The Formula*, but I wouldn't swear to it, as they're all the same. Anyway, in the Scott Grisham books the prosecutor was always the DA, or the Deputy DA, or the Assistant DA, or the Deputy Assistant DA, so I assumed the man rising from the table was a DA of one rank or another. The judge's next words proved that my recollection of Scott Grisham's predictable prose had been spot on.

"Deputy District Attorney McGovern," she said, in a voice dripping with scorn. "I might have guessed. What is the nature of the charge against our distinguished visitor?"

"Your Honour, Mister Ocram is charged with homicide. He was responsible for inflicting wounds on one Olmev Kamogin—grievous wounds to which Mister Kamogin subsequently succumbed."

The judge peered at me over the rims of her gold-framed spectacles—her capacious robes swallowing her frail shoulders.

"Is this true, Mister Ocram?"

I brought myself stiffly erect, and spoke in a voice of majestic authority.

"Your Honour, it is true that I inflicted wounds on a man, and it may be true that the man subsequently died, but . . ." I paused for effect, "I wish the court to take the following factors into account:

"Firstly, the wounds were inflicted in self-defence to avoid either a certain death or a bizarrely improbable plot twist." I went on to explain to the judge how the would-be killer had cocked his gun, and was looking through the window to shoot me, and how I had made a snap decision to kick him in the face, the alternative being to die or to invoke some ridiculous deus ex machina intervention at a premature point in my book, such as an earthquake.

The judge interposed: "That argument is exceptionally well-made, and is exceptionally well-taken by the court. The rightful place for a ridiculous deus ex machina intervention is the end of a book. Where would we be if such plot twists were introduced barely twenty pages in? I must say that this bodes badly—very badly indeed—for the prosecution. Please continue."

"Secondly," I continued, "the prosecution has put forward no evidence whatsoever to prove that the would-be assassin's death was directly caused by the injuries he sustained from my shoes when attempting to shoot me. There has been no post-mortem as yet, and there is every possibility that a post-mortem would reveal he died of entirely unrelated natural causes, especially since the results of any post-mortem would be written by me."

"Is this true?" The judge turned her fiercely admonishing gaze on the Deputy DA, who was floundering among the papers on the table, desperately seeking evidence to support his position.

"Your Honour, it does appear to be true," admitted the flummoxed official.

"If I may, Your Honour . . ." She nodded that I should continue. "The final factor I respectfully ask the court to take into account is whether it is likely that I, a publishing legend, celebrity and foremost exponent of particle physics, would pose a danger to the public or a flight risk? I humbly ask the court to quash, repudiate, annul, and negate the ridiculous charges against me, charges which have been made vindictively without a scintilla of supporting evidence—charges which have been made in clear violation of the rules of the Clarkesville County Legislature and those of natural justice."

A huge wave of clapping erupted from the crowded public gallery. The judge walloped the bench with her antique mahogany gavel to bring order once more to the majestic surroundings of the courtroom.

"What has the prosecution to say?"

The Deputy DA had finally found a key document among his papers, and was now holding it between him and the judge, much as a vampire's intended victim might brandish a crucifix.

"Your Honour, the defendant's argument is that to avoid death his only credible option had been to assault the victim, the alternative being to invoke some plot twist such as the abduction of the victim by aliens—a plot twist too ludicrous, he claims, for him to include anywhere other than at the sensational denouement of his book. I put it to the court that the defendant has a long history of writing ludicrous plot twists whenever it suits him."

A hundred gasps from the public gallery. Cries of No, Shame.

"I have here a copy of the *New Yorker* from June last year. It is a special edition, commemorating the publication of the defendant's record-breaking book, *The Awful Truth about the Herbert Quarry Affair*. It contains a profile of the defendant by perhaps the world's pre-eminent literary theorist, Professor E. Sushing. I would like to quote from page nine of the profile, in which Professor Sushing refers to the defendant's most recent work. *This so-called novel is the final gruesome development of Ocram's warped philosophy of literature. It is no less than a catalogue of bizarre and improbable plot twists from start to end."*

McGovern looked around the court with a smirk.

"A catalogue, Your Honour, of bizarre and improbable plot twists."

I raised a patient hand, one that McGovern had just played right into.

"If I may, Your Honour . . ."

"Please proceed, Mister Ocram."

"Your Honour, Professor Sushing is not an objective authority in this case. It is well-known that he has a long-standing feud with my literary mentor, Herbert Quarry. Indeed, Your Honour, it was in this very courtroom, in the very book that Professor Sushing dismissed as a catalogue of bizarre plot twists, that the Professor lost an historic legal battle with Herbert Quarry. I take it you have read the book in question, Your Honour?"

"I have indeed, Mister Ocram, time and time again."

A smile illuminated the judge's otherwise stern countenance as she fondly patted her copy of *The Awful Truth about the Herbert Quarry Affair* and recalled the many pleasures of reading it.

"Then Your Honour will understand why I repudiate the prosecution's evidence as the work of an embittered axe-grinder who, having failed in his campaign to discredit my mentor, has now directed his resentful attentions to discredit the mentor's protégé."

A series of nods had been the judge's reaction to my speech. I had no doubt that an ally in the cause of justice sat upon the bench. Her next words confirmed the point.

"Mister McGovern, what have you to say to the defendant's cast-iron rebuttal of your pathetic case? And I warn you, Mister McGovern, that the court will brook no Latin obfuscations or other lawyerly circumlocutive tricks. Get to the point."

"Your Honour, it is the understanding of the State that the police arrested Mister Ocram as a matter of due procedure. By his own admission he kicked the victim savagely in the face and the victim subsequently died having not regained consciousness after the brutal pedal attack. There is therefore a prima facie case for the defence to . . ."

Bang, bang, bang, bang, bang. The judge walloped the bench once more—actually five times more—with a gavel of utmost ferocity. Barely containing her wrath, she spoke.

"I could not have been clearer to the prosecution that obfuscating Latinities were not to be uttered in this courtroom, and yet only fifty three words into your remarks you blatantly disregard my instructions. I have never heard such an out-rageous example of contemptuous disrespect for the authority of this court.

"I hereby order that Marco Ocram is released without charge and without a stain on his character. The court also formally admonishes the Chief of the Clarkesville County Police for bringing unsubstantiated charges and wasting court's time. Mister Ocram, you may go."

I bowed deeply to the judge, and, to the cheers of my readers, I left the court a free man.

CHAPTER FOURTEEN

In which Marco suffers an emotional volte-face concerning Como, and hears from two minor characters.

WHEN THE JUDGE RELEASED ME without a stain on my character, she clearly wasn't referring to my large police chief character, Como Galahad. I had a score to settle there. But first I returned to the Clarkesville County Police HQ to sign the paperwork to release my confiscated belongings. After a short wait, I was duly handed my iPhone, my iPad, my wallet, my bespoke Rolex with the face of my Bronx mom on the dial, my writer's satchel, the Barbara Cartland I was reading, my car keys, my haemorrhoid cream, a rubber prosthetic face that Tom Cruise had given me as a memento, and the copy of *Dragon's Claw* I'd taken from the warehouse. I fastened the Rolex upon my left wrist, pocketed my keys and put the rest in my satchel. Now to face that villain Galahad.

The patrolmen were expecting to drive me to Como's, but I politely declined their kind offer. I needed some thinking time, not a run in a smelly prowler being grilled about tau muons. Accordingly, I was ordered a cab, which I entered with the hood of my anorak raised to avoid recognition.

If I had hoped for contemplative calm in the back of the cab, then I should have been more selective in my choice of character for the driver. The species in front of me was garrulous, loud and opinionated.

"Hey, Mac, did you see what was going down at the courthouse?" he asked over his self-satisfied shoulder. "They had that writer guy, Marco Ocram. Said he'd killed someone in Clarkesville. Ha! How can a complete drip like that have killed anyone? Probably can't even tie his own shoe laces. And you know what I heard? I heard he still lives with his mom in the Bronx. Imagine! A grown-up guy, a writer and everything, still living at home with his mom. Jeez, these celebrity bozos. And you know what else? I read his book—you know—the one about that paedo scumbag Herbert Quarry. OK, so the book says Quarry was framed. But how d'you know? How *d'you* know? What if he wasn't framed? What if that bozo Ocram made up a cover story for his old pal? Just to get him off the hook. I'm telling ya, that's what it's like. Hollywood and publishing and all the rest is just one huge big clique where everyone looks after everyone else. And I'll tell you something else I know. All those quotes you see on books, the quotes that tell you how great the book is—all that is made-up. They're paid to write those quotes, and they'll write whatever they're told to write if the price is right. Hey, that rhymes! And you know what else? My cousin Macey wrote a book, and it was a real good book with words and a plot and everything, and he sent it to an agent and they wrote back and said it had no commercial appeal. No commercial appeal. What's that meant to mean? Probably it's just because my cousin Macey didn't go to Yale and hasn't kissed enough assess in the publishing business. It makes me sick the way they write about books in the papers and the like. Honest to God, I wanna puke. Did you read that *Da Vinci Code*? Biggest heap of shit in the world, and yet they go on about it as if it was the best thing since sliced bread. And then did you . . ." blah blah blah blah blah.

I slumped in my seat. I had lost the will to write. I let his bigoted rant wash over me like a . . . like a washing rant of bigotry. I withdrew into the sanctity of my mind and tried to think what to do next with the plot line of Como's disloyalty. I remembered my mentor Herbert saying that writing a book was like playing chess. I'd no idea what he was talking about then, but now I was starting to see the wisdom of his words. In writing, as in chess, you make a random decision about where to go next. The decision looks good at the time, but straight away you see that you've moved into trouble, and you can't go back. I'd thought that getting arrested by Como was a good move, but now I didn't know where to move next. I was beginning to wish that I'd just bitten the bullet and written about three more trips to warehouses. However, as Herbert always said, there was no going back. What was written was written. I'd have to make the most of it, but I was torn in tow, sorry two. More than ever, I wanted to teach Como a savagely unforgettable lesson, but I knew that would make writing the rest of the book even harder. I needed his cooperation. I needed him to turn a blind eye to the fact that I, a civilian, was participating inappropriately in what was ordinarily the preserve of the police. I stared through the untinted window of the cab. We were getting nearer to Como's place. The driver knew our destination . . .

"We'll be there any minute, Mac. Old Como Galahad's place ain't much to look at, but I'll tell you what—that guy's real. He ain't one of those stuffed shirts at City Hall. I knew him before he worked with that Ocram asshole on the Herbert Quarry case and he was real down to earth. He helped me get my boy out of some trouble with drugs. He didn't need to. He coulda just as easy arrested him and had him banged up, but he didn't. He knew what right and wrong was, and he did right and helped me out. I still go over there when there's a game on, and he has his old pals around. We all take over some beers, and Como gets some food in. He's not so hot with his cooking and all that, but we're having such a great time watching the game we never really notice. He's a great guy. Ok, that'll be thirty bucks."

We'd stopped behind my black Range Rover with tinted windows which I'd left on the street by Como's house. His police chief Range Rover with tinted windows was on his drive. I paid the driver, with a pang of regret at his words. I'd been whingeing about Como's disloyalty to me, but I'd been just as disloyal to him. He'd invited me to Clarkesville to watch the game, and instead of embracing the generosity of his offer, I had self-pityingly made him miss the game just to satisfy my need for a story. Perhaps an apology was more appropriate than an admonishment.

With a heavy heart, I walked up the drive and knocked on Como's half-open door. There was no answer. I could hear his TV, so I walked through to his living room. Como was sprawled on his settee, his clothes dishevelled, the room a mess. He looked at me and saluted with a raised hand engulfing a tumbler of what I took to be neat bourbon. He swigged half the contents in a gargantuan glug of extreme alcoholic fortitude, then looked blankly at whatever was on his new TV.

"Como, I'm sorry."

For a reply, he raised his other hand over his head, palm forwards. I walked over and high-fived the huge paw half-heartedly, then slumped on the settee next to him. So here we were, after all that plotting, watching his TV again. I wondered if my readers would appreciate the nuanced echo of the very first scene in Como's house without me having to point it out.

"You're such a fucking asshole, Writer."

I said nothing. He was right.

"I get you down here to watch the game—the first person to watch a game on my new TV. D'you know how special that makes you? Huh? And what d'you do? You make us miss the game, that's what. I don't mind going off after your crazy idea of a murder at the container port, but couldn't it have waited? Couldn't we have taken the call *after* the game?"

He knew the answer was yes.

"And then you make me the dumbass. Dumbass Como does this dumb thing. Dumbass Como does that dumb thing. How'm I meant to have respect? How'm I meant to feel being the dumbass? I wouldn't mind being the dumbass to someone bright, but being the dumbass to *you*—man, that's something else."

"Como, I know, I know. I didn't mean it."

"You want some of this?" He waved the bourbon at me.

"No." I'd drunk too much bourbon once, and the smell made me sick. "You got any superfood infusions?"

"What?"

"It doesn't matter."

It was a stupid question. I should have guessed that Como wouldn't have any superfood infusions. I had some in the car, so I went to get them. When I got back Como was snoring. He was about ten times heavier than anything I could carry, so I didn't even think about putting him to bed. I just took off his shoes, put a cushion under his feet, and turned off the TV.

"I'll see you in the morning," I said, and left the room.

I tossed a mental coin and decided to find a motel instead of crashing out at Como's. There was one a couple of blocks away. I haggled for a decent rate with the guy on reception. To preserve my anonymity, I paid cash, giving my name as Jack Reacher—a character from a hilarious book I'd read. I got Room Eleven. It was too boringly like every other motel room to warrant a word of description, so I decided not to pad out the paragraph by mentioning the plain carpet, the cheap TV, the beige curtains, the noisy air-con, the chipped veneer on the wardrobe, the mouldy stains on the grout in the bathroom, or the prolapsed venetian blind.

I dumped my things and flopped on the bed. I was tired. I'd lost count of time since I first knocked on Como's door. It had probably been several days, so I hoped my readers wouldn't notice that I'd screwed up the timeline and should have booked into a motel pages ago.

I reached for my phone and entered my passcode, 10334628—the number of copies *The Awful Truth about the Herbert Quarry Affair* had sold in its first year. I had two new messages. The first was from my mom:

"Markie. Markie Markie Markie. It's your mom. My poor Markie. I just seen the news on TV. I can't believe they've arrested my poor Markie. It's awful. It's dreadful. All the ladies at the salon say how dreadful it is. And you haven't called me, when I'm sitting by the phone waiting to hear. You've got to call me, Markie. Your useless pop says you'll be alright. That big dolt will be alright, he says. But you gotta call your mom, Markie, I'm worried sick. And I met Mrs. Rosen's daughter today. She'd be just right for you, Markie, just perfect. I told Mrs. Rosen that I can just see the two of you together in a nice apartment in the Bronx with six kids. Give your mom a call, Markie. Give me a call. And keep yourself clean in that jail, Markie. Don't eat any food you shouldn't. Make sure you've got plenty of clean pants. If you don't have pants tell me. I can post the pants. I need the address of the jail. I need . . . what? . . . just a minute Markie— your useless pop's trying to talk when I'm already talking with my boy . . . what do you know about it, you're a useless waster and you'll always be a useless waster . . . I told him, Markie, so call me, you gotta call your mom. Mrs. Leverson said . . ."

But before my mom could say what Mrs. Leverson said, she'd run out of recording space and been cut off. The next was from Barney, my agent . . .

"Heeeeeyyy, Marky baby. I hear the brilliant news. You got yourself arrested for murder! It's inspired. The phones are going wild. I got every newspaper in the world wanting to know what's happening. It's gone viral, Marky. You need to call me and tell me what's what. Tell me about your big new case. We need to line up the movie deals now while the news is hot. I'll get the lawyers down in case they try and release you early. We need to really milk this one, Marky. I can just see the big court scene. We'll get Hanks to be your lawyer. Streep can be the judge. It's gonna be stellar, Marky, stellar."

I killed the call and looked at my watch. Nearly midnight. It was too late for food, so I had a shower and climbed into bed. I remembered that Jack Reacher had a mental alarm clock that always woke him exactly on time, so I decided to give it a try. I set mine for 06:43:18, then went out like a light.

CHAPTER FIFTEEN

In which Marco digresses into Starsky and Hutch nostalgia.

I WOKE IN THE MORNING and looked at my watch. It was nearly eleven. Fucking Jack Reacher.

I ordered coffee, bacon and pancakes, then sat on the lavvy reading my Barbara Cartland. Herbert said Barbara Cartland was one of the most prolific authors in the world—a benchmark of prodigious literary productivity. I doubted she'd match my best of three-thousand words per hour, but we were, after all, aiming at different markets; it would be misleading to compare her highbrow flights of literary fancy with my more commercial output. I also noticed that in her books, no one ever sat on the lavvy reading. In fact, now I thought about it, no one sat on the lavvy reading in anyone's books but mine. I wondered if I was being avant-garder than other authors, or just making another of my giant literary gaffes.

I showered and dressed in time for breakfast, which I downed like a prairie dog gulping a baby rabbit.

Fortified and refreshed, I grabbed my iPad and started the special 'Plot Wizard' app, which lets top authors keep track of plot threads in a developing book. I made a list of all my outstanding questions, such as who had erased the entries on the schedule of container movements to hide the killer's tracks? Who were the mysterious associates whose foto-fit pictures I had drawn with Tsatarin's nice neighbour? What would we find in the other three warehouses?

By the time I'd finished, there were a dozen questions I hadn't the energy to answer. A debilitating wave of ennui swept over me. God knows how my readers felt.

I decided to see how Como was faring after his bourbon binge. I left my key at reception and walked the two blocks to his place. As I got close, I could see him on his drive in his slippers. A breakdown truck was lifting the back of his police chief Range Rover with tinted windows to tow it away. Wow, that was unexpected.

"Hey, Writer," said Como flatly, staring at his car as it was gradually winched to a crazy angle.

I was staring at it too. "What happened?"

"Started it this morning and there's a light flashing on the dash. Looked up the light in the handbook, and it's the one for complete engine failure with gearbox complications. And it's only done ten thou' miles."

I whistled. Complete engine failure with gearbox complications in a Range Rover after only ten thousand miles. It was probably the only realistic scenario in my book.

"I can go back to the motel for mine if you like."

"No, they're dropping another car here in a while. Some old junk prowler probably."

He turned to walk inside, and I followed him to the kitchen.
"You want coffee?"

"Sure."

I was worried about the serious nature of the fault with his car. It was going to screw my product-placement deal with Range Rover. I dreaded to think what Barney would have to say about it. But then, every cloud . . .

As we stared glumly out of the window, drinking Como's rancid coffee, a car transporter came round the corner.

Could it be?

Yes!

There on the back was the Range Rover's replacement—a '74 red Ford Gran Torino with white 'vector' side darts, mag wheels and a 'Huggy Bear' doll dangling from the mirror. Wow! It was the old Clarkesville County Police back-up car—the car that had virtually been our home when Como and I had worked on the Herbert Quarry affair

"Gimme five!" I said jubilantly.

Como put his arms around me, picked me up, and danced a circle.

"Hey, Writer. What d'ya know? We got ourselves a real wicked car for some real wicked policing. C'mon."

By the time Como had put on his police shoes and grabbed his police hat and his police phone and his police gun, the Gran Torino had been backed off the transporter. Como signed for it and caught the keys which the transporter driver tossed to him. He squeezed in and fired the big V8, which throbbed into life and burbled with latent energy. I throbbed into life and burbled with latent energy too. All my ennui had been blown away. We were back in business.

"Where to, Writer?" said Como, sliding back the driver's seat to make room for his enormous legs.

"The industrial estate. And make it quick—we've got three warehouses to visit!"

Como laid monster strips of rubber all the way down his street.

CHAPTER SIXTEEN

In which Marco writes his first car chase, and nearly dies.

COMO DRY-SKIDDED THE GRAN Torino to a stop near warehouse three. I leaped out of the car and bounced over the hood as a short-cut to the pavement—or should that be the sidewalk—horribly bruising my coccyx. Como stood and appraised the building while I winced and rubbed my lower back. As with warehouse two, the place seemed deserted. The staff entrance was locked, and no lights were showing.

"Let's try round the back again."

I followed Como towards the back, wondering if I could get away with writing a scene that was more or less identical to the one that had unfolded at the back of warehouse two, where Como had used a police trick to open the emergency door. I had just decided that I couldn't, when we walked round a corner and saw two men unloading a panel van about a hundred yards away, one of them standing inside the van, passing a cardboard carton out to the other. They saw us as we saw them. The man on the ground dropped the carton and ran to the cab of the van.

"Hey!" shouted Como. "Stop, police."

He pulled his gun and fired two shots in the air in a blatant breach of proper police procedure. But I had no time to admonish him for his inappropriate and clichéd behaviour. The van had lurched forward and round the far corner of the warehouse, its rear doors swinging wildly. I was amazed to realise that I'd teed-up the chance for something I'd always wanted to write—a car chase!

Forgetting all my literary pretensions, I type with immense gusto straight into the present tense.

"C'mon, Writer," yells Como, as he runs for the Gran Torino. Como might be a giant, but he can still sprint. I almost have a heart attack trying to keep up. We leap in the car.

"Strap up tight," he says, firing the engine. The tyres screech like my Bronx mom when my dad's too long in the toilet, and we hurtle down the road.

The van has a ten second start, but we're already gaining.

"All units. All units."

Como has the handset to his mouth. He gives instructions, letting other cars know where we are and what we're doing. We skid out onto a busier road, narrowly missing a huge truck. I'm excited and terrified—mainly terrified. The panel van's a quarter of a mile ahead, twitching between lanes to pass the slower vehicles respecting the limit. We're weaving too, but the Gran Torino is faster—in the clear spots we're hitting a hundred before Como stamps on the brakes for the next obstacle. The gap narrows. The van's close ahead. Its rear doors swing at each twist in its path. I see the man in the rear of the van, hanging desperately to some fixture to stop himself from flinging about. We swerve past another car and there's nothing but space between us and our target. Como floors the pedal. The Gran Torino rockets forward. We're driving straight at the rear of the van. The man in the back kicks out. A stack of cartons topples from the van like huge dice straight in our path, some bursting to spew books like giant literary confetti. I slam my feet on imaginary brakes and close my eyes. Como locks the real brakes solid, and we smash into the boxes in a sixty mile an hour skid, spinning through several circles.

"You OK, Writer?"

"I wanna be sick."

"Well, puke out the goddam window. Here we go again."

We've spun to a halt, blocking the road. The traffic behind has stopped in a startled clot, so there's empty highway ahead. Como floors the pedal and we resume our chase, the back of the car slithering as the tyres struggle for grip.

The tyres aren't the only things struggling for grip—I've no idea what I'm going to write next.

"What's your plan?" I shout, clutching the handle above my door with a terrified clutch.

"Catch them," says Como, twitching the wheel. "What did you think?"

The fight or flight instinct takes over, which is odd because I'm strapped in a car and unable to do either, but you know what I mean. I abandon myself to my primitive authorial instincts and let the action unfold unconsciously.

We're quickly catching the slower vehicles ahead. The panel van's still in sight, still weaving between lanes. It takes a daring right, almost tipping over as it curves past the front of an oncoming truck. Como checks his mirrors and slews round the same turn in a screeching drift.

We're on a narrower road now, alongside a broad open drain perhaps fifty yards across between sloping concrete embankments. The van's three hundred yards ahead, doing sixty and getting faster, but it doesn't have our speed. Como gets us within twenty yards and holds us there. I can't see what he can see, but I guess he's waiting for a gap in the stream of cars coming the other way. Now! Como floors the pedal and again the Gran Torino tears forward. In just seconds we're doing a hundred along the wrong side of the road, passing the van just inches from my window.

There's a long angry blare from a car coming head on, then Como slews across the path of the van, forcing it to veer. And then the van's gone from my peripheral vision! Astonished, I turn. The van's in the air in what seems a long, slow, suspended trajectory, arcing from the road to the far bank of the drain. It hits the concrete embankment with a sickening crump, and bounces round to smack on its side into the murky water.

Como screeches the Gran Torino to a stop in a cloud of smoke from the tyres.

Wobbling with a huge adrenaline overload, I stagger out of the car. The wrecked van sinks slowly in the scummy drain. Waves from the impact slap the bank with a noise like Como glugging bourbon. Traffic stops. People pile out to rubberneck the aftermath. Como's calling for back-up, standing with one foot in the Gran Torino, looking over its roof to where the van settles on its side with six inches showing above the water.

I'm horrified. I can't believe I've written such an inhuman fate for the men in the van. Yes the Bulgarian henchmen were minor characters—hardly more than extras—but even so. In a funk I had surrendered myself to primitive authorial instincts, and this carnage is the result. I feel compelled to atone for my savage scribings.

Tearing off my anorak, I run to the drain. The concrete embankment is steep—the water ten feet below the edge. I sit on my heels and slide down the side like a ship being launched, grimacing as I hit the murky water. Breaking into a powerful doggy-paddle, I make for the van. I heave myself onto it, panting with the effort and the shock of the cold water. The buckled passenger door is at my feet, its glass smashed. The water in the cab is dark, but I see the driver strapped in about three feet under. I yank at the door. Holding it open, I let my feet down into the flooded cab, finding something to stand on, and wondering if I should have said on which to stand. I let the door drop against my shoulder as I reach into the brown water to find the catch for the driver's seat belt. I feel it with frightened fingers and plunge its button to unclick the strap. The driver's body begins to rise.

I will never forget the nightmare sight that emerges from the watery gloom. I will spare you the description in case you are reading this to your children tucked-up in bed—let's just say that the driver is definitely dead.

I climb from the submerged cab. Along the bank people thrill at the drama, many taking pictures or video, but I've no time for celebrity poses. I slop to the back of the van and slide into the water. The back door has dropped shut. Trying to open it pulls me under—I don't have the buoyancy to take its weight. I tread water for a moment, cursing my decision to let the van crash on its side.

I doggy-paddle to the side of the van, probe with my feet and find something to take my weight. I manage to haul the door out of the water. Holding it up with one arm, I angle myself to look inside. In the gloom a rounded shape is breaking the surface—the second man. Copies of *Dragon's Claw* drift slowly out of the van on a small eddy. The body follows them languidly until I can hook my fingers into its clothing. I haul it into the light against the resistance of the water. The head's flopped at a right-angle to the spine. I don't need the years of medical training I lack to know the neck has snapped.

I let the body go. I'm losing strength and cramping in the cold. I can hear the approaching sirens of back-up. The crowd on the embankment gabbles words of encouragement. I try to lift myself out of the water but can't summon the strength. I'm starting to shake, and my breathing's erratic, as if my diaphragm's going into spasm. I'm not sure how much longer I can hold out, and then I'll be joining the man with the snapped neck, drifting dead in the slow scummy water.

I'm starting to get teary at the thought, and wondering how I've written myself into such a mess, when there's a huge splashing noise, and seconds later a voice.

"Take it easy, Writer."

Como heaves himself onto the side of the van, then with one huge hand pulls me up after him.

"Como," I gasp. "You saved my life."

Phew!

It was a touch melodramatic, perhaps, but quite excusable. Had it not been for Como's heroic action, the life of a publishing legend would have been brought to a tragically premature end, as would this book. Evidently the onlookers share my sentiments, as there is a huge cheering from the embankment, and doubtless from my readers too.

CHAPTER SEVENTEEN

In which Marco is taken for two rides.

REVERTING TO THE PAST TENSE, I sat against the wing of the Gran Torino, cloaked in foil and wondering what to write next. I was in my pants and shoes. My wet clothes were with Como's on the roof of the car, steaming in the sun. Likewise attired, Como leant beside me as we watched the retrieval of the van from the drain. It had been less than an hour since the spectacular end to the chase, but to my exhausted mind it seemed a chapter ago. We were at the centre of a circle of emergency vehicles, most with flashing lights that were technically unnecessary but brought welcome drama to the paragraph. Beyond the circle were the satellite vans of the TV stations, then the cars of onlookers.

A commandeered crane had manoeuvred to the edge of the drain, and hooked onto chains around the exposed wheels of the sunken van. As the crane slowly raised its burden, tons of water slid lazily out of its back—the van's back, I mean, not the crane's. Hundreds of copies of *Dragon's Claw* floated slowly towards the nearby sea, back towards the container port where they had started their short but eventful overland journey. We wandered in our foil blankets to where the van was lowered onto the road, still on its side. The body of the man who'd been in the back had already been dragged up the embankment.

"What have we got?" said Como. He started all our investigative scenes that way, and I wondered whether my readers would consider it laziness on my part or adopt it as a catchphrase that would go viral.

One of the officers consulted a notebook. "Vehicle's registered to a Philip Wrath at the Hacienda apartments. Back's empty—everything that was in it's been flushed out by the water."

As he spoke he nodded across to the drain, but I didn't follow his gesture because I was staring at the face of the man with the broken neck, a face with two letters tattooed on the right cheek. AS. Athletischka Sofia.

"Como!" The swishing of foil behind me confirmed he'd heard my call. "Look."

Como examined the tattoo. "A S. Is that the guy from your foto-fit?"

In case you're not following, he meant the foto-fit picture I'd created with Timo Tsatarin's nice neighbour while eating her deadly cookies.

"Could be." I had a thought. "Remember the foto-fit of the other guy—the one with the logo haircut?"

"Uh huh."

"I wonder if he's the driver."

"We'll see soon enough."

With the help of the crane, the van was being toppled onto its wheels. Once it had settled, Como told no one in particular to 'open her up.'

Two scene-of-crime officers attended the task. One opened the driver's door and the other took photographs of the body that flopped half-out towards the tarmac, dripping water and blood. The face was horribly disfigured by the crash, but the back of the skull was undamaged, and there was the logo. I had a distracted moment wondering why people went to the trouble of getting logos cut into their hair, and the even bigger trouble of keeping them there, before I realised that maybe they never did and it was all just in my imagination. Utterly confused by my dual role of writer and character, I asked Como what he made of it, hoping to give myself time to think.

"You tell me," said Como, unhelpfully batting the ball back. "This case is goin' as crazy as the last one."

He patted the clothes on the car to see if any had dried enough to put on, then he turned and faced me.

"To tell you the Lord's honest truth I'm dreading to think what's coming next. I'd rather be back giving parking tickets than put up with any more of this crazy shit."

I knew how he felt. The most worrying thing was that we still had two warehouses to check. I made a crucial plot decision.

"Como, I'm beat," I said. "Can't we get someone else to check out the two last warehouses?"

"That's like the first sensible thing you've said *ever*," said Como, somewhat unfairly. He swung his foil-cloaked form into the car and grabbed the radio.

"Chief Galahad here. I want Chuengo and Taft to check out warehouse four, and Potowski and King to check out warehouse five. Any persons found present to be detained. I also want a full crime scene detail at each warehouse with a preliminary verbal report in the big conference room at 9.30am sharp tomorrow."

"OK, chief," squawked the dispatcher, after repeating Como's instructions word-for word.

That was a relief. Spared several pages of tedious prose about two more warehouse visits.

I looked at my bespoke Rolex with the picture of my Bronx mom on the dial. Nearly two. We still had an afternoon to fill. I was wondering what to write next when my phone rang in my anorak pocket. It was Barney.

"Hey, Markie babeeeey! This is wild. Can you see the TV? They've been showing the crash and the rescue. It's all on video, Markie. This is amazing. This is going to be the biggest deal ever. But listen, Markie—"

"What?"

"They're streaming you now, live, and the pair of you—you and Como—you're just standing there like lemons, Markie. Can't we get some action going? Can't you like dive in the water and write in a drowning kid? C'mon, Markie, this is a big chance. Or get Como to pull a gun and threaten the crowd. 'Tired cop snaps under pressure,' or something like that. Now's a big chance, Markie. Write something big while the cameras are rollin'. Make my day, Markie. Markie!"

"I can't hear you. My battery's going."

I killed the call. It was bad enough having Barney breathing down my neck between books, but to be suffering it while I was appearing in the bloody things was just a step too far. I threw my phone on the seat of the Gran Torino and rested my head in my hands with my elbows on the roof. I desperately needed to think.

"Got some news," chipped in Como. "They've found the name of the lawyer that handled all the leases on the warehouses."

Just what I needed. A new lead to add to the eleven I hadn't followed up.

"Who is it?" I asked.

"A guy called Horgan—his office is out at Assumption Springs."

Horgan? Harry-Rex Horgan? Wow. Harry-Rex was a character from my last book. A portly, middle-aged lawyer, he was a fearless litigator with a brutal work schedule, a brutal drink problem and three brutal ex-wives. He was also as bent as a box of paper clips.

I suggested to Como that we drive to Assumption Springs, but he had to file an accident report, so we agreed I should go alone. Even better, I thought, since I'd been alone when I'd visited Harry-Rex in my last book; with a bit of luck I'd be able to copy and paste the entire scene and make a few tweaks.

Como detailed an officer to take me to the motel, where I could pick up some clothes and my black Range Rover with tinted windows. I got into the officer's prowler, wrapping my foil cloak around me so it didn't catch in the door.

"All set?" asked the patrolman.

I said I was all set, and he nosed us out into the traffic.

"Gee, Mister Ocram, I read your book about that Herbert Quarry business. Was he really a sick paedo scumbag? I can't see Chief Galahad helping a sicko like that. Did he really do it?"

"Well," I said, not really wanting to talk about it. "It's a bit complicated."

"You betcha. I read the book like four times and I still couldn't make sense of it. I thought your other book on tau muons was easier to understand, and I didn't understand a word of that."

I couldn't take any more.

"Excuse me," I said. "I need to make an urgent call."

"Sure thing, Mister Ocram."

I put my phone to my ear and pretended to be speaking with someone so I could avoid talking with the tiresome patrolman. I made up my half of the conversation at random, just as if I were writing a book.

"Marco Ocram speaking. Can I speak to the head of the FBI about an urgent matter? Yes, I can wait, provided it's not too long. (Pause.) Is that the head of the FBI? Good. I want to tell you about a matter of extreme national importance. (Pause.) Yes. I'm currently working on a case in Clarkesville. (Pause.) Yes, that's the place. It involves a conspiracy to take the entire container port out of action, thus bringing a large proportion of America's trade to a halt. (Pause.) Yes, and you'll know that Clarkesville is the port through which the country's supplies of bio-toxins and nuclear materials are sent, and that it's all kept secret so as not to alarm the local populace? (Pause.) Yes, well, perhaps you can give me full details of your fall-back arrangements. (Long pause.) Yes. (Another long pause.) I see. (Yet another long pause.) Go on."

About ten long imaginary pauses later we'd reached the motel. I thanked the imaginary FBI chief and killed the imaginary call just as the prowler came to a stop at the front door.

"That was lucky timing, Mister Ocram."

"Yes, spooky, wasn't it? Thanks for the lift."

"No problem, Mister Ocram. Any time."

I walked regally in my foil cloak to the reception and got my key. Within fifteen minutes I'd showered and changed, and within sixty more I was parked at Assumption Springs—a sleepy town about forty miles down the N66—sparing my readers a long, irrelevant description of the trip.

I found Horgan's office and entered the plush reception, upon the walls of which were various framed certificates and citations and one of those clocks that shows where it is night and day all over the world. I was peering at it, trying to see how dark it might be in the Bronx, when a shapely receptionist appeared from a back office.

"How can I help you?" he said.

"I'd like to see Mr. Horgan."

"Do you have an appointment?"

"No, but I'm sure he will want to see me," I said, wondering why the receptionist hadn't recognised me. He must be blind, I thought. Then I realised—he was blind.

"My name's Marco Ocram, by the way."

"Marco Ocram the famous physicist and publishing legend? Gosh, it's so amazing to see you, Mister Ocram," he said, metaphorically of course. "Do you want Mister Horgan to help you with the murder at the container port? He's a brilliant litigator, and it would make a change from the queries about warehouse leases that we normally deal with."

I closed my eyes for a moment in an attempt to figure how on earth I kept managing to write myself into these misunderstandings.

"No, let's just say that I have a legal matter that I'm hoping Mr. Horgan will be able to clear up quickly for me."

"Mr. Horgan never clears up legal matters quickly, but I'll see if he's available."

I was shown to Harry-Rex's expansive office, admiring a beautiful young paralegal who was leaving just as I entered.

"Good to meet you again, Mr. Ocram," said Harry-Rex, rising to shake my hand in his reassuring lawyerly grip. "It's not often we get such distinguished visitors twice in our little town."

I turned down the corners of my mouth in a gesture of humility. "That's understandable," I said, to show that I empathised with how he must feel being trapped in a dead-end town with few opportunities to talk about tau muons with knowledgeable celebrities.

"How can I help you?" he asked, gesturing to me to take a seat at his conference table, behind which expensively bound legal tomes covered an entire wall, thereby saving me the task of describing anything more imaginative.

"If I can be frank, Mr. Horgan."

"Please," said Harry-Rex, taking a sly swig from a quart of bourbon hidden behind some court papers.

"I appreciate that members of the American Bar Association operate to the highest and most unbending ethical standards, but I wondered if, for the right consideration, you might shed some light on a recent unusual property transaction in Clarkesville."

"Well, as you have pointed out, Mr. Ocram, our ethical standards are rigid, so it takes a lot to bend 'em. What had you got in mind?"

"Five thou' and first refusal on the legal work to secure the film rights for my new book."

"Done." Harry-Rex took the five thou' I forgot to mention earlier when I picked up my belongings at the police station, and locked it in a desk drawer. "What can I tell you?"

"Through your office, five warehouses in Clarkesville were recently leased by a company registered in Panama. The police will be liaising with the Panamanian authorities for information about the company, but as we both know, the Panamanian transparency laws are somewhat opaque. You are clearly an experienced man of the world, Mister Horgan, so it crossed my mind that during the negotiation of the leases you might have picked up some knowledge about this Panamanian company that could be useful to us."

"Well . . ." Harry-Rex drew out his pronunciation of the word as if to indicate an internal struggle with his ethical standards, a one-sided struggle as it turned out. "I can tell you two things that were unusual about the transactions. The first was that money was no object. And when I say no object I mean it. The company was prepared to pay any price to get the lease of five buildings at short notice. It was as if, Mister Ocram, they had so much money at their disposal that it meant nothing to them. And the implication of that is . . ."

". . . that the company represents a rich individual." I finished his sentence for him, obviously.

"Correct. Only a very rich person with a very important personal objective spends so much money in so carefree a way."

"And what was the second unusual aspect of the transaction?"

"Look around my office, Mister Ocram. What do you see?" While I looked around, Harry-Rex took another sly swig. "I will tell you what you see. You see the signs of a moderately successful small-town law practice. What if I were to tell you that my business is one of the largest law firms in the state?"

"I'd say you do a good job of hiding the fact."

"Congratulations, Mister Ocram. That is the answer of an intelligent man."

Hear that—an intelligent man! I was starting to think that I ought to spend more time with people like Harry-Rex, and less time with taxi-driving bums and patrolmen.

"It takes an intelligent man to know an intelligent man, Mister Horgan."

"Harry-Rex," said Harry-Rex. "Please call me Harry-Rex."

"Harry-Rex," I said, wondering if this were the first book in the world in which the words Harry-Rex had appeared five times so quickly in succession.

"If you were to look in the law year book, Mister Ocram, you would see that there are five hundred and eighty two firms registered to practice in this State. What few people know, Mister Ocram, is that I own almost all of them."

I had no idea where this was going, but didn't want to look foolish, so I said nothing and hoped my silence would pass for knowingness. Had I a cigar, I would have blown a cloud of smoke and eyed him keenly through it. As it was, I fiddled with the buckle on my satchel in a knowing man-of-the-world sort of way.

"You might ask why I am telling you this," he continued, and he was damn right there. "Let me just say that it has a bearing on your question. You see, Mister Ocram, by maintaining a large number of seemingly independent law firms, I find that I harvest a greater share of my clients' business than they would be inclined to devote to a single supplier. They think they are spreading their legal eggs across several baskets, whereas the baskets all belong to me."

"Isn't that rather sharp practice?"

"It might be, Mister Ocram, but in truth wouldn't you prefer to have the 'sharp' lawyer on your side rather than, shall we say, the unimaginative one who puts conforming with the rules ahead of the interests of his clients?"

"Possibly—provided that he put those interests ahead of his own also."

"Your point is well made and well taken," he said, blatantly copying dialogue from my earlier court scene. I let it ride, however, as I didn't want to draw the readers' attention to it.

"And what is the relevance of this to my question?" I asked.

"The Panamanian company that took the leases for the warehouses through this office, simultaneously took a lease to another property through one of my other companies, believing themselves to be dealing with an entirely independent law firm."

"Sharp practice again, Mister Horgan?" It didn't seem right to call him Harry-Rex when I was accusing him of sharp practice.

"When I said 'believing themselves' I chose my words carefully, Mister Ocram. They reached the conclusion as a result of inadequate research. I don't hide my ownership of the other law firms, I just don't rub it in people's faces. If the Panamanians believed the other firm was not under my ownership, that's their fault entirely. I was under no ethical obligation to disabuse them."

"No?" I said doubtfully.

"No, Mister Ocram. Had they been up front with me and told me they had a separate transaction that they wanted handled by an independent law firm, then I would certainly have ensured they did not place that business with one of my subsidiaries."

I doubted that too, but said nothing.

"But they said nothing to me about it. They merely placed the other transaction with one of my other companies. At first I didn't notice the connection; but when the staff from that firm said they had a new client spending money like water I naturally took an interest."

"Naturally."

"And I was interested to note that the company had taken a lease for another type of building altogether."

"What type of building?" I asked, wondering what on earth could be coming next.

"A datacentre, Mister Ocram."

A datacentre? My buckle-fiddling became more frenetic.

I decided I needed a new chapter to give myself time to think.

CHAPTER EIGHTEEN

In which a major development of the plot is teed up.

"**A** DATACENTRE?"

"More precisely, Mister Ocram, a vacant datacentre."

"A *vacant* datacentre?"

Now I was even more confused.

"Yes. The client was quite specific that the building must have all of the underlying facilities of a datacentre—air-conditioning, fallback power-generation, suspended floors, superb security, and so on—but no actual IT equipment or networking was required. I took it that the client was to provide their own IT, presumably because . . ."

". . . your client had something to hide."

"Exactly."

I pondered why an extremely rich individual would want to rent five warehouses to stock copies of an unpublished thriller, and a vacant datacentre. I had no idea, so I'd have to park the question for now, and return to it when I'd had more time to make sense of the plot.

"And what is the address of this mystery datacentre?"

Harry-Rex looked at me slyly.

"When you pressured me to bend my ethical standards a fraction, you asked if I could 'shed light on' a property transaction, and that is what I believe I have already done. Divulging a detail as specific and fundamental as an address seems to me to be going far beyond the mere shedding of light, Mister Ocram."

"Are you saying that your ethical standards are incapable of being bent to such an extent?"

"No. I am merely stating an established principle of physics: the greater the bend to be achieved, the greater the force required to achieve it."

"How much greater?"

"Another twenty thou'?"

"Ten."

"Done."

Harry-Rex leant forward to shake my hand, then took the extra ten thou' as neatly as a trained seal taking a tossed fish.

"The address is Unit D, Browndan Industrial Park, Clarkesville. But you never heard that from me."

"Of course," I concurred, in my best man-of-the-world voice.

"Then I believe our little business is concluded, Mister Ocram, unless there are any other legal services I can provide?"

I wasn't entirely sure that the service he had just provided was legal, but I knew what he meant.

"No, Mister Horgan. You have dealt with my needs comprehensively."

"Very well. Let me show you out."

I followed Harry-Rex to the main door.

"I hope you enjoyed your visit to our little town. It might appear sleepy on the surface, but there is plenty to keep a businessman entertained, if he has the right connections."

"I'm sure," I said, not really being sure.

On the point of stepping out of the building, I turned to face him.

"One last question, Mister Horgan. Is the datacentre easy to find?"

"You can't miss it. It's right by the container port."

CHAPTER NINETEEN

In which various literary seeds are sown.

"COMO, COMO, LISTEN."
I was back in my motel room. Como had been unavailable on each of the twenty seven occasions I had tried him as I drove back from Assumption Springs in an excited rush. Now that he'd finally answered I was desperate for him to hear my news. "I've just got back from seeing Horgan, and guess what."

"What?"

"That Panamanian company. It leased a datacentre. And listen to this—the datacentre's right next to the container port!"

"I know."

"What?"

"I know."

"What d'you mean 'I know'?"

"I know. About the datacentre. What's up with you? Of course I know about the datacentre. I'm the freaking Police Chief."

"But how can you know? I've only just bribed Harry-Rex to tell me."

"What do you mean, bribed him to tell you? You don't need to bribe anyone to tell you. All lease transactions are recorded on the State land register. You can see them on the Internet."

"But I've just paid . . ." My voice failed as I realised I'd just paid Harry-Rex Horgan fifteen thou' for information I could have got from the Internet.

"What've you just paid?"

"Nothing. It doesn't matter." I didn't want Como to know that I'd been taken for a spectacular ride by one of my characters. "Hold the line, Como—I'll be right back."

I put down my phone, clenched my fists in the air, and paced around the room, cursing Harry-Rex Horgan, cursing Harry-Rex Horgan's mother and father for giving him a life, cursing the American Bar Association for their sloppy enforcement of ethical standards, and cursing every lawyer in the world and all their mothers and fathers for giving them lives. When I'd got my frustration sufficiently out of my system, I picked up the phone.

"The other thing he told me was that the Panamanian company's probably representing a mega-rich person with more money than sense."

"You mean someone like you?"

"Como!" I bleated.

"Only kidding, Writer. That's good work. Narrows things down to just the folk who are mega-rich with more money than sense. Can't be more than a hundred thousand in this beautiful country of ours."

"Como, let me tell you something—you've become a real cynic since you became Police Chief."

"Correction. I've become a real cynic since I read what you were paid for our last book."

I rolled my eyes. Not that it did any good, since we were talking on the phone, so Como couldn't see me. My income from *The Awful Truth about The Herbert Quarry Affair* had been a continuing source of resentment for Como. According to his twisted logic, since we had each played a part in solving the case, we should each have benefited equally from the spoils. What he overlooked, of course, was the relative importance of our roles. When George Soros made a billion from currency speculation, he didn't share it equally with the person who cleaned his mousepad.

"Well, anyway," I said. "What are we going to do about it?"

"If you mean what am I going to do about it, then the answer's sweet Fanny Adams, at least until tomorrow. I've got a game to watch tonight. Which reminds me. If I have a minute's interruption because of you, Writer, you'll be back in a cell looking at intimate tattoos again, so help me God."

"Well, I only hope the Clarkesville County Fire Service is more diligent than the Clarkesville County Police. 'Sorry, madam, your house will have to burn down—we're watching a game tonight, but if the fire's not out by the morning feel free to call back.'"

"Yeah, but a fire's a real emergency, not some made-up shit. I've got the datacentre under observation, so nothing's gonna happen that we won't know about. Anyway, I ain't got time to chew the fat. Call me when you've something important to discuss."

With which he hung up.

So much for immutable bonds of comradeship and mutual respect. I threw my phone despondently on the side table, and myself despondently on the bed. I lay with my hands behind my head, staring at a stain near the top of the opposite wall, trying to decide what to write next. I was sure there was something I'd meant to do. Think, Marco, think.

That was it—the book!

I'd meant to have a closer look at *Dragon's Claw*. I got the copy from my satchel, and settled myself on the bed to read it.

It was about three inches thick. The cover was dark brown. The title and author's name were in a corny font that reminded me of *Star Trek* for some reason, and between them was a weird Chinese dragon figure, holding what looked like missiles in its claws. The first few pages were plastered with gushing reviews and recommendations from leading international newspapers, A-list celebrities and well-known intellectuals. They seemed to suggest the book was even better than *The Awful Truth about the Herbert Quarry Affair*. Ha! Just as if.

I read them one by one:

'A startling new talent. Every paragraph is a rich heady literary treat. The language flows like cream.' Salman Rushdie.

'Quite possibly the finest literary mined of our generation.' Dan Brown.

'A wizard read.' JK Rowling.

'Devastating plot, devastating style, devastating denouement—it's a devastating debut by a remarkable writer.' New York Times.

'The best book I have ever read.' Marco Ocram.

'Better than anything that . . .'

MARCO OCRAM!!!!

I looked at the front of the book again. No, I was sure—I'd never read it. I flicked through some more of the fawning blurb. Perhaps none of the quotes were true. I made a note to check them out, and there'd be hell to pay when I got to the bottom of how my name had been abused to furnish a misleading endorsement.

I let my blood pressure subside a little, then read on.

There was the usual page of meta-data and disclaimers, which I reproduce here in breach of goodness knows how many copyright laws:

First published by Peluxes Press 2016.
This work must not be lent, re-sold, copied, or
converted into any other form without the
express written consent of the publishers.
Printed in 12-point Attrocia by Inventemente SA, Sofia.
ISBN: 9870248308371
Denis Shaughnessy asserts his moral right
to be known as the author of this work.
Enquiries for film, musical, stage and other rights
to be made to Peluxes Press, Pyongyang.
The characters in this book are fictitious.
Any resemblance to any real person
living or dead is entirely coincidental.

So the publisher was based in North Korea. Wonderful, absolutely wonderful. As if Panama's transparency laws hadn't been opaque enough. I scratched my crotch meditatively. What could a North Korean connection signify? A straightforward outsourcing arrangement to a part of the world with cheap printing costs? An author with a love of badly built automobiles and corny propaganda songs? A conspiracy financed by shadowy Russian and Chinese billionaires to bring about cultural upheaval in the West through the dissemination of subversive ideas? A Bond-style plot, in which a nerve agent is impregnated in the pages of the books and absorbed through the fingertips of the readers? No, I mustn't compromise the authenticity of my work with crazy ideas. I returned my attention to the book and began to read it properly.

It was about eleven when, with a cavernous yawn, I dropped *Dragon's Claw* on my lap. It had been an old-fashioned thriller, a bit like the stuff that Tom Ludlum and Robert Clancy used to churn out, but written in a more literary style. The plot was some nonsense about nuclear weapons and independence for Hong Kong, most of which I'd forgotten before I'd finished reading it. There was one clever bit about how the baddies bombed the Houses of Parliament—the ones in London—which I thought I might copy in my next book, but otherwise it was unremarkable. Quite why there should be millions of copies of the thing in warehouses around Clarkesville was a complete and utter enigma of a mystery inside a whatsits, as Churchill said. I thought about calling Barney, but it would be midnight in New York and he'd be out schmoozing celebrities for book endorsements. I decided to turn in.

CHAPTER TWENTY

In which the Mayor bemoans Marco's mayhem.

I PARKED MY BLACK RANGE Rover with tinted windows at the Clarkesville County Police HQ, and headed for reception.

"Good morning, Mister Ocram," said the gorgeous young officer manning the desk. "It really is an amazing thrill to see you."

"My, you are a pretty little thing," I said, mentally twirling the points of my non-existent moustache in a disgracefully sexist manner. "Call me Marco."

"Oh . . . Chief Galahad said I was to show you straight to the big conference room, Mister Ocram."

She scrambled from her desk and showed me down the corridor to a room at its end. Opening the door, she gestured me in.

"Writer, it's good of you to join us for our 9.30 meeting . . ." Como consulted his watch . . . "at 10.07. Please take a seat."

I took a seat, nodding benevolently to all around the table. Como's full squad was present. Some were hard-bitten detectives—veterans of a hundred cases—others were new to our difficult game, and seemed awed but excited—reactions I would have attributed to my stellar presence were I not modesty personified.

"Right," said Como. "Listen up. We're going to go through everything we've got. We're going to look for links and gaps. I want everyone focussed, and I want no one drifting off topic. That clear?"

The subsequent silence showed that it was clear.

"Good," said Como. "Any questions before we start?"

I put up my hand. "How did the game go last night?"

"For fuck's sake, Writer, I said no drifting off topic. Any other *sensible* questions?"

I thought that was a bit unfair, as he'd said any questions before we start, so I'd assumed that meant any questions before we start not drifting off topic. I said nothing, however, and let his high-handed ill-treatment of a publishing legend speak for itself to his shocked team.

The next dozen or so paragraphs feature Como leading his case conference. You know the kind of thing—where the detective adds photographs to a big screen and draws arrows between them to highlight crucial links in the hope of elucidating the solution to the mystery. I'll leave you to decide whether you want to read them. Personally I found them incredibly tiresome to write—no jokes, just a load of boring police details, which goes to show what happens when you let Como dominate a scene. That said, they do pad out a page or two. In fact, I can see why the police procedural market is so crowded, because they're a doddle to write. Those of you without the appetite to read formulaic police procedure should skip down to where you see 'return here' in bold print. The rest of you can carry on . . .

"OK," said Como, unimaginatively calling us to attention. "To start we have a dead body found squashed between containers at the port." He stuck a photo of the crime scene on the glass wall of the conference room.

"The body is that of Timo Tsatarin, an agency driver living in the Hacienda apartments." Como added photos of the victim, the agency and the apartment block, and drew arrows to show the links between them.

"The victim's known associates are . . ." Como gave their names, stuck their photographs on the wall and drew more arrows. "I want us to find everything there is to know about these people. Their friends and relatives, their bank accounts, where they last worked, their favourite TV shows—everything."

I wrote 'Friends, rellies, banks, jobs, TV shows' on my iPad to show that I was keeping up.

"The victim drove a black Lancia Monte Carlo, with foreign plates ending one four eight." Como added a library photo of a black Lancia Monte Carlo. "We need to find that car, and when we do I want full forensics, and I want any prints from it matched against State, federal and international databases.

"The car is registered to Philip Wrath." Como put up a picture of an anonymous silhouette with a question-mark over it, and drew an arrow to the car. "Who is he? What can we discover about him? Brix and Lundt, I want you to find out.

"The movement schedules for the container that squashed the body were erased by someone without the permission of Harbour Master McBeany or her deceased IT manager. We need to know who did it, and how and why the IT manager died." Como put up the ISO symbol for erased movement schedules, a picture of McBeany—which reminded me of how nice she was—

and a picture of the deceased IT manager, then drew a whole sheaf of arrows linking them to the other things on the wall.

"The victim and his associates are linked to five warehouses and a datacentre." Como added six more pictures and twice as many arrows. "McGee, Tutu—I want door-to-door interviews with all the neighbouring businesses. Find out who has been coming and going at those locations.

"The warehouses contain one thing and one thing only—the book *Dragon's Claw*." Actually that made it about ten million things, but I didn't want to interrupt Como's flow. He put a picture of the cover of the book on the wall, with arrows to the warehouses. "I want to know how all those books got into the warehouses, how they were transported, where they were printed, and so on." He drew some more arrows.

"I want full forensics from the crashed panel-van and the deceased inside it, and I want to know how they were linked to Tsatarin and the other suspects from the gym." Como added three more photos and twelve arrows.

Return here.

Having added all the photographs to the big board and drawn arrows between the related ones, Como stepped back to view the overall picture.

It was an indescribably tangled mess, with everything connected to everything else, reflecting the feeling of utter confusion that had settled on myself and the other members of the team. I put up my hand.

"Yes, what is it?"

"You haven't said anything about the book itself," I said.

"What book?"

"*Dragon's Claw*—the one from the warehouse," I added, in case any of my readers, like me, had lost the plot.

"That's your department, Writer. We can talk about that separately. OK everyone, what are you still sitting here for? If you've no questions let's get . . ."

"Chief, Chief!" A breathless police officer burst into the room. "Mayor needs to see you right now about the container port being disrupted and about all the nuclear waste and everything."

"Nuclear waste? What nuclear waste?"

"It's all in the papers, Chief, and on TV." The policeman handed a copy of one of the local papers to Como. I could see its huge headline: 'Ocram in Nuclear Waste Exposé.'

"What's this shit?" Como read from the paper, "'Unnamed sources at Clarkesville County Police have confirmed that publishing legend Marco Ocram has blown the lid off secretive shipments of nuclear waste through the Clarkesville container port. We can reveal that Ocram is in close contact with the FBI as panic spreads at news of a plot to block a major US trade artery.'" He turned to look at me. "Are you out of your fucking mind?"

It was a good question. If I wasn't now then I might soon be if there were any more of these farcical digressions.

"Como! It's . . . it's not my fault. Someone on your force can't keep their mouth shut about my confidential telephone conversations."

"You're having confidential conversations with the FBI about nuclear waste going through Clarkesville and a plot to block the container port?"

"Well, not confidential conversations exactly. Monologues."

"Confidential monologues?"

"No, just one confidential monologue."

"OK, so that's now crystal clear. You're having a confidential monologue with the FBI about nuclear waste going through Clarkesville and a plot to block the container port?"

"I . . ." I breathed out heavily, momentarily lost for words. I decided to make a relatively clean breast of it. "I wasn't talking to anyone, Como. I was just dictating ideas for another book into my phone. Someone must have overheard it and got the wrong end of the stick."

"A fucking big stick that will have my ass on it," said Como, with a good deal of exasperation that wasn't entirely unjustified. "OK, you're coming with me to see the Mayor, and let's see you explain it."

Ten minutes later we were in the Mayor's office . . .

"And so you see, Mayor, it was all a simple misunderstanding."

"I quite see, Mister Ocram. But I have to say," the Mayor turned to Como, "that a simple misunderstanding has led to a major public relations disaster, owing to a lack of discipline within the Clarkesville County Police Department that resulted in Mister Ocram's words being released to the media. Have you any mitigating justification whatsoever for the wanton betrayal of a confidence by one of your men?"

Como shuffled his considerable weight from one foot to the other.

"Well, have you? Speak up, man!"

"No, Mayor."

"'No, Mayor,'" said the Mayor. "Your department sets the world's biggest hare running and all you can say is 'No, Mayor.'"

"Sorry, Mayor."

The Mayor made a noise I don't know how to spell, like hmmmph. I closed my eyes and clutched the edge of the conference table—like Bertie Wooster did in that story about Sir

Roderick Glossop and the sweet-peas—waiting for the Mayor to bust Como down to patrolman, and wondering how I would be able to look Como in the eye again when she did.

"Well, Galahad," I heard her say, "I suppose you have had a lot on your plate with this container port murder, and you have been telling me repeatedly that you're short-handed, so perhaps it's time I allocated more funds so you can take on the extra people you need to get that department of yours under better control. In the meantime I'll get my PR people to put this little fire out so it doesn't take up any more of your limited time."

I opened my eyes and found myself inspecting the intricate grain of the Mayor's tropical hardwood conference table and wondering if I'd really written what I thought I'd just heard.

"Thanks Mayor. I hope business stays good."

I looked up to see Como shaking hands with the Mayor, and holding the Mayor's hand a fraction longer than would be usual. Call me paranoid, but it crossed my mind that Como might have some kind of hold over the Mayor, or at least some common bond of loyalty. I wondered what kind of bond or hold would be strong enough to stop the Mayor from busting Como right down to the bottom of the pile, something I would have done in a heartbeat given his recent behaviour. It had to be something very improper. Disguising my unspeakable disappointment, I rose and made my cordial, if somewhat stiff, goodbye to the Mayor. Como followed me out.

"OK, what have you got over the Mayor, Como?"

"What have I got? What d'you mean 'what have I got?'?"

I stared at the double question-mark, just to check it was right. It was. That gave me an idea . . .

"You know what I mean, Como. You should have been busted down to patrolman for what happened on your watch, even if I did trigger it, and yet the Mayor gives you more money.

Doesn't that tell you why I'm surprised by you standing there saying 'what d'you mean "what have I got?"?'?"

Yes! Three separate question marks in a row. Surely a first in literature. If that doesn't impress the Nobel Prize committee, then my name's not Marco J Ocram.

"Listen, Writer. You just thank your lucky stars I wasn't busted down to patrolman. If we got any half-sensible replacement Police Chief here, the first thing he'd do, even before he sat at his desk, would be to ban you from taking any part in this container port case. So don't ask questions it's not in your interest to have answered."

I was rather horrified by his patronising and sexist assumption that a new Police Chief would be a he, but I let it ride, as we needed to get back to some fast-paced action. My phone rang.

"Excuse me," I said to Como. It was a voicemail from Barney, who sounded about to pop with excitement.

"Markie baby! I just seen the incredible news. Nuclear waste! The FBI! Now you're talking. We've hit pay dirt here, Markie, I'm telling you. No one's going to remember that paedo scumbag Quarry once this story hits the presses. But you gotta call me, Markie. I need you in New York. We've got deals to sign. This is gonna be huuuuge. Call me."

I killed the call and turned to Como. "Como, I . . ."

I stopped because Como was on the phone himself, and it sounded like important news. When he finished the call, he replied to my expectant look.

"They've found Timo Tsatarin's car. It's down at the data-centre by the container port."

CHAPTER TWENTY ONE ALREADY

In which Marco revises his back-story to solve a problem.

WE BURNED RUBBER IN THE Gran Torino all the way to a burger bar, grabbed grub and then headed for the datacentre. It was a low building with no windows, set at the end of a quiet road on an industrial estate next to the container port. It had a car park to one side, and a scrubby patch of stunted trees at the back, beyond which was the port's chain-link fence. A black Lancia Monte Carlo was the only car in the car park, apart from an unmarked police car, and now our Gran Torino of course.

Como did his usual thing and walked to the unmarked police car, leant on its roof and spoke with the officers inside.

"Good work, Archer. See anyone around?"

"No, Chief, only the car. Looks like it's been there a while."

"OK. Get Nyquist here quick."

Como did a quick double tap on the car's roof, a gesture I took to mean that he was pleased, then walked over to the black Monte Carlo. He eyed it with his experienced Police Chief eye, while I looked through the driver's window. There was some paperwork on the passenger seat that seemed to be in a foreign language—Bulgarian presumably. I pointed it out to Como.

"We'll need the forensic guys to get the car open," he said. "Let's go look at the building."

I wasn't sure why we needed the forensic guys to do something as simple as breaking into a car, but I went along with Como's assertion, not wishing to undermine the credibility of one of my characters in the minds of my readers. Unlike the warehouses, the datacentre was bristling with security. It had more cameras than the red carpet at the Oscars. I wondered if we were being monitored. The main door was steel, with an iris scanner and a keypad. I examined them with an increasing sense of impending failure.

"Know what they are?" asked Como, thus teeing up an explanation for non-technical readers.

"Yes, it's a form of digital lock. The camera thing is an iris scanner, and it and the keypad are connected to a computer. To get in you need to have your iris scanned and punch in a passcode. Unless the passcode and the fine structures of your iris match authorised details in the computer you can't get in."

"Never mind that crap—we'll break our way in."

"I suppose you just happen to know some police trick for getting through steel doors with digital locks." I raised a sarcastic eyebrow at the thought of such a corny plot twist.

"No, but I know there's a plant-hire outfit two blocks down."

Twenty minutes later we'd visited the plant-hire outfit two blocks down, where Como commandeered a twenty ton excavator with a percussive chisel attachment. We trundled it to the datacentre, Como steering and me shouting at him to avoid things. Como lined it up by the doorway, jerkily manoeuvring the point of the chisel to rest just above the door, then he pushed the lever that started the percussive action.

Wow! I hadn't been sure what to expect, but the chisel pushed through the wall at the first tap, followed by more or less the entire arm of the machine. With his usual heavy-handedness, Como pulled the levers that made the machine track backwards, and the whole door came away, as did its frame and about five tons of surrounding masonry. In his excitement, Como forgot to look behind, and no one was less surprised than I when he backed the huge excavator into the unmarked police car.

"Shit," said Como as we stood alongside a startled Archer and looked at the impact twenty tons of excavator could have on an unmarked police car. Or, rather, a previously unmarked police car.

"Never mind that," I said. "The milk has been spilled. There's nothing you can do about it. I, on the other hand, have an entirely new topic to master. C'mon."

My words referred, of course, to the forthcoming scene where I'd have to write loads of stuff to do with computers. I'd been worrying about it ever since Harry-Rex Horgan had introduced the idea of a datacentre. You'll have noticed that, aside from the occasional mention of my iPad, there hasn't been anything about computers in any of my books. There are two good reasons for that. One is that computers are dead boring. The other is that I hardly know how to switch them on, let alone explain what they do. However, ignorance had never stopped me from writing about boring things, and I wasn't going to let it now. If I could write a sentence with three question marks, then deciphering a screen or two of computer program wasn't going to phase me. I threw back the shoulders, shot the cuffs of my anorak, and strode fearlessly into the datacentre.

Well, not that far in, actually, because just the other side of the gaping hole that had been the door was a sort of turnstile, with a waist-high sheet of glass blocking the way, and another digital lock next to it. I bent to examine the sophisticated mechanism, assessing it with a scientist's eye. Hmmmmm.

"If I'm not mistaken, Como, this security barrier requires us to present a special token with a near-field wireless activation chip and double-encrypted asymmetric bypass keys. I've read about them in a Dan Brown book. They can take weeks to decipher."

"Is that an occupational hazard with you writers?"

"What?"

"Making up shit."

With which, Como vaulted over the glass security screen in a blatant display of police high-handedness. I followed him more slowly, with an awkward personal moment when a part of me got caught as I was straddling the glass. Ooohhhh.

We were now in the ante-chamber before the main server room, the doors to which were firmly locked. I tried desperately to remember some details from the Dan Brown book, so I could copy them to explain how we might break in; understandably, however, I'd skim-read most of it, and for some reason the only bit that came back was about a special alarm fitted to the protagonist's Range Rover.

To give me time to think, I decided to leave the action to Como. He walked straight to a fire alarm panel and smashed the glass with a huge knuckle. A painfully loud siren sounded from the ceiling, overlaid by a recorded voice saying "This is not a test. Please leave the building by the nearest exit. This is not a test, please leave . . ." and so on. I was about to leave the building by the nearest exit, when Como hooked a finger in my collar and spun me round. The fire alarm had triggered the doors of the server room to unlock. Hmmmm. Another of Como's tricks.

"Hold this open," he said above the din, meaning the door.

I held it open.

Como stomped off somewhere, and after a minute the fire alarm stopped. I was still holding the door when he came back with a fire-axe. I was worried about what he might do with a fire-axe, but he just used it to wedge the door open, so that was alright, if a bit of an anti-climax.

"OK, Writer, we're in. Over to you."

I looked around. The room was full of servers, unsurprisingly, with a few screens and keyboards here and there. I sat at the nearest keyboard and flexed my fingers in preparation for an astounding display of IT-nerd typing skills. Como, meanwhile, was wasting his time somewhere else, presumably on some boring police procedure like dusting for prints.

As I flexed my fingers, ideas were forming in my mind, vague and disconnected at first, but slowly coalescing. I was building an IT back-story for myself, so that I could plausibly hack into the servers and discover the baddies' plot. Ideally I would have gained my IT experience somewhere famous. I waited for something to come into my head . . .

CERN! That would do. CERN was the renowned centre for experimental particle physics. I'd heard they use big computers there, and it would complement my role as the physicist who had famously postulated the existence of the tau muon.

OK, so, on with developing the back-story . . .

Brilliant young PhD, Marco Ocram, is developing computer code at the Department of Theoretical Physics at the

University of Geneva. He is modelling the scattering distributions from 'warm' neutron collisions with heavy nuclei. The results suggest the existence of a Jekyll and Hyde particle, sometimes acting as a tau and sometimes as a muon. Could there be a chimera particle ... a ... a tau muon? He is disturbed from his train of thought by his kindly professor. Marco, there is a call for you from CERN. Monsieur Peter Higgs wishes to speak to you.

Distractedly, Marco hurries to the phone.

"Brilliant young PhD Marco Ocram speaking. How can I help you?"

"Doctor Ocram, I'm sorry to interrupt your brilliant work. You realise that I would not have done so were it not for a matter of supreme international importance. The Large Hadron Collider has been generating data at a rate that has exceeded our wildest expectations, so much so that the computer program that analyses the output has failed to cope. Unless drastic action is taken, the entire project could be at risk. Our brightest computer scientists have been unable to find a solution. You are our only hope."

The Large Hadron Collider!

That reminds me—those dopey physicists at CERN are meant to be kings of precision, and yet they can't even give their biggest-ever experiment an unambiguous name. Is it supposed to mean the large collider of hadrons, or the collider of large hadrons? Idiots. They think it's tough getting counter-rotating beams of protons to collide at 99.9999999998% of the speed of light in a 30-mile-long vacuum tube under the Alps. They ought to try writing a crime book.

Where was I? Oh yes . . .

"Never fear, Professor Higgs. I will drop everything and come at once."

Changing to the first-person, I tore down the N66 to Lucerne in my battered old Citroen, never dreaming that one day it might be changed for a black Range Rover with tinted windows.

When I got to CERN I wasn't recognised by the receptionist, and nor was I mobbed by her colleagues with questions about tau muons, as I had yet to become famous, and tau muons were still just a jiggle in my neurons. Peter Higgs came rushing from the gents' toilets, a heavily-annotated copy of The Racing Post—no, make that The Journal of Physics—under his arm.

"Ocram. Thank heavens you are here." He stubbed out his cigarette. "Please come this way."

The careworn physicist led me to his office, where a 72-inch screen newly-affixed to one wall was showing real-time results from the giant particle accelerator under the mountains. Sorry, I mean the giant accelerator-of-particles under the mountains, of course, not the accelerator of giant-particles under the mountains. The screen showed a succession of images, each featuring an indescribable tangle of particle trajectories, an arrangement almost as complex and bewildering as the arrow diagram drawn by Como on the wall of his conference room.

"Somewhere within the tracks on that screen, Doctor Ocram, may well be evidence of the boson that bears my name. But our computer program has proved unable to distinguish the needle of signal from the haystack of noise, if you understand my expression. Our best brains have failed to spot the flaw in the program's logic, but now that you are here . . ."

His failing words were an unwitting metaphor—the time for talk was over. It was now time for action.

"Bring me a print-out of the flawed computer program," I said, even though the time for talk was over.

"I have one here, ready for your arrival."

He passed to me several sheets of paper, closely printed with the obscure symbols of the programmer's art. Yes, it was just as I suspected. My face set in an iron mask of disapproval for only the second time in the book.

"I think you will find that this is the problem."

The point of my propelling pencil hovered above a 'goto' statement—the notorious programming short-cut that inevitably led to computer glitches.

"Can you . . . can you . . . fix it?" The Professor looked at me with pleading eyes.

"I will see what can be done. I will need a terminal, a keyboard, and access to your most-powerful server. Oh, and if you have it, there's a book called 'Programming for Dummies' *that might be useful too."*

"Certainly. I will see that you have everything you need."

It was a tense night that followed, and more than once I almost despaired of finding a solution; but I worked on. Courage, Marco, I said to myself, you mustn't fail the world of science. After hours of intense intellectual effort, with the sky pinkening over a distant Alp, I was ready. The new computer code had been written and compiled. I had mounted the magnetic tape on the spool. All that was needed now was . . .

"Cracked it!"

It was Como, interrupting my thoughts.

"Cracked what?" I assumed he meant the glass of his iPhone, or some other unfortunate item that had fallen victim to his clumsiness.

"The computer set-up, dumbass."

"What?" I pushed back my wheeled chair and went to where he was sitting at another computer, dabbing at a dwarfed keyboard with his giant fingers. "Since when did you know how to work computers?"

Como gave me one of his looks.

"Don't you remember *anything* you write from one book to the next?"

"Some things, Como. I admit probably not everything, but the main things—my characters' names, and so on. Why?"

Como gave me another of his looks.

"Surprised I cracked it huh? You think you're the only one with the brains to do something like this? In the last book, before you roped me into all that Herbert Quarry crap, I was leading the cybercrimes unit at the Clarkesville PD. I can do this stuff with my eyes shut."

I wished he'd reminded me before I wasted all that effort on my IT back-story. I pulled up a chair next to his.

"Whatcha got?"

"Look at this." Como brought up a list of names on the screen:

AMAZON
BARNES_&_NOBLE
BOOKS_A_MILLION
CHARTER_BROWN
ELLIOTS
JACOB_AND_DOYLE
POWELL_BOOKS
PRESTON_BOOKS
TEXTS_ONLINE
XYZ_BOOKS

"Bookshops!"

"Not just bookshops, Writer. These are the top ten online booksellers in the USA. Between them they handle more than 98% of all new book sales. Now look at this."

He then showed me what seemed like page after meaningless page of names, addresses, dates, and numbers.

"Talk to me, Como. What are we looking at?"

"Credit card details. Stolen credit card details."

I was glad he said it twice—it was an important pivot in the plot and I didn't want readers to miss it.

"Wow. There must be hundreds of them."

"Ten point four million," corrected Como.

"Ten point . . ." My words morphed into a long whistle. That was a lot of stolen credit card details. I put my thoughts to Como.

"That's a lot of stolen credit card details."

"Uh huh. And what does ten point four mil remind you of?"

I thought. The population of New York? The advance on my next book? A thousand times what I'd paid to that swindling corrupt asshole Harry-Rex Horgan? It could be anything.

"You tell me," I said.

"Who's the dumbass now, Writer? Think."

"I've thought. I don't know. What's it meant to remind me of?"

"*Dragon's Claw?*"

I looked at him, hearing the resonant metallic sound of a huge penny starting to drop.

"Getting it now, Writer?"

"*Dragon's Claw!*"

The forensic guys had counted the books in the warehouses—there were ten point four million copies of *Dragon's Claw*.

"Uh huh. Now look at this." He showed me something else on the screen—page after page after page of what I assumed was computer writing. None of it meant anything to me.

"Como, if you're trying to prove that you know more about computer writing than I do then you've made your point. Can we please stop this pointless point scoring, and get back to the point."

"OK. I'll take you through it real slow. This is the first part of the computer program. Notice anything?"

I looked at the hieroglyphics on his screen . . .

try{
r=function(a){a=a.$;delete   this.Vi[a];this.$&&delete this.$[a]};s_.equals=function(a){if(!a||this.constructor!=a.constructor)return!1;for(var f=s_1Va(d),g=s_6v(this,e),e=s_6v (a,e);if(d.Zj()){if(g.length!=e.length)return!1;for(d=0;d<g.length;d++){var   k=g[d],l=e[d];if(f?!k.equals(l):k!=l)return!1}} else if(f?!g.equals(e):g!=e)return!1}}return!0};
BOOK.NAME = DRAGON'S CLAW
url");window.open(b,"_blank","menubar=no,left="+((window.screenLeft||window.screenX||0)+Math.max(0,((window.innerWidth||document.documentElement.clientWidth||document.body.clientWidth||0)-

"It mentions *Dragon's Claw* on the sixth line!"
"Well spotted. What about this?"

D("aspn");s_F();}catch(e){_DumpException(e)}try{s_E("s y247");var   s_ZVa=function(a,b,c){this.ka=a;this.Nh=b.name|| null;this.$={};for(a=0;a<c.length;a++)b=c[a],this.$[b.$]=b};s_ ZVa.prototype.getName=function(){return this.Nh};var
USE STOLEN CREDIT CARD DETAILS

445)/2))+",top="+((window.screenTop||window.screenY ||0)+Math.max(0,((window.innerHeight||document.docume ntElement.clientHeight||document.body.clientHeight||0)- 665)/2))+",width=445,height=665");(a=a.getAttribute("data- ved"))&&google.log("","&ved="+a)};

"It's using the stolen credit card details!"
"Correct. And now this bit . . ."

1:this.ma=!0}this.ha=c.defaultValue};s_0Va.prototype.g etName=function(){return this.Nh};var

*s_ee("aspn",{init:function(){s_Hh("aspn",{ota:s_F7a},!0)},dispose:function(){s_Jh("aspn",["ota"])}})s_*

BUY COPY OF BOOK.NAME TEN POINT FOUR MILLION TIMES FROM BOOK.SELLERS.LIST
s__Va=function(a){a=s_cb(a.$);s_3a(a,function(a,c){retu rn a.$-c.$});return a};var s_0Va=function(a,b,c){this.$=b; this.Nh=c.name;this.Ea=!!c.Lr;this.Wa=!!c.required;this.ka=c. mj;this.qa=c.type;this.ma=!1;switch(this.ka){case 3:case 4:case 6:case 16:case 18:case 2:case s_1Va=function(a){return 11==a.ka||10==a.ka};s_0Va.prototype.Zj=function(){return this.Ea};s_0Va.prototype.aAa=function(){return this.Wa};var

"It's buying copies of the book ten point four million times from the book sellers!"
"Correct. Someone's programmed these servers to buy ten point four million copies of *Dragon's Claw* using the stolen credit card details."

CHAPTER TWENTY TWO

*In which what appears to be padding is
an important trigger for a crucial event.*

"**B**UT WHY WOULD THEY DO that?"

"Beats me, Writer. I don't make up this crap."

We were driving back to police HQ in the Gran Torino, having left Nyquist and his forensic team to make a meticulous search for evidence. I stared out at peaceful, sleepy Clarkesville. How could such a major crime have come to happen here, of all places? As Como had said on page two, it was the kind of thing you'd expect a really crap writer to dream up, and yet I had written it. How were we to make sense of it?

Como read my thoughts. "How are *you* gonna make sense of it, you mean. Aren't you forgetting something?"

Probably.

"What?" I said.

"Tomorrow's Sunday. You can work Sundays if you like, but Clarkesville PD only pays overtime on Sundays for murder, arson or matters of international security, so unless something even weirder than this week's shit crops up, I'm gonna be taking the day off."

I could do with a day-off myself. I hadn't seen my Bronx mom or Barney for almost a week, and the pair of them were hounding me with texts and voicemails, my Bronx mom worrying that I was getting into too much trouble on TV, and Barney worrying that I wasn't getting into enough trouble on TV.

"Como, do me a favour and drop me at the motel. I think I'll go back to New York for the rest of the weekend. I can get back for Monday."

"That's a shame."

"What?"

"You gettin' back for Monday."

"Como!"

"Don't blame me. We were having a peaceful time till you showed up. You've been here three days and I've missed the game, nearly died twice, been chewed out by the Mayor and marked an unmarked police car with a twenty ton digger. And you won't believe the forms I'm gonna have to fill to explain the busted door on the datacentre and the dead guy in the Chevy and the two dead guys in the panel van. It's ok for you. You come down here wreaking havoc and it's me that has to clear up. A day off? I'll need a year off by the time you've finished."

Which reminded me . . .

"So what's going on between you and the Mayor?"

"Nothing."

He said it in the kind of voice I used to use when I was ten and my Bronx mom asked me what I'd been up to in the closet with Rebecca Goldman from next door.

"Como, in spite of what you think, I'm not completely stupid. There must be something going on or the Mayor would have busted you down to patrolman for what you did."

"For what *you* did, you mean. It wasn't me who made up all that crap about nuclear waste."

"No but it was you who . . . who allowed a culture of sloppiness to develop in your department which resulted in a patrolman blabbing about my made-up crap to the local papers. Whoever owns the local papers must be rubbing their hands with . . ."

I had a thought.

"OK, Como. Scouts honour. Does the Mayor own the local papers?"

"Might do."

"Hummf."

So that was it. The dressing down by the Mayor had just been a cover. The patrolman who overheard my made-up call to the head of the FBI had probably told Como about it, and Como had probably leaked it to the Mayor himself so the Mayor could publish a sensational story to boost the sales of her local paper. Corruption was everywhere. You take a nice little town like Clarkesville and you lift the lid a little, and you find the same dirty crooked deals you find everywhere else. I felt dirty myself, as if I needed a shower.

"OK, Writer. This is it."

We'd got to the motel. I stepped out of the car and watched Como burn rubber all down the street. He probably had a relative selling tyres to Clarkesville PD.

CHAPTER TWENTY THREE

In which Barney gives some good advice.

I CRASHED OUT IN THE motel for the night and drove up the N66 to New York the next morning. As I stared through the tinted windows of my black Range Rover, I puzzled over the mysterious case I'd uncovered in Clarkesville. There were so many confusing questions. Why would someone hire a datacentre to buy ten point four million copies of a book with ten point four million stolen credit card details when they've already got the ten point four million copies of the book stockpiled in a warehouse next door? Well, five warehouses really, but that didn't change the question.

I parked in the basement of the Seventh Avenue tower where Barney lived and took the express elevator to his penthouse apartment. Even though I'd rung ahead, I had to buzz the buzzer a few times before he opened the door.

"Markie babeeey! Great to see ya. Come on in."

I went in.

"Great to see you too, Barney."

"How's my boy? I gotta tell you, Markie baby, the world's gagging for your next book. Gagging for it." We walked to his big lounge overlooking the city. On one of the many settees was a young plump blonde in nothing but a satin dressing gown. She looked as if she'd just got out of bed.

"Felicia, go and get that filing done." He slapped Felicia on the butt as she traipsed past. "Felicia does some filing for me."

I wondered why the person who did his filing came to work in a satin dressing gown, but I didn't say anything. If Barney wanted to let his staff take liberties, that was up to him.

"Now, let's get some drinks. Champagne?" He didn't let me answer. "Champagne it is for my star boy. You settle down and I'll get us some fizz."

I didn't settle down. Instead I paced Barney's familiar apartment. There had been a few changes in Barney's life since we'd published *The Awful Truth about the Herbert Quarry Affair*—the apartment for one. He'd also picked up many more clients, as he was now officially the world's most successful literary agent. There was a framed certificate from the Guinness people citing his phenomenal success at exploiting the various rights to my work. Of course, that was good news for me too. As Barney often pointed out, our contract gave me ten cents of every dollar he brought in, so the more he earned, the more I earned.

I looked at the framed photographs along the wall that he called the rogues' gallery (or maybe the rogue's gallery would be more appropriate). The central one, of me with my Bronx mom, was the biggest. His newer clients were either side: Rushdie, Brown, JKR, King, and so on. They reminded me of the celebrity endorsements in *Dragon's Claw*.

And then I came to the end of the gallery, where a hook and a lighter patch of wall showed that a small photograph had once hung there. I asked Barney about it when he returned with the fizz.

"That? That was nothing really—just an old photo of Herbert Quarry."

Herbert Quarry—my mentor and closest friend in the world—had been Barney's first big client. When I wrote *The Awful Truth about the Herbert Quarry Affair*, Herbert had urged me strongly to find another agent. I never got to the bottom of his motive—I assumed some kind of professional jealousy was at work.

"Why did you take it down?"

"Why did I take it down? Come on, Markie, what sort of question is that? He was a sick paedo scumbag. I got tired of telling you. I can't have a picture of a bum like that with my other star boys and girls. Here—have some fizz."

"So where's Herbert now?" I'd lost track of him. Since the success of my last book, he hadn't been in touch.

"I sent him to the Christian Brothers' place in Pasadena. Best place for him."

"The Christian Brothers? Can they cure his paedophiliac tendencies?"

"No, but it'll make 'em stand out less. Cheers." Barney clinked my glass of fizz.

I mentally assessed the number of sales I might lose by alienating the world's Catholics with my cheap joke at the expense of the Christian Brothers. Maybe I'd break my golden rule and edit that later.

"So Markie, don't keep Barney in suspense any longer. Tell me all about the new book." He shepherded me to one of the settees.

"To be honest, Barney, I don't know how it's going to end yet," which was God's literal truth. "I went down to Clarkesville to see Como, and there's something really strange going on there."

"Como! How is that big lug? I never knew he was still on the scene until I saw the pair of you on the TV news. By the way, Markie, that was sensational. Did you see all the footage? Some kid with a phone took a real sweet video of you diving in for the big rescue. Shame those bastards had died so you weren't able to pull anyone out, but even so—it's huge, Markie. Huuge."

"Yeah, Como's good, he's good." I didn't add that he'd become a power-crazed, self-important asshole.

"Great. But what about the story, Markie?"

"Well, we found a dead guy down in the docks squashed under some containers . . ."

"Brilliant!"

". . . and then it all sort of spiralled out of control."

"Out of control. Great."

"We thought we had a prime suspect, but he turned out to be the dead guy."

"Wow! Great twist."

"Then me and Como got slugged and they were going to kill us."

"Kill you!" Barney got up from his chair and started to fret around me.

"Yeah, but it's OK. Como killed the guy who was driving us. I've never seen anything like it. Almost took his head off, and the car rolled right over at least once—maybe a few times—then this other guy tried to finish us off with a gun until I kicked him in the face."

"He's the one you got arrested for, right?"

"Yeah. But that was just Como messing about." It was odd that I now thought of it as messing about. It hadn't felt like messing about at the time.

"Messing about? That wasn't messing about, Markie—that was inspirational PR. I don't suppose you saw the effects, being locked in the slammer, but in the outside world it was crazy. The media went bananas. It was the only thing on the TV news. They had to close down Twitter for three hours because it couldn't cope with the load. Your hashtag was incandescent, Markie, and I mean hot."

"Well, it didn't seem so hot inside." I sipped my fizz. "You ever been in jail, Barney?"

"Never mind all that. Don't you go listening to all those people, Markie. They're just jealous liars. Now what happened next?"

"That's the thing, Barney. It all got weird after that. The bad guys have these warehouses, and they're full of copies of some book called *Dragon's Claw* by a guy called Denis Shaughnessy. You heard of him?"

"Naaah. Sounds like some complete bum."

"Anyway, we found there were ten point four million copies of this book, and a scam to sell all of them with stolen credit card details."

"Ten point four million copies? What was that guy's name again?"

"Denis Shaughnessy." Barney got me to spell it, and he wrote it in his black book. "The weird thing was, Barney, the book was covered in celebrity endorsements, including one by me, and I swear I never read it even. So how does that happen?"

"Kid, I hate to tell you, but you're one big dope sometimes." He moved next to me and put an arm around my shoulder. "The celebrities that give those endorsement—they don't actually read the books. Think about it, kiddo. Think of all the millions of crap books that get published year in and year out, all with bullshit endorsements on the front. What kind of celebrity's got the time to read all that crap?"

It all made sense now that Barney was explaining it, so I'd been right to come to New York to see him. "So how do the endorsements get there?"

"Here, have some more fizz." He topped me up. "That's what agents do. You don't want to be bothered with all that crap, so we agents handle the sweat work."

"So did you put the endorsement in *Dragon's Claw*?"

"Must've done, but don't ask me when, kiddo—there's endorsement requests coming in as fast as losers leaving bookies. I got girls that deal with all that."

I hoped my readers would forgive his rampant sexism. "But why do you do it?"

"Why do you do it? Why do you do anything, Markie? You do it to earn a turn."

"A turn?"

"Sure. I get, maybe, one cent for every endorsement on every book, so if your *Dragon's Claw* sells ten point four mill copies and I've got ten endorsements in that baby you're looking at a cool mill for Barney."

"Well, it's not going to be selling ten point four million copies anymore."

"What?" Barney backed off from me. "Don't go joking like that, Markie—my ticker isn't so good, what with all the stress I take looking after you guys."

"I'm not joking, Barney. Como busted their operation, so the books are just going to stay in the warehouses until someone pulps them."

Barney put his fizz down on the table and stared at his hands before looking at me. "But that's crazy, Markie—we lose a mill! You . . . you . . . could have got ten thou for yourself out of that. Markie, think of what you could have done with ten thou. Can't you go back and get Como to forget all about busting their operation, and cover his tracks?"

I thought of the dead Bulgarians, the smashed panel van, the destroyed datacentre door, the crushed unmarked car, the headlines about nuclear waste, the hours of TV news coverage. No, I didn't think Como could cover his tracks.

"Sorry, Barney. No can do. But when I write it all up in a new book we'll make even more money, right?"

Barney's face brightened. "Right, kid. Have some more fizz. I've got some contracts I need you to sign. You just wait right here."

He went off, and I paced around his huge apartment, feeling a bit dopier than usual because of all the fizz. I noticed another certificate from the Guinness people—this one was for my book, *The Awful Truth about the Herbert Quarry Affair*, which it officially certified as the fastest-selling paperback ever, with total sales of ten point three nine million in a single year. As I stared at the number ten point three nine million something in the very back of my mind tried to get my attention, but then Barney came back in.

"Here, kid, let's get this paperwork out the way, then we can go and hit town. Don't worry about the details—you leave those to me. Just sign where I've put the crosses and let good old Barney worry about the rest."

CHAPTER TWENTY FOUR

In which Marco introduces a pivotal character.

AFTER I'D SIGNED A LOT of contracts and left the rest for good old Barney to worry about, we hit town for lunch. Barney took me to the newest, hottest restaurant where there were queues round the block. We went through the VIP channel with the velvet ropes and were quickly shown to Barney's permanent table. We talked business over the menus.

"Kid, I might have a few more writing jobs for you. You know, like that hush hush stuff for Rushdie."

"Sure, Barney. Whatever. I've got my iPad with me most of the time so fire it over when you like."

"You're a good kid, Markie. Never let anyone say you're not a good kid. Now—isn't that Herbert's big friend?" He pointed with his menu at a slight, elderly gentleman who was being shown to a table on the other side of the room, next to the aquarium with the giant squid.

"Sushing!" I stared with a touch of resentment at the man who'd been slagging me off in special editions of *The New Yorker*.

Barney clicked for a waiter. "I heard he's worth a hundred billion. Must be handy having that sort of dough. Think he needs an agent?"

"I doubt it, Barney. He's meant to be one of the most intelligent people in the world. An autodidact too."

"He can spout as much about cars as he likes, but he might still need an agent. Why don't you go and ask him to join us."

"I'm not so sure about that, Barney. He's not exactly a fan of mine."

I told Barney about the critical article Sushing had written.

"Jesus, Markey, don't be so thin-skinned. Guys like that have opinions about everything, but they don't let them get in the way of good business. Go ahead, ask him."

I left my menu and walked across to the famous billionaire, who was pencilling some calculations on the back of his menu while a waiter hovered uncertainly nearby.

"Professor Sushing?"

He looked up.

"Doctor Ocram. I didn't expect to see you in New York. What a pleasant surprise. I have continued to follow your promising work on tau muons, although I must say that your latest concept of an entangled quantum state of a tau and a muon seems fundamentally unsound. Fundamentally unsound."

I thought it was fundamentally unsound myself, so that wasn't news, but I was surprised that he'd said it twice. "If you are lunching alone, would you like to join me and my companion?" I waved vaguely at Barney who was smiling greasily at us from the other side of the room.

"Ordinarily I would have been delighted, Doctor Ocram, but I have some issues I must resolve as a matter of urgency, for which I need uninterrupted concentration. You may have read the distorted reports in the press about the advice I have been giving to the Republic of North Korea in connection with their ambition to build an inter-continental ballistic satellite launcher. I have one or two calculations that must be checked and sent to them within the next two hours, so I am afraid you must excuse me and pass my sincere apologies to your companion."

"Of course, Professor. Forgive my interruption."

We exchanged final pleasantries and I returned to Barney. "He's too busy with some calculations for North Korea. He said to pass on his apologies."

"I've heard some excuses in my time, kiddo, but calculations for North Korea is a new one. Is he talking about the nukes he's been helping them with?"

"They're not nukes, Barney. He's just helping them make a rocket that can launch satellites. He told me himself."

"Satellites schmatellites. It's all the same, so don't kid yourself, kid. I played golf with Trump yesterday, and we had a bite and a drink or two after. And you know what he said?"

"No, Barney, I don't know what he said."

"He looked me in the eye and he said, Barney, you know that Sushing says he's only helping the North Koreans launch satellites. Yes, I said. Well, answer me this, says Trump. What if those Koreans launch a satellite? And what if they put it in a geo-stationery orbit over Washington DC, you follow me? Sure, I follow you, I said. So what if, says Trump, what if the Koreans put a nuke in the satellite, and one day they send a signal up, and two bomb-bay doors open in that satellite and the nuke drops straight down on the White House. What about that then,

Barney boy? That's what Trump said. So what about that, Markie boy?"

"Barney, that's crazy."

"Crazy? You're telling me Trump is crazy? That guy's worth a billion or two, so he can't be that crazy."

"No, I mean it's literally crazy. Even if there was a nuke in the satellite, and even if they opened a bomb bay, for God's sake, the nuke wouldn't drop out."

"It wouldn't drop out? What are you talking about, Markie—of course it would drop out. That's what bombs do, for crying out loud."

"No it wouldn't, Barney. It's physics. The satellite's in orbit, so the nuke's in orbit too. It's weightless in the satellite, like the astronauts floating around in the space station. If you opened the bomb-bay doors the nuke can't fall out because it's weightless."

"Well, you're saying that, but how can you be so sure? Huh? You won't get me into DC if the Koreans ever put a satellite over it, that's for sure."

My phone blipped. It was a text from a reader saying that geo-stationery shouldn't be spelled with an e. So much for my subtle dig at Trump's literacy.

Over lunch, Barney blabbed on about the latest publishing gossip. I wasn't listening—I was wondering why the Professor had said he was surprised to see me in New York.

CHAPTER TWENTY FIVE

*In which Marco's visit to his caricature
Bronx mom finishes with stunning news.*

AFTER LUNCH WITH BARNEY, I decided to visit my caricature Bronx mom. I drove my black Range Rover with tinted windows over to the building in the Bronx that was the family home. I climbed the familiar stairs to the familial apartment and rang the familiar bell. My mom opened the door.

"Oh my God it's Marci. It is Marci. I knew it. Everyone come and look. It's Marci, I knew it."

"What do you mean you knew it, mom? Who's everyone?"

"Oh Marci, I knew it. I knew you'd be home today. I got everyone round for a little party. Come on, everyone. It's Marci. He's home, just like I knew he would be."

I was dragged by my mom into the living room where a gang of her friends from the hairdresser's were waiting in party hats. They all cheered and let off party-poppers when I came in. There was party food everywhere—my mom must have been cooking for days. Mom dragged me into the middle of the room, covered in paper strands from the party poppers (me that is, not my mom). I waved at all the friends of my mom's I recognised. They were all really thrilled to see me. Mrs. Hiram came over and offered me a plate of matzos.

"Oh Marci, you're looking so grown up now. Your mom had a premonition you'd be home this weekend, and we all told her it was nonsense, but she said no, she knew her Marci and she knew he'd be coming home. So we've been cooking and baking all week for you."

It wasn't much of a premonition, really—I went to my mom's every weekend, but her memory was going, and she'd always been a bit dramatic.

Most of my mom's friends from the hairdresser's were too old or infirm to stand, so they stayed on the sofas talking and eating. My mom introduced me to all of them, as if I didn't know them already.

"This is Mrs. Angelman, Marci. She has three really beautiful daughters and none of them is married yet. I said to Mrs. Angelman that you ought to meet her daughters, Marci. One of them might be just right for you. Say hello to Mrs. Angelman, Marci, like a good boy. Isn't he handsome, Mrs. Angelman? I can just see him with one of your girls in a nice little apartment in the Bronx with six children."

"Mom!" I objected, but she still dragged me along past the front of the sofas to meet all her friends.

"These are Mrs. Hartman and Mrs. Silver—you don't need to speak to them, Marci, all their daughters are married already. And this is Mrs. . . . ."

It went on that way for another twenty minutes, with my mom introducing me to all her friends and telling them how good it would be if I were married to any one of their many daughters in a nice apartment in the Bronx with six kids. After she had introduced me to the last of them and was about to start all over again with Mrs. Angelman, I pulled her into my old bedroom.

"Mom, I don't want to get married just yet."

"What are you saying, Marci? Are you one of those homosexual boys? Tell your mommy, Marci. We can get you treatment."

I winced at her offensively homophobic crack. "Mom, I'm not homosexual, but I just don't want to get married yet. I'm too busy writing."

"Oh, you're writing again! Oh Marci, more writing, that's just what your mom wants to hear. What a sweet surprise for your mom. What are you writing about, Marci? Are you writing about a nice Jewish family with a flat in the Bronx and six nice kids, and . . ."

"No, mom. I'm writing about a criminal conspiracy down in Clarkesville."

"What? Are you crazy? Why do you want to go writing about sick things like that?"

"Mom, I can't explain now. Where's dad?"

"Whaddaya mean you can't explain? No time he has for explaining to his sweet old mom, but he has time to ask about his waster of a father. I don't know why I bore you for nine months, and all that pain when this big head of yours was trying to pop out, but no, he doesn't have time to explain to his poor suffering mom, he's too busy . . ."

"Mom! Just tell me where dad is."

"Where he always is, in the park playing chess. I told him he was a lazy bum and he was getting in the way of our baking so he storms off and I say, what about Marci, what's Marci going to say when he gets in and finds all his mom's friends are there but not his bum of a dad. And he says, Marci's not coming home, so don't kid yourself, and yet here you are, you came to your mommy, Marci, you came to your poor old mommy. Here . . ."

She went to give me a big slobbery kiss.

Luckily my phone rang.

"Como. I thought you were taking the day off."

"So did I, Writer, so did I."

"What's brewing?"

I thought back to the list of things for which Clarkesville PD paid overtime on Sundays and wondered which of them to use as the reason for Como's call.

"Arson."

"Arson?"

"Yeah. Someone's set fire to all the warehouses."

Wow!

"Don't move—I'll be right there." I was speaking metaphorically, of course. It was going to take me hours to drive down the N66 to Clarkesville, even in a top-of-the-range black Range Rover with tinted windows.

"Mom. I've got to go. There's been a big new development in the case. Como needs me."

"But Marci, you can't go now. You can't leave your poor mom with all that food. And you haven't really spoken to any of the guests. And Marci, when can I get you to see Mrs. Angelman's beautiful daughters if you keep going off in cars like this, Marci?"

"I'm sorry mom, I've got to go." I raced through the living room, waving at mom's friends and catching up a couple of slices of matzo as I went.

CHAPTER TWENTY SIX

In which things get serious.

WHEN I GOT TO CLARKESVILLE I didn't need the sat-nav to find the warehouses—I could just drive towards the huge palls of smoke hanging over the industrial quarter of the sleepy town. To simplify the plot, I wrote that Como was at the first one, overseeing the liaison between the PD and the fire and rescue service. He was standing in the road talking to one of the fire crew. I walked up and waited behind him until he'd finished, then put my hand on his broad back.

"How's it going, Chief?"

"How d'you think it's going? It's hot and it's wicked and it's dusty as hell."

Even though the flames had been put out, there was still an amazing heat from the smoking ruins of the warehouse, where bent and twisted skeletons of shelving were draped with thick blankets of ash and burned paper. The heat had whipped up eddies of scorching air laden with soot and smuts. Everything within sight was coated with ash like grey snow, including Como's face. It was strangely lined where drips of sweat had cleared away the ash coating.

"When did it happen?"

"First calls came through about two pm. Warehouse three was torched first. While we were all there trying to put it out, the rest got done. We don't have enough fire trucks to handle them all. I've got every police officer helping out. I've even roped in the retired ones that are fit enough to lend a hand, but we still don't have enough. The US marines are sending over teams from Fort Chandler, but it'll be another hour maybe before they arrive."

I stared at the charred tangle of girders that had once been a building. It seemed such an enormous step for anyone to take, and I struggled to imagine a motive for what I'd written. Although looking on the bright side, it had got me away from my mom and her friends.

"Do you think they were trying to destroy evidence?"

"That's what I don't understand. We've had forensic teams crawling all over the warehouses for nearly a week. If the torcher was trying to destroy evidence they've left it too late. We've got all the evidence we need back at police HQ."

I nodded to show I understood his logic, which, unusually for Como, made perfect sense. Why would they have done this when all the evidence was back at police HQ?

Back at police HQ!?!!!

A thrill ran through me, bringing me keenly alive after the tedium of typing three chapters of mainly dialogue. What if the fires were a diversion?

"Como! It's a feint! The real target's police HQ!"

"Huh?"

"Don't stand there huhing. Can't you see? They've torched the warehouses to get all hands over here putting them out. Who's left at HQ?"

"No one."

"Exactly! C'mon. They'll be torching that next."

"Shit!"

We raced for the Gran Torino, and Como was laying rubber before I'd even shut the door. Luckily, the Sunday streets were almost deserted, so we treated them like our private race track, the roar of the big V8 booming back at us from the fronts of the buildings we passed.

"Aren't you going to radio for back up?" I said, carelessly omitting a hyphen from back-up in my excitement.

"We won't need back-up. If they've torched it we'll be too late, and if they haven't I'll stop them."

There was menace in Como's words. He was the king. Police HQ was the heart of his kingdom. No one was going to take it away from him without a fight.

We were getting close. I could see the radio tower of HQ above the roofs of the surrounding buildings.

"There's no sign of smoke, Como. Maybe we're in time."

Como's reply was to put the Gran Torino into a long, screeching tailspin round the corner into Main Street. He floored the pedal to tear past City Hall, then locked the brakes to skid us to a stop just feet from the steps of the main entrance to police HQ.

"Como, the door!"

The door to HQ was open, one of its glass panels smashed.

Como pulled his semi-automatic from his waistband as he stepped from the car. I followed as he ran up the steps to the door. I didn't have a gun, so I pulled my iPad from my satchel, switched it to video mode, and held it in front of me with maximum menace. The reception was empty. Como nodded me to the doors to the south block. I stepped lightly to the left-hand door and held the handle for further orders. Como nodded. I opened the door, shielding myself behind it, and Como whipped his gun round into the gap.

The corridor beyond was quiet. I spotted an opportunity for a minor cliché, and went back a sentence. The corridor beyond was quiet, too quiet. We stepped down it together, Como fanning his gun across each doorway we passed, I fanning my iPad. We were heading for the forensic suite, where evidence was kept pending assessment or trial. As I wrote these words, I realised that anyone trying to destroy our evidence couldn't just torch the forensic suite. They'd have to check what evidence had been found, and make sure that nothing crucial had been passed to the prosecutor's office, or still be in transit from Flora Moran's labs. That was going to take time, and that explained why such a big diversion had been needed. I was amazed to find one of my plot twists actually making sense. There was a good chance, then, that we would find the ruthless arsonists in the act.

As we crept further down the corridor, I thought of Lieutenant Steve McGee, whose extended family had featured so negatively in my last book. Could he be behind this? I didn't have time to make up my mind, as the doors to the forensic suite were now directly ahead. Como motioned me to repeat the sequence we'd followed earlier. I snatched open the left-hand door, and he whirled round it. There was no one in sight, but someone had obviously been disturbed, as the contents of filing cabinets had been scattered on the floor, and, much to my disgust, one of the computer screens had been left logged in, in clear breach of the Clarkesville County PD usage policy and all the established tenets of good IT security. We stepped in silently.

The forensic suite had a dozen or so rooms off either side of a central hall. The perp, or perps, could be in any or none of them. Como told me to stay put and went to check them one by one, cautiously pushing open each door with his foot while standing to one side of the opening. I walked slowly round the tables and desks in the main hall, videoing the mess made by the intruder. Discarded evidence and documents lay everywhere. Fingerprint cards, hand-written testimonials, knives, guns, drug samples, some in pouches, others wrapped in clingfilm or left unwrapped and tagged.

I was so engrossed with what I was capturing on video, I didn't see a gun that was slowly raised to point at me from a half-open doorway about twenty feet behind my back. I didn't see the subtle movement of the hand that meant the gun was about to be fired, that bullets were about to speed across the small gap and smash into my torso.

But Como did.

"Writer, no!"

It was a huge bellowing roar of fury and concern. From nowhere Como strode to where I stood and pulled me violently behind him. I heard three shots, incredibly loud, then Como staggered back, knocking me to the ground before toppling backwards onto me, his body carrying the bullets that had been meant for mine.

I stared at my iPad. We were in for two chapters of serious shit. I hoped my readers would be able to cope . . .

CHAPTER TWENTY SEVEN

In which Marco creates an episode of pathos entirely out of keeping with the frivolous character of the book.

"COMO! COMO!"

My voice was a desperate scream. I twisted round on the floor and pulled myself from under his legs. He lay on his back, blood pooling beneath him. There was an indistinct movement behind me and I turned just as a figure in black dived through the glass of a window to the car park beyond. In a hot explosion of wrath, I clawed at the gun lying by Como's twitching hand, and I ran to the window. The black figure was opening the door of a silver car. I pointed the gun and pulled the trigger again and again and again and again and again and again and again until it just clicked in my hands. I threw the gun down and ran back to Como, skidding onto my knees.

"Como, Como." I patted his face, just as I had done twenty five chapters ago when he had a fit on his settee at the thought of working with me again. His eyes opened.

"Writer."

It was all he said. I ran to the deserted dispatcher's office. The radio kit was on, voices from the warehouses sounding from the monitors. I picked up the handset, just as I'd seen the dispatchers do on my countless VIP visits to police HQ.

"All officers. All officers. This is Marco Ocram. Your Chief is down. I repeat your Chief is down. We are at the forensic suite. Chief Galahad has taken three shots . . ." My voice started to break as I thought of what Como had done for me . . . "I repeat, he has taken three shots. We need emergency medics NOW!"

A buzz of outrage came from the monitors as the combined staff of the Clarkesville emergency services reacted to my announcement. I listened to enough of the ensuing traffic to be sure that help was on its way, then ran to the first-aid unit, a small office just off reception. I grabbed an armful of swabs and bandages, then raced to the forensic suite.

To my horror the pool of blood had grown. I didn't have any first-aid training, and I usually fainted at the sight of blood, but I had a lifetime's adrenalin surging through me. I wrote what people always wrote when someone had been shot. I ripped open Como's police chief shirt and pulled up the police chief tee-shirt he had underneath. There were two red holes oozing blood. One of the shots must have missed. I felt with my hand under Como's body to check if there were exit wounds, but I just felt unbroken skin. If the bullets were still inside, that might be good news. I tore open packs of the biggest swabs and pressed them gently down on the bullet holes, not sure how much force to use.

I was still there holding them in place and calling Como's name when help arrived.

CHAPTER TWENTY EIGHT

In which Marco is shocked by his previous chapter.

"**Y**OU DID REAL GOOD, MISTER Ocram. You did real good."

I was with Taft and Fovantski, two of Como's most senior detectives. They had led me from the forensic suite, and I'd walked with them unsteadily to the toilets where they'd washed Como's sticky blood off my hands. They took me to the canteen where they'd made me sit with a coffee, although my hands were still too shaky to pick up the cup without spilling it.

"How's he going to be?" I asked.

"Fine. Doc Marten says he's gonna be fine. Now we need you to tell us everything you can remember. What happened?"

"I don't know. I didn't see everything. We were in the forensic suite, and . . ."

"Let me stop you there, Mister Ocram. Why were you in forensics, and why's it all messed up like that?"

"The fires at the warehouses were just a feint. A diversion. Whoever lit them just wanted everyone out of the way so they could break into police HQ and destroy evidence. We caught them in the act. They shot Como!"

The shock of what had happened was starting to hit me.

"They? You said they. Who were they?"

"I didn't mean they. I only saw one person."

"What did they look like?"

"I don't know. I didn't see them."

"The Chief's gun's on the floor by the window, and all the slugs are gone. Did he shoot them?"

"No. I . . . I shot Como's gun. I saw someone break out of the window, the person who shot Como, and I grabbed Como's gun and ran to the window and just fired and fired."

"Did you hit them?"

"I don't know. I didn't properly look. They were trying to get in a silver car, an Audi I think."

"Where was the car?"

"It was over to the right, near the big tree."

There was a big old maple in the middle of the car park. People at HQ were always moaning about how it dripped sap on their cars.

Fovantski nodded at Taft to go and look.

"So how did the Chief get shot?"

"I was videoing the mess in the main hall, just by where you found us. There was evidence everywhere. Como was checking out the side rooms to see if the intruder was still in the building. I heard him shout my name, then suddenly he was there, and there were shots and we fell over and he was bleeding."

"OK, Mister Ocram, you're doing great, but let's just take that last bit again, real slow. How many rooms had the Chief checked when all this happened?"

"I'm not sure. I think he'd done all the ones on the right."

"Which right?"

"The right if you're standing with your back to the entrance."

"OK." She wrote stuff on her pad. "So you hadn't checked any of the rooms on the left?"

"No. I don't think so."

"OK. So where was he, exactly, when he shouted?"

"I don't know. I wasn't looking at anything then except my iPad so I could see what I was videoing."

"But you know roughly where he was?"

"He must have been coming towards me from the last of the rooms on the right, I guess. He'd be crossing over to the rooms on the left."

"And why did he shout?"

"He must have seen that someone had a gun. He was warning me."

"So why didn't he just shoot the guy with the gun."

"I don't know. I guess he might have seen the gun and not had a clear shot of the person holding it. Or maybe he just didn't think it was right to shoot."

Fovantski gave me a look as if to ask whether I was talking about the same Chief Galahad that she was talking about. She was right. My comment about Como not thinking it was right to shoot was nonsense. Como would shoot an armed assailant in the blink of an eye if he could.

"So could the person with the gun have been in one of the rooms on the left, and maybe the Chief could see their arm with the gun but couldn't see enough of the rest of them to give a decent target?"

"Maybe." It sounded as plausible as anything I would have made up, so I went along with it.

"So where was the Chief relative to you when the shots were fired?"

"He was right next to me, but kind of behind me. I was videoing stuff on one of the tables. I guess he saw that someone was going to shoot and he got himself between me and the guy with the gun to protect me."

Fovantski nodded now. That was more like the Chief she knew.

"OK. So the Chief is down. You see a guy going through the window. You grab the Chief's gun and shoot after the guy. Then you drop the gun and radio for help."

"No I didn't radio for help right away. I went back to look at Como first."

"And how was he when you went back?"

"He was fading. There was a lot of blood. He opened his eyes and said my name then passed out."

"He said your name?"

"No, I mean he said 'Writer.'"

My eyes started to moisten again as I recalled the whispered word.

"OK Mister Ocram. Take it easy. You're doing fine. At your own pace."

"I'm OK," I lied. In all my life I'd never found myself writing such an upsetting and unfunny scene.

"So that's when you radioed for help."

"Yes. I knew I couldn't save him by myself, and I thought everybody would be out at the warehouse fires, and that you'd all know what to do if I just radioed to say that he was down."

"That was the smart thing to do, Mister Ocram. You were right on the money there."

Taft came back. "There's lots of glass in the car park by the tree, but no obvious signs of blood."

166

Fovantski looked at me. "You hit the car at least. Not bad shooting from that distance if you're not used to using a gun."

I was gutted. I'd hoped I'd killed the bastard.

"Useful too," added Taft. "Shouldn't be hard to trace a silver Audi with fire-arms damage."

"Better get out a report on that now," said Fovantski.

Taft said OK and left us again to issue a report. I wasn't sure what sort of report they meant, but I guessed it would be a broadcast to look out for a silver Audi with bullet holes.

Just then I saw movement through the doors of the canteen. It was a gurney being wheeled past. I knew Como would be on it. I chased after it, catching up just as it reached an ambulance. Como was bandaged but awake. There was a drip in his arm. He looked at me.

"You saved police HQ from being torched, Writer. I owe you one."

I watched as Como was man-handled into the ambulance— the paramedics straining with his huge weight—then the doors were slammed and it eased off with full lights and sirens. I waved farewell until the ambulance disappeared from sight.

I stared numbly into space, trying to make sense of my emotions. I'd been so used to thinking of Como as a pain in the ass that I'd never realised that he actually meant something to me. And I'd allowed him to get shot just to save my skin. What kind of writer was I? One thing was for sure—someone was going to pay for this. I checked my watch. My mom's face on the dial looked fondly up at me. It was a good thing she hadn't been at police HQ tracking the perp with me and Como. It would have given her a heart attack to see the mess the perps had made.

CHAPTER TWENTY NINE

*In which Marco surprises even
himself with the turn of events.*

I WALKED WEARILY BACK TO the forensic suite. The sight
of its double doors reminded me that the last time I'd
approached them, I'd been wondering whether to implicate
Steve McGee in the break-in. To my mind, a leopard's nephew
had just as many spots as the leopard, more or less. In my last
book, Steve McGee's uncle had tried to murder Como and me,
having murdered defenceless Lola Kellog and framed Herbert
Quarry for her grisly death. With an uncle like that, what were
the chances that Steve McGee's record would be spotless? And
besides, he'd inflicted a nasty hand shake on me, so there was a
score to settle there, too.

Pushing through the doors, my keen author's eye alighted
on the computer that had been left logged-in in breach of the
most basic rules of computer security. I would have sharp words

to say to Como about this once he was well enough to discuss it. In the meantime, I decided to exploit it for an opportunistic plot twist.

I pulled over a chair and peered at the screen.

The computer showed a message that said: *'Hello McGeeSJ.'*

Hmmmmm—my suspicions seemed well-founded. If McGeeSJ wasn't the computer-name of Steve McGee, then I'm not the unpredictably inventive author that my readers know and love. There was one way to be sure.

I clicked a link labelled 'My Account.'

The screen refreshed, and there was the proof I needed—a page listing the personal details of McGeeSJ, which included the surname McGee, the forename Steve, the rank Lieutenant, and, most telling of all, a mug-shot of the villain himself.

On a hunch, I paged down to see if there was any other incriminating detail, and guess what I saw.

Car: AUDI (SILVER).

Ha! So the silver Audi I'd shot was Steve McGee's. I knew it would be.

I also knew what would be coming next—what perps always did when their cars were implicated in a crime. Any minute now, Steve McGee would report that his car had been stolen, so that when it was found full of bullets he could say it was nothing to do with him. Or better still, he'd get his wife to report it, so it looked less obvious, with some crummy story to explain why it had only just been reported. It was the oldest plot twist in the book (so far, anyway). I wagged my head at the thought of how predictable it all was. If that was his plan, I'd write a pre-emptive strike and go round to his house and confront him about it.

I read his home address from the 'My Account' screen.

Back in the car park, I made a convenient continuity error and climbed into my black Range Rover, hoping my readers wouldn't remember that I'd left it at a burnt-out warehouse three chapters ago. I punched McGee's address into the sat-nav, then pootled slowly out of the car park. I didn't feel like burning rubber when Como wasn't there to enjoy it.

As I slavishly followed the sat-nav's unimaginative instructions, I thought about the horrendous corniness of the unfolding events. I reckoned that the 'stolen car' excuse appeared in at least half the episodes of Wallander in the boxset my Bronx mom got me when I was bed-ridden with a bad verruca. It was practically the first dodge a crime-writer learned, and yet still there were villains like Steve McGee who seemed to think they were being clever by using it. Well, he'd met his match this time.

When the sat-nav told me to get out of the car and walk up Steve McGee's drive, I looked through my tinted windows to get a feel for the neighbourhood. It seemed a respectable area, with no obvious street-crime, prostitutes or drug-pushers—quite different from my Bronx mom's place. McGee's house had a well-kept lawn and a garage to the far side. I walked up the path and pressed the buzzer at the front door. This was going to be good. I couldn't wait to hear them trot out their lame excuse about their car being stolen.

A sobbing woman opened the door, an emulsion of tears and mascara dripping down her cheeks. Ha!

"My name's Ocram. I'm here on the authority of Police Chief Galahad."

"But . . . but . . . how can you be here so quickly? I've only just phoned the emergency line."

So, she'd rung-in the pathetic lie already.

"Let's just say that I suspected something might have happened, and I knew Chief Galahad would want me to be here to offer support in the moment of your loss." I could be just as melodramatic as she about the whole sorry charade.

"Oh, you're so kind." She lunged at me, and clung to me, her head on my chest, heaving with sobs. I admit her histrionics were an unusual twist. If that was the way she wanted to play it . . . I patted her hair soothingly.

"It must have been a terrible shock."

"It was. It was like a nightmare."

"And the car's definitely gone?"

"Yes," she wailed. "What am I going to do? What about the poor children?"

They can walk to school, I thought—get some weight off them. "Do you know when it happened?"

This is where she'd come out with some story to cover the fact that the car hadn't been reported stolen earlier.

"No. I've been at my parents' house all day. I've just got back. The children are still there, and they don't know anything about it. How can I tell them?" She started wailing again.

"I don't suppose you have an idea of who might have done it?" Of course she wouldn't.

"No! No! I can't believe anyone could do it. They must be sick, or on drugs. It's inhuman."

"Of course. How did you find out it had happened?"

"I walked back from my parents' and I saw the garage door open, and I walked over, and . . ." She burst into incoherent blubs and gasps.

"Can I see?"

Unable to speak, she answered with tearful nods. I headed to the garage. Apart from the over-acting, which was actually quite convincing, it had been a textbook example of the corny my-car-was-stolen routine. I wondered what other nice touches they might have prepared for me at the garage—perhaps they would have bent the door a bit to make it look as if someone had broken in.

I reached the garage and looked in.

The body of Lieutenant Steve McGee was roped to a chair in a pool of congealed blood.

CHAPTER THIRTY

In which Marco plays for time.

I CLUTCHED THE GARAGE DOOR and muttered a choice oath. For a few seconds I was incapable of thought, let alone a meaningful sentence. This should have been my moment of sarcastic triumph, the moment in which I would put a series of questions to Steve McGee that proved beyond doubt that he had shot his Chief, made his getaway, then invented a stolen car story to explain the bullet holes in his silver Audi. I'd had it all prepared. I'd even imagined the ironic tones in which I would have sympathised about the low-life who had pinched his car. And now . . .

Now, all that thinking was wasted. That would teach me for failing to follow Herbert Quarry's advice. I should have just written the first thing that came into my head. Well, I wasn't going to make the same mistake twice . . .

THE AWFUL TRUTH ABOUT THE SUSHING PRIZE

I swivelled my eyes systematically, playing them over the interior of the garage like powerful searchlights. Resisting the temptation to pad out a paragraph with irrelevant details of the garage's contents—such as the four bicycles, two of which were touchingly the bikes of young children who would now tragically miss their daddy; the cans of paint, lubricants and fuel; the ladders, golfing equipment, extension leads, Christmas lights, galoshes (or wellies if you're reading the English version), old newspapers, a lockable chest-freezer (lockable, note) with heavy boxes stacked on top (heavy, note), power tools, spare fluorescent tubes, an odd bent bit of weld-mesh that must have once been used for something, empty cat-litter tray, cat-box, vice, work-bench, pressure-cleaner, trays full of fasteners sorted by length and diameter, car-cleaning sundries, wheel-barrow, lawn-mower, lengths of chain, a snow shovel, paint brushes, sand-paper in various grades of abrasiveness, a half-used bag of cement, drainage pipes, buckets, pressure-cleaner, sorry I've already said pressure-cleaner, watering can, gardening gloves, sledge, inflatable boat and paddles—resisting, as I say, the temptation to pad the word-count by listing such things, I focussed on a black sports bag on a shelf at the back.

I'd seen a sports bag just like it twenty three chapters ago—the one Como found full of money in Timo Tsatarin's apartment.

Using my propelling pencil to avoid leaving fingerprints, I pulled the zipper open and eased the bag's sides apart. Yes—there was a smelly old towel, just as there had been at Tsatarin's. I lifted it out with my pencil, wrinkling my nose at the whiff, and . . . no, there was no money underneath. Bummer. Mind you, who would be stupid enough to leave a bag full of money in a garage? I should have known better.

My self-recriminations were interrupted by the wailing of sirens. The emergency responder team had arrived in response to Steve McGee's wife's emergency call. I walked out of the garage to find a young patrolman pointing his pistol at me.

"Gee, Mister Ocram, you gave me a shock. I thought you might have been the perp."

"I'm sorry, Collins," I said, in a kindly avuncular way, for I was fond of the young man. "I'm afraid the perp is long gone. The body's in here." I nodded over my shoulder at the garage. Collins holstered his gun, and we went in together.

"Jeez," said Collins when he saw the body. He apologised for his blasphemous ejaculation, "Sorry, Mister Ocram."

"Quite alright." It was only natural that an impressionable young police person should express startled emotion at a gruesome sight the hardened thriller-writer barely noticed.

Collins put on plastic gloves and carefully examined the body. McGee had been killed with a knife, after some preliminary work on his fingernails, presumably with pliers that lay near the chair. Someone had tortured him.

Collins stumbled outside and was sick in Steve McGee's dahlia bed. I knew how he felt—the cliché count was making me nauseous too.

"You OK?"

"Yeah. Sorry, Mister Ocram. I guess Chief Galahad doesn't react like that when he sees dead bodies."

No, but he has plenty of other objectionable behaviour traits, so don't be too hard on yourself, I thought, but didn't say.

"Poor Nancy," he said, looking to where Steve McGee's wife was still sobbing on her front step. "I better get back-up."

Collins radioed HQ, giving a precis of the circumstances and requesting various types of support.

Ten minutes later, the various types of support were providing various types of support in and around the McGees' place. Conveniently, one of them was Fovantski, thus saving us the bother of a completely new character. The three of us— Fovantski, Collins and I—were in the garage speculating about what might have happened. I switched to 'movie-script mode' to make it easier to show who was saying what:

FOVANTSKI
So, as I see it, the perp or perps must have had a gun. Steve McGee wouldn't have sat in a chair for no one, knife or no knife.

COLLINS
(Nodding absently.)
That's true.

MARCO
(Points finger in the air in a clichéd gesture announcing a thought.)
Unless he was drugged or sapped first.

COLLINS
(Nodding absently.)
That's true.

FOVANTSKI
No. There's no sign of a blow to the head, and McGee would be a bit heavy to move if he was drugged. I don't buy the drugs theory.

MARCO
(Staring blankly at corpse, waiting for inspiration, says
nothing.)

COLLINS
(Nodding absently.)
That's true.

FOVANTSKI
The more I think about it the more I think two perps. McGee's
a wily fox. He ain't gonna let someone tie him to a chair, gun or
no gun. Someone with a gun gets close enough to Steve McGee
to tie him to a chair, that someone ain't gonna have the gun
much longer, that's for sure.

Marco places hand over Collins' mouth to stop him saying
'That's True.'

MARCO
Could be. Though I definitely saw only one perp at police HQ.

FOVANTSKI
That doesn't stop there being two perps here. Perhaps one of
them went to torch the warehouses. Or here's an idea for you—
perhaps you only saw one perp crash out of the window
because the second perp's still there at HQ.

Close-up on Marco's perplexed face as he considers Fovantski's
remarkable suggestion.

MARCO
(Thinking in voice-over.)

Could there still be someone hidden away at Police HQ? Might they have sneaked out while I went radioing for help? Perhaps it had been a police officer—they could have come out when back-up had arrived, mingling with colleagues. This is going to take more working-out than I can manage.

Fovantski crouches to inspect Steve McGee's tortured fingers.

FOVANTSKI
Either way, we need forensics.

MARCO
(Says next thing that enters head, hoping subconscious will come up with way forward.)
That's true.
(Looks bitterly at Collins.)

FOVANTSKI
Where the hell's Nyquist?
(Checks time on watch.)

MARCO
(Remembering that Nyquist is the forensic specialist.)
When Nyquist arrives, get him to check that black sports bag for prints.

Fovantski and Collins exchange troubled looks.

MARCO
(Sternly.)
Is there something wrong, gentlemen?

COLLINS
Gee, Mister Ocram, we're not sure that's possible.

MARCO
(Looks around for a desk to thump.)
Nothing's impossible when I'm investigating a murder.

FOVANTSKI
(With trepidation.)
It's just that . . . Chief Galahad has issued orders not to let you interfere anymore in the case.

MARCO
Ha! He has, has he? We'll see about that. Very well, gentlemen. I will not insist. However, let me tell you that Chief Galahad found an identical black sports bag in Timo Tsatarin's apartment—a bag containing more than twenty thousand dollars. I suspect that the Chief will be very disappointed indeed if he finds that his officers have not spotted the link and have failed to take fingerprints from the matching bag here.

FOVANTSKI
Thanks for the heads up, Mister Ocram. We'll get the bag printed, but it would be great if you didn't let the Chief know you asked us to.

COLLINS
(Nodding absently.)
That's true.

CHAPTER THIRTY ONE

In which Marco uses a conversation with Como to recap the latest events for the benefit of his struggling readers.

I BOUGHT GRAPES AND HEADED for the hospital. I wondered how Como would be. My nightmare scenario was that the two bullets have taken out his kidneys, and he's found to have some rare genetic condition that means only one person in a million is a suitable donor, and they ask for volunteers to be tested, and I volunteer just to show I care, and they find that I have the same condition, and Como's only chance of living a normal life is if I give him one of my kidneys, and I agree to do it, and the operation is a success, and when I come round from the anaesthetic I find I have to convalesce for two weeks in the bed right next to Como's. That would drive me nuts.

However, when I got to his ward, Como was sitting up watching a game, a bandage tight around his middle.

"Hey, Writer."

We high-fived, or fist-bumped, or thumb-twingled, or whatever the latest thing is.

"I brought you some grapes."

"Right." Como looked at the almost bare stalks where I'd absent-mindedly eaten most of the grapes on the drive over.

"How're the wounds?"

"They'll heal. What happened after I went down? I heard shooting."

"I saw the perp jump out of the window, and I let him have it with your gun."

"Is he dead?"

"Not exactly."

"Is he alive enough to talk?"

"Could be."

"Could be?"

"To tell the truth, Como, I'm not completely sure I hit him."

"Shit, Writer, I heard six shots. You didn't get him with any of them?"

"No, but they think I hit his car."

"Good shooting. Next time I need to hit a barn door from ten paces I'll ask you along for advice."

"It's easy to be sarcastic, but don't forget I've never used a gun before."

"That's true. At least you worked out which was the shooty end. Could have been messy otherwise. They found the car?"

"No, but we think it's Steve McGee's."

"Steve McGee? Don't give me that shit. I told you before— I'd trust my life to Steve McGee. He might have wanted to shoot you, granted, but there's no way he would have shot me."

"No, we know he didn't do the shooting, Como—he's dead."

"Dead?" Como gave up trying to find the few grapes left, and stared at me. "Dead?"

"Yeah. And not just ordinary dead. He was roped to a chair, tortured, and had his throat cut."

"For fuck's sake, Writer. All that's going on, and you got me in here with bullet holes? I need to be protecting my people."

"You can't, Como—you need to rest. If you move too much you could start to bleed internally. And then gangrene could set-in. Or you might get some flesh-eating superbug." There'd be a lot of flesh to eat, mind you.

"You're a big comfort."

"Anyway, you can put me in charge, and I'll make sure everything runs smoothly in your absence."

"Ha. You couldn't make a ball-bearing run smooth in a barrel of grease. There's no way I'm leaving you in charge."

"But Como . . ."

"Don't you go 'but Como'-ing me. I already told you, when you wanted to do the 'good cop, bad cop' routine with old Chief McGee—you're not a cop, you're a writer. You sure forget things in a hurry."

I hadn't forgotten. In my last book, I'd wanted to play the bad cop in the 'good cop, bad cop' routine when we interviewed one of the baddies, but Como pointed out that I was a writer, not a cop, so we ended up doing the 'good cop, bad writer' routine, with me as the bad writer, which had caused no end of cheap jokes at my expense. You don't forget a thing like that easily.

"Anyway," said Como, ignoring my pained look. "I put Kojak in charge till I'm out of here. He knows what's what."

"OK, have it your way. But there's one thing I need to check in McGee's garage. I need to look in his lockable chest freezer with heavy cartons stacked on the lid."

Como looked at me with less than utter respect. "And why, exactly, do you need to go looking there?"

"McGee was killed in his garage. His car's missing. Someone used his account to log in to the police evidence database, so he was probably tortured for his password. But why would they pick on McGee if he wasn't already involved in some way? According to Fovinski—or was it Fovantski?—McGee was tough, so he wasn't a guy you'd pick if you just wanted to steal a car and get someone's password."

"That's true," said Como, sounding disturbingly like dozy Collins from the last chapter.

"I found a black hold-all in McGee's garage that was exactly the same as the one you found in Tsatarin's house. It even had a sweaty towel."

"Two black hold-alls with two sweaty towels aren't going to convince a jury, Writer."

"I know, I know. I've been thinking about it ever since I left the garage. Suppose McGee's been in on the scam. Maybe taking protection money. Tsatarin hands it over in black sports bags. Where's McGee going to hide it?"

"You tell me."

"In the chest freezer. Why else would you stack a whole pile of heavy boxes on a chest freezer? It's a classic hiding place, straight out of Wallander."

"Straight out of a fucking fairy story, more like. Listen. Steve McGee is a McGee, which means he's related to half of the most important people in Clarkesville. He's been tortured in the line of duty. His wife will be out of her mind with grief. You start implicating him in the *Dragon's Claw* crap now and you're going to have every vigilante in town after your sorry ass. There's no way I'm going to sanction a search of McGee's freezer without more evidence—heavy cartons or no heavy cartons. You wanna search it—that's up to you, but don't let anyone catch you doing it, because police officers get mighty protective when one of their kind's been killed, and they won't take kindly to you stirring up mud."

"When did I ever stir up mud?"

CHAPTER THIRTY TWO

In which Marco writes the first act of a set piece,
not yet knowing how the second will unfold.

IT WAS DARK. I WAS parked by the McGee house. There were no lights inside. The scene-of-crime team had finished their preliminary investigation. Nancy McGee had been sedated and driven to Steve McGee's parents' place. The garage was taped off with police crime scene tape.

I donned a black balaclava and black gloves—it was a freezing night. I slipped out of my black Range Rover with tinted windows, having first spent half-an-hour puzzling over the handbook to find how to stop the courtesy lights coming on when I opened the door.

After leaving Como looking for the last grape, I'd called at an all-night army surplus store and bought some equipment, including the latest fourth-generation night-vision device, which was now strapped to my head. I padded over the street and up the McGee's drive. I felt oddly self-conscious, because the bright view afforded by the night-vision headset made me think I was standing out as clearly as my surroundings. I went up the path beside the house and found the side door of the garage. It was unlocked. I eased it open and stepped inside, closing it behind me.

McGee's body had gone—probably to Flora Moran's lab— but a circle of his blood was congealed like a huge scab on the concrete floor. I went to the freezer and started to shift the boxes from its lid. They were a dead weight. Full of books, I imagined.

I'd shifted four of them before I made the connection— books!

I was getting slow. I pulled one of the boxes open and wondered if any of my readers would be surprised that it was neatly filled with copies of *Dragon's Claw*. Ha! It's amazing really. I honestly hadn't thought of putting the *Dragon's Claw* books into the boxes until right now when I typed it. That's the power of Herbert Quarry's advice.

I moved the rest of the boxes, then lifted the lid of the freezer. At least I tried to—it was locked. Now in full cliché mode, I opened the utility pouch strapped to my thigh and removed the latest fourth-generation freezer-lock gun. I inserted its delicate probe in the key-slot and pumped the handle until the over-ride valve clicked. Then I turned the gun to open the lock.

The next thing that happened is that I nearly blinded myself. A light inside the freezer flared in my latest fourth-generation night-vision goggles like a nuclear blast. I tore off the goggles and stuffed them in my utility pack, then started to empty the freezer, tears streaming down my cheeks.

The freezer was full of the highly processed food that fuels America's obesity tragedy. Resisting the temptation to make a long and stupid list of the food-stuffs, having recently done something similar with the contents of the garage, I worked my way down through the layers of the freezer's contents. I forced a gap between some boxes of pizzas, and there was the white floor of the freezer.

There was only frozen food. No money.

I cursed. How could there be no money? Who stacks heavy boxes on the lid of a lockable chest-freezer unless there's something dodgy in it? If not money, then at least there should be weapons, or body parts, or the blueprint for a nuclear sub, or a stolen Picasso—something other than just frozen food. Then I remembered something from *The Sopranos*, or was it *CSI Miami*? I looked among Steve McGee's tools until I found a tape. I measured the depth of the freezer on the outside, then on the inside. There was an eight-inch difference.

Yes! I punched the air.

I took out everything that was in the freezer, stacking it in stacks on the floor. I could see a definite gap between the inside bottom of the freezer and its sides. I got a screwdriver and prized open the gap, lifting a false floor away. Underneath the false floor was money, lots of money, sealed in clear plastic bags. I pulled one out and wiped the frost off the plastic. The notes were tens. There must have been nearly a million dollars. Wow! I wondered if my readers were as excited as I was.

I got my iPad and videoed enough to show the false bottom with lots of money underneath, then I put everything back in the freezer, re-locked the lock, and stacked the cartons of *Dragon's Claw* back on top. Quite why I did all that, rather than leaving the freezer empty, was a bit of a mystery to be honest, but it was the first thing that came into my head, so at least I didn't waste any time on pointless planning.

I put on my fourth-generation night-vision goggles, suddenly realising I should have done it two sentences ago so that I could see to re-lock the freezer. For a moment I wondered if I should break my golden rule and go back to re-write the sequence. No— any readers pedantic enough to be worried about mistakes like that would have thrown away the book chapters ago.

I eased open the side door and stepped out of the garage. A car was slowing to a stop at the bottom of the McGee's drive. A car with its lights off. I froze in the deeper darkness at the end of the walk-way between the garage and the house. Two dark, swarthy-looking men got out of the car and walked towards me. I did the first thing that came into my head, and slipped back through the side door into the garage.

I think it was at this point in my writing career that I first seriously questioned Herbert Quarry's mantra about writing the first thing that came into one's head. I had just put myself inside the very place that the two swarthy-looking men were likely to be headed—two swarthy-looking men who might have tortured Steve McGee with pliers. I looked around for ideas. I didn't find any. There was no key, so I couldn't lock the door. Trying to barricade it would make too much noise and take too long. Running out of options, I decided to stand where I'd be hidden behind the side-door when the swarthy-looking men opened it.

Quite what I was going to do after the swarthy-looking men opened the side-door I never found out, because they opened the main door instead.

CHAPTER THIRTY THREE

In which tension mounts unbearably.

THROUGH MY NIGHT-VISION GOGGLES I saw a crack opening under the main door, then I saw the feet and legs of the two men. Before the door rose higher, I did something sensible for a change and dodged behind the inflatable dinghy leaning against the back wall of the garage. Behind my rubbery nautical shelter I opened my mouth wide to minimise the noise of my gulping breaths. I was more scared than I ever had been in my entire life. The pliers they'd used to torture Steve McGee might have been taken away in an evidence bag, but when I thought of all the remaining tools that could be put to effective use by a pair of imaginative sadists, I almost pooped.

I heard the treads of the men as they came inside, then whispering that sounded something like this:

"Porolskoy portendyabr ilgul dent racht."

"Nah—djutfresco rnadlent deep freeze jhgeslot."

"Karprut chenasksy dredenyag opritchelvi nskapul *Dragon's Claw.*"

"Schtup?"

"Darah, darah!"

That decided, they heaved all the cartons off the freezer. I wondered whether the freezer lock would stop them. A cracking noise, of the sort made by a freezer lock and crowbar, told me it wouldn't. After further whispered consultations, I heard the packets of frozen food being lifted out and dropped on the floor.

I was just starting to think there was a chance they'd find the money and leave without spotting me, when my Bronx mom called my mobile. *Que Sera Sera* burst from my anorak pocket, sounding like a hundred decibels in the suspenseful silence of the garage.

They say that when you are about to die your life flashes before your eyes. Not true. What flashed before my eyes was a catalogue of plot twists that might have helped me avoid being tortured to death by interrupted Bulgarians. For example:

"A sink hole?" Como took one of my proffered grapes. "Steve McGee's garage fell down a sink hole?"

"Not all of it, only the front half."

"Jesus." He picked out the pip from his mouth and looked at it before dropping it into a vase of flowers on his side table. "I ain't never heard of a sink hole in this town before."

"The City engineers say it was caused by a chronic leak from the water main to the McGee's house. It had been undermining the front of the garage for years. They said it was a miracle it hadn't happened earlier."

"And there were two Bulgarian guys found in the hole?"

"Yeah. Weird, isn't it."

"I think your weird and my weird are two different things, Writer. And the Bulgarians are dead?"

190

"As dodos. The garage had pre-cast concrete rafters that fell on top of them. Flora thinks they died instantly." Which was a shame, since a bit of suffering would have been nice.

"And tell me again, what exactly were you and the Bulgarians doing in the garage?"

And that was one of the less bizarre and improbable, so you can imagine what the rest were like. But before I could decide whether sinkholes were a better bet than the arrival of an alien craft from planet Zog, something else happened.

Without thinking, I tried to kill the call from my Bronx mom, and my elbow banged into the inflatable dinghy, toppling it with an almighty slap onto the garage floor. The light from the open freezer overloaded my night-vision kit, and to the thundering chorus of *Que Sera Sera* I stepped blindly forward to meet my doom.

Above the noise I then made by falling into the inflatable dinghy, the baddies shouted what I took to be Bulgarian expletives too coarse to be printed in full:

"M*******a t**********y!"

"C***e ! B**j z***q!"

Banging my shins on the rim of the dinghy's transom, I shouted a few expletives of my own, then courageously curled into the foetal position in the bow of the boat.

"Don't torture my fingers! Don't torture my fingers! Please don't torture my finders! I need them for . . . for texting my mom."

I screwed my eyes tight shut, along with another part of my anatomy best left nameless, and strained my ears for indications of the baddies' intentions.

I heard running steps heading away down the drive! Were the baddies going to get their tools of torture from the trunk of the car?

I heard the car doors open and close! Had the baddies climbed inside for a private conference about the best way to torture a mega-selling writer?

I heard the car screech off! Were the baddies going for reinforcements?

After a minute's silence, I raised a puzzled head over the bow of the boat, hardly able to believe I was alone, alive, and with fingers intact. Slowly I worked out what had frightened the baddies away. With my night-vision head-set, my clumsy blinded gait, and my outstretched arms probing ahead of me, I must have tottered out of the dark like the worst possible combination of Frankenstein's monster and Robo-cop. No wonder they'd screeched off. Suddenly needing to find a toilet, I got into my own car and screeched off too.

CHAPTER THIRTY FOUR

*In which Marco tees up a visit to
Professor Sushing in Panama.*

"OK, PEOPLE, LISTEN UP. LET'S hear what Ocram has to say. Over to you, Writer."

We were in Como's private ward at the Firearms Injury Unit of the Clarkesville County Hospital. Como had called a case conference. He was sitting in bed in pyjamas. Around him his team sat or stood—hardened and capable veterans waiting cynically for the news I was about to write.

I got up from the wheelchair in which I had been sitting for sympathy, and went step by step through the logic that had led me to suspect Steve McGee, beginning with his blood-ties with the disgraced murderers from my last book. At first my words met with the resentful looks of a tight fraternity hearing criticism of a brother, but the cumulative impact of my evidence became too compelling to doubt when I described the black hold-all—now confirmed as bearing Timo Tsatarin's finger-prints—and the damning significance of the money in the locked chest-freezer covered with heavy cartons.

What really got them on my side, however, was the news of how I had bravely tracked two Bulgarian felons into the garage, then frightened them off. The revelation prompted a round of spontaneous applause—a tribute I acknowledged with typical humility.

Como interrupted my high-fiving with the team.

"OK. I want fast action. I want a full forensic analysis. We need prints and DNA from everything in that garage, and then we need to see what they match, including the databases of Interpol, Europol, and Bulgaropol. Is that clear? Good. Now, Fovinski, what have we found about the deceased from the panel van?"

"Both Bulgarians, Chief," said Fovinski, in a continuation of my disgraceful racial stereotyping. "Here with tourist visas. Living at an apartment in Barton Hills. The apartment's leased by Invenmeste EDF, the same Panamanian company that leases the warehouses. Their IDs are fake, but good fake. Their cell-phones were what we normally call burners, but to spell it out for Mister Ocram so he can explain it to his readers, that means they were bought for cash with no contract for service. The history shows they were mainly used to call other burners, but there were some calls to landline numbers in Panama and North Korea, which we're trying to trace."

Good luck with that, I thought.

"Taft," said Como, "what's the latest from the container port? Have they found who erased the movement logs for the container that squashed Tsatarin?"

"Not yet, Chief. They need a software upgrade to get an audit module added to the system, and the Port Authority has to go through an open tendering process because the module's going to cost more than twenty five thou."

"How long will that take?"

"They're fast-tracking it, Chief. Should have it done in . . ." Taft consulted his notes . . . "nine months."

"Jeez." Como picked frustratedly at his bandages. "What other leads have we got?"

In the tumbleweed silence that followed, the team picked at its fingernails, examined the soles of its shoes, wiped smudges from the screens of its iPhones, and so on.

I filled the vacuum. "It seems to me, Como . . . er . . . Chief, that the only concrete leads are Investmente EDF in Panama and the Peluxes Press in North Korea."

"That's a big comfort."

I ignored Como's unhelpful sarcasm. "I know someone with interests and connections in both those countries." I went on to explain my relationship with Professor Sushing, the famous billionaire polymath, feeling a growing respect from the team as I did so.

"Think he can help?" said Como.

"It's our only hope."

There was a minute of silence as Como and his team absorbed the solemnity of my words.

"Where does this Sushing guy hang out?" said Como.

"He has bases all over the world, but his HQ is in Panama."

"Panama? Shit," said Como, lowering the tone I had been slaving to raise. "It's hard enough to get the Mayor to pay for gas for the prowlers. I don't see her agreeing to pay for flights to Panama so we can chase the world's weakest lead on the world's weirdest case."

I couldn't believe what I was hearing, even though I'd just typed it. Here I was, halfway through what had the makings of a mega-seller, and the whole project's threatened by the parsimony of a petty local bureaucrat. No wonder the country was going to the dogs.

I put up my hand.

"Yes, Writer? You got something good to tell us for once?"

"To relieve the Clarkesville PD of the financial burden of overseas travel, I was going to offer to fly to Panama myself to see if I can wheedle information out of my contact."

Como clapped his hands for action.

"What are we waiting for, people? I want Mister Ocram at the airport five minutes ago."

CHAPTER THIRTY FIVE

In which Marco pontificates.

IT TOOK COMO'S PEOPLE SLIGHTLY longer than minus five minutes to get Mister Ocram to the airport.

I had to go to the motel to pick up some clothes and use the loo, and my mom called and I answered without realising who it was. She gave me a hard time about killing the call she'd made while I was hiding behind the rubber dinghy. When I told her about the two murderers and the million dollars in the freezer, she thought I was just making up rubbish for another of my stupid books, which was unusually perceptive of her. In the end I told her I had to catch a flight to Panama, which triggered another five minutes of lectures about clean underwear and foreign food before I managed to shush her with twelve 'bye mom's. Then, just as the cavalcade of police cars and motorcycle escorts was sweeping me into the drop-off area of Terminal Four at Clarkesville International Airport, I realised I'd left my passport at the motel, and we had to cavalcade back for it, using cavalcade as a verb for the first time in publishing history.

By the time I'd settled into the VIP lounge, I needed the soothing ministrations of the attentive staff, who kindly made me a superfood infusion. While I was sipping it, I texted Barney to let him know that I was heading to Panama to see Sushing, then flicked through the various local and international newspapers provided for the VIP short of intellectual stimulus. My activities were front-page news in most of them. 'Ocram Thwarts Million Dollar Heist', was a typical headline, above stories that described how I had single-handedly fought off a gang of Bulgarian hard-men. There were quotes-a-plenty from Barney, who exhorted the public to read the true story when my next book was published.

My next book . . . with all the excitement I'd forgotten that I'd been meant to be writing my next mega-seller. I looked at my fellow VIPs seated here and there in the quiet spacious lounge, most re-reading their well-handled copies of *The Awful Truth about the Herbert Quarry Affair*. How was I to follow that brilliant debut? I opened my satchel and searched for my most treasured possession—a framed photograph of Herbert signed in his own hand 'To my friend Marco. Never forget—always write the first thing that comes into your head.' It was advice that had never let me down before, and it gave me new heart now.

Inspired, I looked up to see the Pope walking through the automatic doors, his passport and tickets in one hand and a drink in the other. I had met him in Valparaiso, where we had a dinner over which we discussed *The Awful Truth about the Herbert Quarry Affair*, its many implicit religious messages, and how it had given him new insights into humanity's role in the world. He saw me and came straight over, lighting up the lounge with that smile of his. I stood, and we shared a long, warm embrace of genuine affection.

"It is a pleasure meeting your supreme holiness again."

I acknowledged his words with a shrug of humility.

"Where are you travelling, my friend?"

I told him I was bound for Panama.

"What a holy miracle. I am heading there too. What seat do you have?"

We compared our seat numbers and found we were in separate rows. He spoke crossly in Latin to his entourage, then said in English, "They will sort it so we can sit together, my friend. I have so many questions to ask about your book, and about tau muons, of course. Ah, but they are calling our flight already. Come, come."

We made our way through the duty-free, where the Pope picked up some perfume—for 'a friend'—and a bottle of Jack Daniels in case we got thirsty on the flight, then we settled into our seats in the first class cabin.

"So tell me, my friend, is it true that you are at work on another book at last?"

"I'm about half way through, doing some research for the second half."

"Ah yes, the research. That must be very important. The book has to be accurate and convincing in its details, yes?"

"Absolutely. It is one of my golden rules. Credulity is like an elastic band."

"In what way, my friend?"

"You can only stretch it so far, and then it breaks." Actually, it was one of Herbert's golden rules.

"Ah, very good. It is good to have golden rules. I have some myself, but you have to break some now and again, eh?" He patted the bottle of Jack Daniels and gave me a broad wink.

"Could you tell me, in secrecy of course, anything of your new book?"

I gave him a summary of the strange events since my breakneck dash to Clarkesville—the warehouses full of books, my escapes from death, my rescue attempt in the river, and how I had scared off a horde of swarthy Bulgarian henchmen hell bent on stealing a hoard of cash from Steve McGee's freezer.

"I do not wonder your books sell so well, when you lead such a daring life, my friend. But the greatest mystery to me is the books in the warehouses. How do you explain their existence?"

It was a good question, and I admitted my doubts to the puzzled pontiff. "I don't have a theory yet that fits with all the facts," which was the under-statement of the millennium.

"Do not worry too much about facts, my friend. Facts are all well and good, but we need a little faith too. And with faith things can be believed, eh?"

"That's true," I said, wondering if my readers would appreciate the nuanced echo of patrolman Collins.

"I will let you into a secret, my friend. I too would like to write a bestseller. I have written a synopsis and three chapters. Perhaps you might like to show them to your agent?"

"Maybe I should read them first." I wasn't sure that introducing the old rogue was such a good idea—heaven knew what he might get up to with Barney.

The Pope snapped his fingers then murmured something into the lowered ear of a flunky—evidently an order to fetch his manuscript, since the flunky reappeared a moment later bearing a sheaf of papers covered in double-spaced type.

"Here." The Pope handed his work to me. "It is sure to be a bestseller. It is about a charismatic religious leader, known and loved all over the world. In his extensive international travels, he picks up the scent of a global conspiracy involving the governments and secret services of many countries, and the vested interests of the multinational manufacturers of arms, chemicals and pharmaceuticals. He faces a crisis of conscience when he has to seduce a number of extremely beautiful women in order to avert a global crisis. It is very dramatic, with a strong moral theme. As the old saying goes—you should always write about what you know."

"You mean, strong moral themes?"

"No, I mean global conspiracies and beautiful women. Ha ha ha ha ha."

"Ha ha ha ha ha." We laughed heartily at his witty quip.

"Here, miss." His Holiness signalled one of the cabin crew. "Bring us two glasses, my child. Bless you, bless you," he added when she put them on our tables.

"Not for me, thanks," I said, as he went to pour a slug of bourbon into my glass.

"No? Well, you know best, my friend, but a man cannot drink alone, so I will drink for you. Salute." He knocked back his bourbon in a gulp, Como fashion. "And how is your mother? Does she still try to match you with her friends' daughters?"

I admitted that she never stopped trying to match me with her friends' daughters.

"But you don't like the idea?"

"Not really, not just yet anyway."

"You want—how do you say—to sow the wild oats, yes?"

"Not so much that, but . . . I'd like to enjoy being a free man for a while longer."

"Good on you, my friend. You should join the church. I could have you made cardinal. We could paint Rome red, and talk about books and tau muons all day long. Ah, dinner."

Our urbane conversation was diverted by the arrival of the various courses of food that were designed to distract the first-class passenger from the tedium of a long flight. By the time the last was cleared away, the Pope was somewhat tired and emotional, and his talk became more and more desultory until it was replaced by contented snoring. I eased the empty tumbler from his hand and turned out the light over his seat. I was tired myself, but my head was full of thoughts about my book. What the hell was I going to write next?

CHAPTER THIRTY SIX

In which Marco is distracted by a beautiful woman.

AFTER A CONGENIAL BREAKFAST ON the plane, the Pope and I stood together in the baggage hall watching for our luggage on the velvet-covered conveyor of the first-class carousel. With alarm I clocked the Pope seeming to watch the approach of a black hold-all exactly like the ones in McGee's garage and Tsatarin's apartment. Surely it couldn't be . . .

"Ah, here is mine."

I closed my eyes as the Pontiff leaned over the moving baggage. I summoned all my willpower to stop him from picking up the black bag. I wasn't sure that Catholics would be completely happy with the gently spoofing nature of my last chapter, so heaven knows how they would react if I wrote their supreme leader into a shady international web of conspiracy involving North Korea, Panamanian lawyers and the deaths of several Bulgarians. I almost clapped with relief when he reached beyond the black hold-all to lift out a suitcase in cardinal red leather, embossed with a fetching but unusual cross-key motif.

My relieved eyes continued to follow the black hold-all as it slid past the other passengers. It was hooked out by a beautiful, elegantly-dressed woman in dark glasses. I had to follow her. I made my farewells to the Pope, promising to read his sample chapters and to send his love to my mom, then pushed my baggage trolley innocently towards the Panamanian customs.

The beautiful woman was three places ahead of me in the line. She was evidently a regular passenger, as she flirted disgracefully with the customs officers, with much tasteless talk about strip-searches, which seemed entirely out of place in a humorous thriller. I lubricated my own passage through border control with a ten thou' note between the pages of my passport, and aside from being asked to sign the officers' copies of *The Awful Truth about the Herbert Quarry Affair,* my entrance into Panama was unimpeded.

Luckily the beautiful woman was still in sight as I left customs, as she had lingered to powder her nose. As I approached, she picked up the black hold-all and made for the canal-side exit where the famous Panamanian gondoliers plied their watery trade. She hailed a gondola, and asked for the Grittiani, the opulent hotel overlooking Panama's Grand Canal. Yes—this was more like it. Time for some Cary Grant/Audrey Hepburn capers in a luxurious tourist trap, instead of climbing stacks of containers in dingy old Clarkesville.

To avoid notice I threw up the hood of my anorak, Cary Grant fashion, and hailed a gondola, giving the gondolier a hundred dollar bill and instructions to follow the gondola that had just left. "And don't lose it," I added, meaning the departed gondola, of course, not the hundred dollar bill.

I settled back in the embroidered damask cushions, and took in the sights, sounds, and sadly smells, of the Panama Canal. Amid the bustling water-buses, water-taxis, water-trams and gondolas, the larger ships moved majestically—cruise liners, oil tankers, bulk carriers, and container ships.

Containers—I'd had enough of them to last a lifetime. I wondered whether I might have received a text from Como with news about the case. I checked my phone. Nothing but a message from my mobile service provider kindly letting me know that now I was in Panama, texts sent to me from my mobile service provider would cost $684.37 each, and they would send me reminder texts to that effect every hour until I returned home. That was a relief.

We went under the romantic Realto—the bridge upon which the merchants of Panama once gathered to discuss the state of the property market—then rounded a tight left-hander, and there were the famous minarets of the Grittiani. With nifty oaring, the gondolier brought us alongside the hotel's private jetty only seconds behind the gondola bearing the beautiful woman. Just as I was stepping out and handing over another generous tip, an argument broke out between the woman and her gondolier—a burly ruffian with features as dark and swarthy as the Clarkesville Bulgarians. They were speaking in Panamanian, of course, but it seemed remarkably like Spanish, so I was able to get the gist. The ruffian was demanding a higher tip than the woman thought appropriate for the quality of his gondoliership.

Pausing only to confirm that gondoliership was indeed a new word, with not a single hit on Google, I sprang neologistically to the lady's side.

"Can I be of any assistance?"

"Only if you can get blood out of a stone," said the ruffian. "She's as tight as a leprechaun's condom." Or words to that effect—he was speaking Panamanian, don't forget.

The beautiful woman looked at us both with scornful eyes. "That's right. Stick up for each other. I spit on all men."

And spit she did, before stomping off to the hotel.

The gondolier gave a fatalistic shrug, while I tried to figure out where I'd gone wrong with my last three sentences. I gave up. It was too hard. I saw that in her wrath, the beautiful woman had left the black hold-all in the gondola. With the help of hand-gestures, my rudimentary Panamanian, and a fifty dollar bill, I got the gondolier to hand over the bag, which I carried with my own towards the reception of the hotel. A porter in the famous ostrich-plumed regalia of the Grittiani emerged to take my luggage, and followed me into the cool of the building.

Inside the hotel there was a developing scene. The beautiful woman had realised her bag was missing and was simultaneously accusing some staff and guests of having stolen it, while urging others to help her find it, with considerable overlap between the two sets of people involved. I had prepared my lines, and in a Roger Moore voice was about to say, 'Perhaps this is what the lady is looking for'—a cleverly ambiguous statement that could refer to the black hold-all or to the sudden appearance of a suave hero—when she spotted the bag in the porter's hand, ran to him, and planted a hugely relieved kiss on his mouth.

"My hero," she said, along with other murmured cooings that I couldn't quite catch.

I'd had enough. It was time to re-assert my celebrity status. I threw back the hood of my anorak, and slapped my passport on the reception counter.

"Señor Ocram!" said the astonished receptionist, pressing the VIP alert button under the counter-top. "What a pleasure to have you here."

She was waved away by the manager, who had sprung from the back office, alerted by the VIP buzzer to the possibility of huge tips.

"Señor Ocram. What a pleasure to have you here. And a most unexpected pleasure." That was true—I wouldn't normally have chosen to visit a dump like Panama. "We have all read your book, *La Verdad Terrible*, and it is so profound, so moving, so dramatic, and so exciting. I have worn out four copies reading it. You wish to stay with us I hope?"

I said I did wish to stay.

"Then you must have the presidential suite. It is reserved for another guest, but . . ."

But the reservation will be over-ridden in anticipation of a huge tip, he needn't add.

"The presidential suite sounds fine," I said. "Let's get this predictable padding over with, shall we?"

"Of course, of course." He clicked his fingers to have my bag whisked away, then took me via the lift to the suite on the top floor, all the while with a fawning commentary that mixed, in roughly equal measure, name-dropping, flattering hyperbole about my last book, and the usual questions about tau muons. "Here, Señor Ocram. I hope you will not be disappointed."

He opened the doors to what appeared to be a slightly smaller version of Versailles, then showed me round the bedrooms, cinema, jacuzzi, gym, film studio, office, bondage dungeon, and other facilities of the presidential suite, before inviting me to sign its crimson-bound guestbook. I flicked through its pages, noting the names of other literary giants with the misfortune to find themselves in Panama—Archer, Blyton, Cartland . . . a veritable ABC of great writing.

I thanked the manager and shooed him out. I needed time to think. I flopped on the huge presidential four-poster bed and stared vacantly at the splendid views across the canal. I had come to Panama to see Professor Sushing. Should I focus on my original plot, or write a digression about the beautiful woman? But what if the visit to the Professor turned out to be a digression, while the real plot concerned the beautiful woman? I realised I was making my old mistake—thinking. I smiled. What would Herbert Quarry say if he knew? Thinking is the devil in a writer's head, he used to tell me; great writers know to ignore the devil. I must not think, I must write.

I decided to follow-up the beautiful woman—if nothing else it would keep my Bronx mom happy. I called reception and invented a suitable story to elicit her details. She was Donna Maria Triabla de Medici, Room 604. Did she have any favourite celebrities? There was a consultation at the other end of the line—the staff weren't sure, but they thought her favourite film star was Tom Cruise. Ha! I thanked them with hints of a huge tip.

Tom Cruise—I had met him many times since he bought the film rights to *The Awful Truth about the Herbert Quarry Affair*. From my satchel, I took the rubber prosthetic face he had left as a memento—the rubber prosthetic face that he wore in films to hide the fact that he was now looking really old. Thirty minutes in the make-up department of the presidential suite's film studio and the mask was in place. Now we would see about Donna Maria.

Casting caution and credibility to the wind, I went straight to Room 604 and knocked smartly on its door. Donna Maria opened it, wrapped in a towel.

"Señor Cruise!"

"Pardon me," I said in a passable Tom Cruise voice, with perhaps shades of Bill Gates. "I must have the wrong room. I'm sorry to have disturbed you, Miss . . .?"

"Donna Maria Triabla de Medici." She held out her hand, causing her towel to droop in a way that almost had my eyes popping from the prosthetic Tom Cruise face.

I took the proffered hand and kissed it. "A thousand apologies, Miss Triabla de Medici. To compensate for the inconvenience, perhaps I might invite you to dinner?"

"Si, Señor Cruise. It would be my pleasure."

"Let me collect you here then, at six."

I completed my farewell and left her, wishing only that I'd suggested lunch instead of dinner. I was famished. I returned to my suite, unglued the mask, ordered food from room service then called Como for an update.

"Hey, Writer. You seen Professor Sushi yet?"

"It's Professor Sushing, and no I haven't. I have been pursuing other hot leads." I told him about the beautiful woman with the black hold-all. He poo-pooed my initiative.

"Those black hold-alls are like KFC—they're everywhere. The chances that someone you met at Panama Airport is involved in this just because she's got one of those bags is like a million to one."

"Exactly. That's just it. It's always the person you least expect."

"By that stupid logic you might as well make it the Pope. Anyway, I've got some news. You had a lucky escape at Steve McGee's garage, Writer."

"How d'you mean?"

"It collapsed."

"What?"

"It collapsed, or at least the front half of it did. Fell into a sink-hole. City engineers say it was caused by a leaking water pipe, and it was a miracle it hadn't collapsed earlier."

CHAPTER THIRTY SEVEN

*In which Marco writes himself
into an embarrassing predicament.*

I KNOCKED PUNCTUALLY ON THE door of Room 604.
Donna Maria Triabla de Medici opened it wearing a dress
that hid less than her drooping towel had. Within thirty minutes
we were stepping out of the stretch limo I had ordered and being
greeted by the maître d' at Panama's most exclusive restaurant.

"Good evening, Senor Cruise. This is truly an honour for us.
Our most exclusive table is already prepared for you and
your . . . ahem . . . dining companion."

The maître d' bowed us to walk ahead of him—either as a
gesture of deference or an opportunity to peak at some part of
Donna Maria's anatomy—and we were shown to our table.
Donna Maria perused the menu, while I wondered how the
maître d' had known we were coming, given that I hadn't
booked anything. Perhaps the driver of the stretch limo had

phoned ahead to tip them off—that kind of thing probably happens all the time.

"You are much taller than I expected, Señor Cruise," crooned Donna Maria.

"Call me Tom, please."

"And your hair—I never knew it was so red and curly. You must dye it for your films, yes?"

"No, it is dyed now, Donna Maria. I am in Panama on a mission, so I have disguised my appearance just a little. We must be very discreet."

"Ah, I am always very discreet. What is your mission—is it a mission *impossible*?"

"Ha, ha, ha, ha, ha."

"Ha, ha, ha, ha, ha."

After we'd wiped away the torrents of tears triggered by Donna Maria's hilarious quip, I made up something Tom Cruise might well be doing right about now. "I am looking for possible locations for my next film."

"Your next film! That is so exciting. What is it called?"

"The Awful Truth about the Herbert Quarry Affair."

"Oh! That is such a brilliant book."

"You have read it?"

"Who has not, Señor Tom? I have read it in English and in Panamanian. It is so dramatic, so human, so exciting, so . . ." You can imagine the rest. "What part will you be playing?"

"Marco Ocram."

"Ah, the writer. It is strange that he has written such a famous book, and he invented those tau muons of course, but I have been told by a person who knows him that he is . . . how do you say it . . . a complete asshole."

I put down my menu markedly. "You interest me," I said. "Who is it that knows Ocram?"

A tear welled in Donna Maria's shark-like eye. "He is dead. He was a man who helped me and loved me too. A man I met in Clarkesville."

"And his name?" I asked, dreading what might be coming next.

"Stephen McGee." She pronounced the cG in a guttural Panamanian way, but she could have pronounced it as QZJPIT for all I cared as I tried to rally from the shock announcement.

"Steve McGee?!"

"You know him, Señor Tom?"

"Well . . . no. But the name McGee is familiar."

"Yes, we all know the name McGee, thanks to Señor Ocram's book. Stephen used to say that Ocram brought shame on all the McGees in the world."

That was hardly my fault. All I did was expose the fact that virtually every member of the extensive McGee clan in Clarkesville had had a hand in framing Herbert Quarry for the murder of poor Lola Kellog. It was the McGees themselves who performed the shameful acts. However, this was neither the time nor the place to go into questions of fairness with Donna Maria.

"And how did Steve, sorry, Stephen McGee, know about Señor Ocram?" I asked, smelling a large police-chief-shaped rat.

"His . . . how you say . . . his boss man, the big chief of police, was the man who really solved the Herbert Quarry affair, and he says that this Ocram just got in the way yet took all the credit for the case."

"He did, did he?"

"Yes. Poor Stephen, he say that he go to the big chief's house to watch the game on TV, and they hardly get to hear any of the game because the big chief he drinks plenty of whiskey then he goes on and on and on and on about the asshole Ocram."

Ha! There would be withering words when I was next in the ward with Galahad. I thought it time to change the subject. "And how was Stephen helping you?"

"I tell you this in confidence, Señor Tom, yes?"

"I swear it, Donna Maria. This is just between you and me." And the half-billion readers of my next book, I added under my breath.

"I have a very sick sister, Señor Tom. She needs a big operation to live life like a normal person, but I have not the money to pay for her care. It would be thousands of balboas, or dollars as you say. But I hear of a . . ." She looked around, and lowered her voice. ". . . a conspiración. You know the word, Señor Tom?"

I nodded to show I knew the word. "A conspiracy."

"A conspiracy. A conspiracy, yes. I am working for a company with interests in Panama and Clarkesville, Señor Tom. The work they make me do is very mysterious to me. The mystery makes me want to know what is going on. So I use my eyes and my ears to find out."

"Yes?" I prompted breathlessly. I could hardly believe that after almost forty chapters, a minor character might be just about to blow the lid on the centrepiece of my plot with huge chunks of expositional dialogue. I was also excited at the possibility that this might be the only book ever printed in which 'a conspiracy' appears three times on the trot.

"My job is very simple, Señor Tom. I have to be a courier for a company here in Panama. A . . ."

I cut her short. "And the name of the company?"

"Invenmente EDS is its name."

"I see." I wondered if my readers would remember that Invenmente EDS was the company that leased the warehouses, or whether I should remind them—I decided not to. "And may I ask where their office is?"

"I cannot tell you, Señor Tom."

I gave her a reproachful look. How could she not trust me?

"It is nothing about trust, Señor Tom. I cannot tell you because I do not know where their office is."

"But that's ridiculous. You play games with me, Donna Maria."

She leant across the table and stroked my hand fawningly. "No, no, Señor Tom. I cross my heart. I get my instructions on the telephone. I collect and deliver to a box at the post office in Panama City. My wages are left there also."

"I see," I said.

"So I act as courier. Is easy work, and pays me well. But I know that the work is, how you say, dark?"

"Shady."

"Yes, the work is shady. Something goes on. The men I deal with in Clarkesville, none of them is American. They have something going on in warehouses there. I know in my heart it cannot be a good thing, but what can I do, a beautiful woman all alone?"

"What did you do?"

"One night I am in Kelly's Bar and Diner in Clarkesville, and some nasty men they pester me. But one man, he comes, a hero, and he scares away the nasty men. I do not know it then but he is a policeman. I see he loves me. He asks why I am in Clarkesville and why I am all alone and why I am so sad. I tell him about my sister, and how I need money, and that I know about the conspiración, and he say he will help me if I trust him. So together we go to the warehouses, and it is very strange because the warehouses are full of books all the same. So Stephen, he investigates, and he finds the truth about the books, and he says that a very, very rich man has the books there for a secret reason, and the very, very rich man will not want the world to know the reason, and if we promise to keep the reason secret the very, very rich man will give us money to pay for my sister's operation."

"I see." So that's what the rogue was up to. "What happened next?"

"What happened next was that Stephen tell me to trust him, and to leave things to him. And just two days ago, when I am on my next courier trip, Stephen call me to say that he has got the very, very rich man to pay us the money for my sister's operation. Fifty thousand dollars, Señor Tom, and that he was going to give it all to me. We were meant to meet in the car park of Kelly's Bar and Diner, but he did not turn up. There were big fires that day—all the warehouses were on fire—so I think that maybe he is helping with the fires. But then I don't hear from him. And the next day in the papers there is news that he is dead. Murdered! I am sure, Señor Tom, that the bad men get to know that he has the fifty thousand dollars for my sister's operation and they take it from him. And now my sister will never live a normal life."

She withdrew her hand and sobbed, tears dripping all over her miniscule dress.

"Don't cry, Donna Maria. I am sure I can pay for your sister's operation."

"You can?!"

"Yes, but please, tell me first. Did Stephen tell you why the very, very rich man had all the books in the warehouses?"

"Yes he did."

At last. Here would be the answer. I was about to ask her why, when something else came into my head. Over her shoulder I saw the door of the restaurant open. Someone came in while his minders fought off the paparazzi. Now I knew why the maître d' had prepared the table. Staring towards me with a particularly mean look was the real Tom Cruise.

CHAPTER THIRTY EIGHT

As if that wasn't embarrassing enough . . .

"Excuse me, Donna Maria. I just need to go to the men's room. I'll be right back."

Throwing up the hood of my anorak, I hurried to the back of the restaurant with my head down. I could already hear the noisy expostulations of the startled maitre d'. Glancing over my shoulder, I saw Tom Cruise's minders heading towards me like tigers after a baby goat. Expostulations wasn't really the right word, but I was in a panic.

It was as I dived into the corridor to the toilets that a brilliant idea came into my head. I would go into the ladies'— that would throw the minders off the scent. I entered a long narrow room decorated in pink, with stalls off to the right and a full-width mirror across the far end. A woman with her back to me was leaning towards the mirror to apply her lipstick. For a moment her eyes caught mine via the mirror, then I slipped sideways into the sanctuary of one of the stalls. I would be safe here.

Deciding to make hay while the sun shone, I lowered my trousers and made myself comfortable on the throne. I would do my business, wait until the tumult died, then sneak out the back way. I heard the lipstick woman snap the catch on her handbag and trot out into the corridor.

"Tom Cruise! Tom Cruise is in the ladies! Tom Cruise is in the ladies! Wow!"

I stared down at the boxer shorts stretched tautly between my ankles and wagged my head in a slow wag of despondency. Bloody Herbert Quarry. It was true that writing the first thing that came into your head did introduce a certain degree of entertaining unpredictability for the reader, but it was a nightmare for the author, or for this one at least. Before I could even stand, the door to the ladies' was barged open by burley bodies, and seconds later three Tom Cruise minders were staring angrily over the door of my stall.

"Get out of there, buddy. Now!"

"There's been a mistake. I can explain."

"There's been a mistake, alright. A big one, and you made it. Now get out now before we lift you out by your hair."

"But I'm Marco Ocram, the writer."

"Yeah, and I'm Hillary Clinton, the president. Get out."

I plucked ineffectually at the rubber prosthetic face mask. It was glued tight, and I didn't have any solvent with me.

"OK, buster. You asked for it."

They pushed in the door of my stall, ripping out the thingy that held the lock and bruising my left knee quite cruelly.

"Right, boys, let's show him what we do to jokers who take the piss out of the boss."

THE AWFUL TRUTH ABOUT THE SUSHING PRIZE

So saying, they turned me upside down and dangled me by my ankles into the bowl of the toilet, then flushed it. For a moment I reflected upon the fate of the poor interns waterboarded by the CIA at Guantanamo. No wonder the CIA was unpopular, if that's the way they treated potential employees. Then I thought fuck the CIA interns, and started to scream. Or at least I tried to scream but my mouth filled with the flushing waters from the cistern.

"Haw haw haw haw haw."

The laughing minders dragged me out to the corridor and dumped me on the floor, my trousers still around my ankles. I could imagine nothing more ignominious.

"Haw haw haw haw. Let's throw him on the street, boys."

Now I could.

"No, no, leave me, no, no."

My pleas were in vain. Streaming eau de toilette, I was carried through the restaurant and out onto the street where I was dumped at what instantly became the centre of a semi-circle of paparazzi, who took insensitive shot after insensitive shot as I tried to pull up my trousers with one hand while failing to preserve the privacy of my parts with the other.

CHAPTER THIRTY NINE

In which Marco meets Professor Sushing,
after first learning of an enormous prize.

IT TOOK ME MORE THAN an hour to get back to the Grittiani, skulking down the darkest alleys. I'd hoped to sneak to my suite unobserved, but I'd lost the key. There was an awkward moment—actually quite a lot more than a moment—when I had to present myself at reception and prove that I was me. When I finally got the key, I could have cried.

However, crying never got anyone anywhere, so I pulled myself stiffly erect and walked with all the dignity I could muster to wait for the elevator. By this time, the rubber prosthetic face was peeling visibly at the edges, especially around the eyes and mouth, which might explain why so many of the guests were taking pictures and video. I waved hellos at them, signed copies of *The Awful Truth*, and was just about to correct a Venezuelan man's misunderstanding about the role of the tau muon in 'warm' neutrino scattering experiments, when thankfully the lift came.

I awoke the next morning with the sun blazing into my room through the oily haze above Panama City. I fumbled for my bespoke Rolex with the face of my Bronx mom on the dial—nearly ten o'clock. I padded into the nearest of my many bathrooms and stood under the shower for ten minutes, symbolically washing away the horrors of the previous evening. The rubber prosthetic face was still in the bowl of the toilet where I had thrown it with disgust twelve hours ago. Bloody Tom Cruise.

Back in my room, I checked my iPhone. Its battery was dead. I knew exactly how it felt. I plugged in its charger and it slowly beeped to life. I had ten text messages—one from my mom, eight from Barney, and one from my mobile service provider to let me know that I had nine other messages. Almost seven grands' worth.

The text from my mom said I was a heartless boy for not ringing her, and what was I doing in Panama anyway, and she'd really, really found the right one for me this time. Mrs. Goldfarb's middle daughter was just right for me, and I had to call home at once.

The eight texts from Barney were all variations on 'ring me'. I rang him.

"Hey, Markeeee. How's the boy, Marky baby? You seen the news yet?"

I told him I hadn't seen the news yet.

"But you can guess, right?"

"If it's about me with my trousers down in a Tom Cruise mask . . ."

"Well there's that for sure. Every goddam front page on the planet has that story. Brilliant. Ocram Spoofs Cruise. Tom's a bit bitchy about it, but he'll calm down. I said it was a promotional stunt to help the *Awful Truth* movie at the box office. Not that it'll need help, mind you. It's gonna be huge, Marky, huuuge."

I said but what about my dignity as an author and a scientist.

"Dignity? Dignity? Since when have you had dignity? Let me tell you something, Marky, in this business you can have success or you can have dignity. What would you want dignity for?"

I let it ride. I wasn't sure Barney was the right person for a conversation about the angst of the tortured artist.

"Anyway, Marky, that's not the really big news. Are you sitting down?"

I wasn't, but I told him I was.

"This is the real big news—your special friend Professor Sushing has announced that he's sponsoring a new prize of ten million dollars for the best writer of commercial fiction. Of *commercial fiction,* Marky. Only one guy qualifies in my book for a prize like that, and his name's Ocram. And don't forget, Marky, you get ten percent of everything—*everything.* That means a coooool mill."

I pointed out to Barney that he was counting his chickens and reminded him that Sushing was an outspoken critic of my work, and thus hardly likely to be awarding any prizes to it.

"Chickens schmickens. Look at the timing. You're down in Panama to see Sushing. The very day you touch Panamanian soil Sushing announces a prize with your name written on it. Think about it. He's sending you a message, Marky boy."

"Maybe, Barney, but maybe it's a different message. Maybe he's taunting me with a prize he knows I won't win."

"Jeez, Marky, don't be so negative. Why would be do that? More like he's trying to bribe you not to spill any more beans about him in your books. Get real, kid. Anyway, the winner's gonna be announced at the games, so we'll know soon enough."

"The games? What games?"

"What games? What games? Don't tell me you've forgotten about the Literary Games. What other games could they be?"

"Sorry, Barney, I thought you meant something else."

"Listen, Kid, you better get your brain into gear. If you're meeting the Professor today you need to be razor sharp. Keep the ears pricked for anything he says between the lines, impress him, and whatever else you do, *don't say anything to upset him.*"

I promised I wouldn't upset the Professor, and we ended the call.

I realise that I haven't previously mentioned the Literary Games, and as I result I might have left myself open to the accusation of a last-minute plot twist invented off the top of my head. Absolutely not. Yes, ordinarily, I write the first thing that comes into my head, but it so happens that the Literary Games came into my head ages ago, and I'd agreed with Barney that he could represent me as a professional entrant, and then I'd forgotten all about it, so I better just explain it now.

The Literary Games had been announced about a year ago by a new foundation with shady backers in places like Panama. They were going to be held every two years, filling the gaps between the Olympics and the soccer World Cup. The first was going to be held in the Bahamas for some reason, at Nassau. After that, countries were going to be able to bid to host them, thus giving huge opportunities for back-handers to the shady foundation. If you're interested, here's the Literary Games entry in Wikipedia . . .

The Games will span the literary spectrum, covering all established genres. Individual events will be scored by the 'weighted speed' method, in which the score is the quality of the written work (as rated by a panel of judges) divided by the time taken for its completion. Thus competitors will face a tactical choice between gaining extra points through higher quality or speedier execution.

The 14-day programme is expected to include:

Short verse forms, including haiku and limerick. These to be in knock-out rounds each of eight contestants, culminating in a final with four contestants.

Short-stories. To be between 1,995 and 2,005 words. Initial rounds to be in specific genres, with a cross-genre 'Grand Final'.

Long verse-forms. Length of the work to be at the choice of the competitor; however, the scores will be weighted by the number of words produced.

Non-fiction. Works to be full-length on topics specified by the judges ten minutes before the event.

Pentathlon. Authors compete in short verse-form, short-story (two genres, selectable by the competitor from a list published by the judges on the day), non-fiction (freestyle), and long verse-form. Winner decided by normalised cumulative scores from individual events.

The Blue Ribbon event is the full-length novel. To avoid cheating through the re-use of prepared material, the genre and synopsis of the novel will be stipulated by the judges and revealed to the competitors two minutes before the starting gun. The most stringent security measures will be enforced to ensure no premature leaks of the specification. Authors will have nine days to complete their works, leaving five days for judging and speculation about the likely winner.

THE AWFUL TRUTH ABOUT THE SUSHING PRIZE

Publishing rights for works produced during The Games will vest with The Committee and will be auctioned to sponsoring publishers to generate funds to re-invest in 'grass roots' literary participation schemes.

Barney had put me forward for the short story event. He said I would have been the natural favourite for the full-length novel, but he didn't think it was in my interests to let the Committee keep the publishing rights to what would almost certainly become another mega-selling book. To be honest, I'd been in two minds about whether to pull out, as I just couldn't face the pressure of it. People imagine that literary megastars have it easy—that all they need do is sit with an iPad when the fancy takes them and tap out a few words, then go swanning to their next interview or photo-shoot before hanging round with their beautiful model girlfriends and going to celebrity parties. What they don't realise is how hard it is to tap out those few words without getting into trouble. Look at the fiasco of my Panama trip. I'd wanted to get away from dingy Clarkesville to somewhere exotic, somewhere I could be like James Bond with a beautiful James Bond girl, and what happens? I get horribly humiliated, and the beautiful woman turns out to be a hard-case who's only interested in getting money for her sister's operation. It was all so hard to take. Writing the first thing that came into my head had made me famous and rich, but it was destroying my sanity and ruining my life. Maybe my next book could be *The Awful Truth about Life in a Buddhist Sanctuary in Tibet* in which I just turned prayer-wheels all day—though knowing my luck the Buddhist sanctuary would get invaded by Chinese commandos and I'd be tortured as a Western spy.

I felt wretched.

But then I saw a copy of *The Awful Truth about the Herbert Quarry Affair* standing proudly amid the lesser books that the management had left in the suite for the pleasure of its occupants, and I remembered my readers. I remembered the millions and millions and millions of people who relied on me to write the words that allowed them to escape from their own feelings of wretchedness. Perhaps it was just the karma of a kindly universe that decided that one person, Marco Ocram, should be wretched in order that millions of others should not.

I wandered to the panoramic windows of my suite and watched the comings and goings of the Panamanian canal traffic, but the sentence didn't lead me anywhere, so I went back and checked my diary. I was expected at Professor Sushing's at noon. I knew the old man was a stickler for punctuation, oops— and punctuality as well, so I'd better get cracking. My anorak was looking too soiled to touch, so I left it with instructions for it to be cleaned and packed everything in my satchel. Grabbing a banana for a mobile breakfast, I headed downstairs.

One of the drawbacks of leaving my anorak for the cleaners was that I couldn't throw up its hood to disguise my appearance, which meant that I was mobbed by fans as I waited for a taxi, and I was plagued with questions from the taxi driver about all the loose ends in my last book. Why were there so many suspects who might have been guilty who were never investigated? Why were there so many leads that were never followed up? Why were there so many inconsistencies in the behaviour of the criminals? How did Como and I manage to make the intuitive leaps across vast gaps in the trail of evidence? I told her again and again that that was the difference between true crime and fiction. In true crime the evidence didn't come in neat little parcels. True crime was always messy. But she wasn't satisfied, and I was glad when she dropped me at the security gates of the Professor's huge research and manufacturing complex.

I stood for a moment, waiting for sufficient imaginative neurons to fire so that I could describe my new surroundings. I gave the neurons a hand by bringing to mind assorted sites of vast human enterprise, real and fictional, that I might use as a model for the Professor's HQ, specifically:

> *A giant oil refinery I'd driven past outside New York one day when I got lost on the way to Times Square.*
>
> *The HQs of the villains in various Bond books.*
>
> *The Ministry of Truth building in 1984.*
>
> *The Range Rover factory in England, where I'd gone on a VIP visit to celebrate my product placement deal.*
>
> *The insides of the Large Hadron-Collider, or Large-Hadron Collider, at CERN, which I'd seen on TV.*

It was all a waste of time, because before I could describe the place, a uniformed guard poked his head out from the security cabin guarding the main entrance and asked me who I was and what I was doing there. I handed him my card and explained that I was to see the Professor by appointment.

I was nodded through a turnstile, then asked to place my satchel and the contents of my pockets into a tray to be put through a scanner, and . . . well, rather than wasting a load of words with descriptions, let's just agree that it was like the security at the check-in at the airport. Except that there weren't lots of other passengers, obviously, and I didn't have a big suitcase, and you didn't need to show your passport or your tickets or anything like that, and there wasn't a big shopping area, and there weren't lots of announcements about will the last three passengers for flight so and so please get a move on because they're holding everything up, and so on, but you know what I mean.

When I got through security, I was invited to step into an open-topped thing like a small electric jeep, which was weird because it had a steering wheel and controls like a normal car but no driver. And the thing drove me all by itself about a mile through the huge complex where the Professor's charitable trust and its various commercial spin-offs were headquartered. We, or rather it, stopped at what looked like a Frank Lloyd Wright house right on the edge of the canal. A man dressed as a butler, who probably was a butler now that I think about it, greeted me.

"Good morning, sir. I trust you have had a pleasant stay in Panama."

Words failing me, I said a non-committal, "Ah."

"If you would walk this way, sir, the Professor has asked if you would be so kind as to wait in his lower study."

Depending on whether you are reading this in English or American, we went in a lift or elevator down to a large, cool, room panelled not just in hardwoods but in exotic tropical hardwoods and filled with innumerable priceless artworks of every conceivable type. Incongruously, the far wall was entirely blank and seemed to be made of a single sheet of frosted glass, like the window of a giant lavatory. The butler pressed a button and the frosting cleared to reveal a huge window into the side of the canal, with sunlight filtering down from the surface of the water some feet above the ceiling of the room. The butler pressed another button, and bright lights penetrated far into the gloomy waters, showing old shopping-trolleys, weed-covered prams, corpses weighted down with concrete, and countless other forms of detritus jettisoned by the good citizens of Panama. It was breath-taking.

"One million dollars, Doctor Ocram."

I spun round to see the Professor had entered the room.

"You were wondering how much it all cost, Doctor Ocram."

"How did you know?"

"It is the common reaction of first-time visitors—especially impressionable unimaginative visitors who have recently read or recalled *Dr No*."

"A million dollars?" I said, unable to think of a wittier riposte with which to impress the Professor.

"Yes, a million dollars, Doctor Ocram. But I am sure you did not come here to talk about the cost of my glazing."

I thought of the wittier response, albeit a bit late. "It must have been a *huge pane* to install. Ha ha ha ha . . ."

My laughter died as I saw the Professor fail to smile at my hilarious bon mot. Hmmm. I could tell that I was dealing with an intellectual opponent as formidable as his reputation, but I couldn't resist a follow-up . . .

"I see that my little joke has not been well received, Professor, to judge by your *glassy* stare. Ha ha ha ha ha. But you'll soon be *putty* in my hands. Ha ha ha ha ha. There's no point pretending to be unamused—I can *see right through* you. Ha ha ha ha ha."

"Doctor Ocram, I am a busy man. If you wish to spout inanities you may do so elsewhere."

"I'm sorry, Professor," I said, dabbing away the tears of my laughter. "I will come quickly to the point."

"Do."

"I understand, Professor, that you have significant interests both here and in the Democratic Republic of Korea."

"I have interests throughout the world, Doctor Ocram."

"Indeed. But it is those two territories that interest me."

"In what way?"

"Professor, I trust that what I am about to say will be between the two of us alone."

A further glassy stare was the Professor's answer. I continued . . .

"I have been investigating certain criminal activities in Clarkesville, Professor—activities that . . ."

"Doctor Ocram, your investigations in Clarkesville have been widely reported by the world's celebrity-obsessed media, so you need not repeat anything that is already public knowledge. Please get straight to the point," he said, selfishly ruling out the possibility that I might pad another few pages by summarising several chapters of plot development in the manner of Hercule Poirot addressing a dinner table of suspects.

"Very well, Professor. What has not been made public is that the mastermind behind the criminal events is likely to be an exceptionally rich individual with immense intellectual powers and influential contacts in Panama and North Korea. You are an exceptionally rich individual with immense intellectual powers and influential contacts in Panama and North Korea—that is, you possess exactly the same distinctive characteristics as the mystery person who is behind the Clarkesville criminal activity. I would have thought it obvious, Professor, that my investigations would lead me here to ask if you knew of anyone else who would fit the profile."

"If I may say so, Doctor Ocram, your powers of deductive analysis are remarkable, quite remarkable."

I flushed with pride at his words. Impress the Professor, Barney had said. I'd get top marks on that count at least.

"I can categorically assure you, Doctor Ocram, that if I recall or encounter another exceptionally rich individual with immense intellectual powers and influential contacts in Panama and North Korea then I shall let you know immediately."

"That is most kind of you, Professor. I shall sleep more soundly at night knowing that you will let me know." As he went to show me out, I spotted another opportunity to impress and win-over the Professor. "Isn't that a *Sörende* vase from IKEA? My Bronx mom has one. She got it for ten dollars in their sale. You and my Bronx mom must have the same tastes. And she *loves* my books." Wink, wink.

Did you see how cleverly I managed it?—impressing the Professor with my compendious knowledge of IKEA product names, building empathy through likening the Professor to my Bronx mom, and then the implication that he should share my Bronx mom's love of my books, thus giving a natural segue to the Professor's big prize! Eat your heart out, Dale Carnegie.

"I think not, Doctor Ocram. The item is a moon flask from the Ming Dynasty, conservatively valued at seventy million dolla . . . *DON'T TOUCH IT!*"

"Ooops! Butter-fingers! Nearly dropped it."

The Professor wrenched back the moon flask and eased it delicately back on its stand. "Forgive me, Doctor Ocram, but the moon flask is literally irreplaceable. In all my years of study I have not seen another like it."

I saw that I'd have to find another way of impressing the Professor.

"So, you study vases. Keeps you busy, does it?"

"It is only one of my interests, Doctor Ocram."

"Good to have more than one, isn't it? What's the other one?"

"Doctor Ocram, if you wish to know more about my research interests I suggest you consult the comprehensive listing on the Wikipedia website. From memory, it begins with Quantum Gravity, Fundamental Particle Physics, Semiotics, Advanced Materials Research, Geo-Political Analysis, Macro-Economics, Comparative Linguistics, Didactic Gradualism, Anthropics, Synthetic Plate Tectonics, Gamma-Ray Lithography, Integrated Circuit Optimisation, Literary Spectroscopy, Climate Change, Quantum Cryptography, Nano-Engineering, Genetic Collage, Fiscal Cyclics Latency, Space Exploration, Quantum Neurology, and Artificial Intelligence. I believe that Rare Oriental Porcelain is somewhere on page five of the list."

I looked at the Professor with narrowed eyes. My Bronx mom always said that people who go on and on about their achievements usually had some big weakness to hide. I wondered what the Professor's weakness was—a massive one, presumably. However, I wasn't going to be cowed. I would show him that he was dealing with a worthy opponent.

"An impressive list, Professor. Almost as impressive as the list you will find in Wikipedia of my literary achievements, which will soon feature a new entry about the first sentence ever to end with three legitimate question marks! I used to dabble in various areas of research myself—you know of my work on tau muons, of course—but nowadays my writing is all-consuming, so, unlike you, I no longer have time to indulge my intellectual curiosity in other matters."

"Ah, yes, your *literary* achievements. You have indeed won many awards since Herbert Quarry took you under his wing."

This was more like it—now for the segue . . .

"Though there are still some prizes to aim for, eh?" I gave the Professor a knowing nudge.

"If you are alluding to The Sushing Prize, I agree that it would seem a natural award for you to receive, given the commercial nature of your output. But you must remember, Doctor Ocram, that regrettably such prizes are not always awarded on merit alone. Inevitably the personal feelings of the judging panel undermine the objectivity of its decision making. Were I an author hoping to win the prize, I would take pains to ensure that my work did not offend the judges. Remember that, Doctor Ocram."

As we reached the front door, my attention was distracted by more of the Professor's artworks.

"You are admiring my triptych, Doctor Ocram?"

"No, but these three paintings had caught my eye. Are they by someone famous?"

"Would it make a difference to you if they were?"

Was that a trick question, I wondered? I decided to play it evasively.

"Possibly."

"They are Bacon's triptych of Freud."

"Really?" They didn't look anything like Sigmund Freud to me. "Are they valuable?"

"That depends upon one's measure of value, Doctor Ocram. The price paid for them was one hundred and forty million dollars, but what is a hundred and forty million dollars, after all?"

"Yes, yes. Quite. My thoughts exactly."

The Professor contemplated his expensive possession with a nostalgic eye. "The artist and the sitter both were students of mine, many, many years ago."

"Really?"

"Neither had a scrap of natural talent, but they were malleable enough—hungry for the commercial success I led them to expect, and very prepared to take risks with their art."

"Both were prepared to take risks?" I nudged him in the ribs. "But obviously Bacon was cut out to be the rasher, ha ha ha ha ha."

"Goodbye, Doctor Ocram. Enjoy your little jokes while you can."

CHAPTER FORTY

In which Marco belatedly meets Herbert Quarry.

CHAPTER FORTY ALREADY, I THOUGHT, with some satisfaction and a good deal of relief. It couldn't be long to the big denouement, and then we could all get back to doing something more useful with our lives. I sat with my fingers poised over my iPad, waiting for whatever was going to come into my head next. I suppose that if there were an obvious criticism of Herbert Quarry's writing advice it was just that—you had to wait for something to come into your head before you could write about it. I heard an old interview with PG Wodehouse where he said he never started writing a book until he'd got the entire story thought through, usually with a few hundred pages of detailed notes. I wouldn't go quite as far as to call that cheating, but you've got to admit that it's hardly cricket. When PG got to Chapter Forty there was no desperate crisis of inspiration—he just looked up what was in his hundreds of pages of detailed notes and transcribed it into the manuscript. It's hardly writing at all when you look at it that way. No wonder he never really got anywhere.

Where was I? Oh yes—fingers poised over the iPad . . .

I picked up my freshly-laundered anorak, checked out of the Grittiani, and took the first gondola to the airport. A fresh chapter, a fresh plotline—that was my motto. I looked at the departure boards. Drat. The next flight to Clarkesville wasn't for another day. What was I to do?

The first departure was to Pasadena. Why did that strike a chord? I pressed the buttons on my iPad to search for Pasadena in what I'd written so far. Yes, there it was—twenty chapters ago, Barney said he'd sent Herbert Quarry to the Christian Brothers' place in Pasadena. That's it—I'd go to see Herbert! It was fate.

I ran excitedly to the ticket desk, bought a first-class ticket, signed the clerk's copy of *The Awful Truth about the Herbert Quarry Affair*, waited while the clerk went and bought five other copies for me to sign for her friends, then hurried to the VIP lounge, checking with a glance from the door that there were no popes or other notables who might hold me up with opportunistic requests for writing advice.

In the VIP lounge, among the various papers showing pictures of the indignities I had suffered as Tom Cruise, there was a paper called the *Times Literary Supplement* which caught my eye. On its front, it had one of those exaggerated sketches—caricatures I think they're called—of me as Gulliver, tied to the ground, with little people from Lilliput standing round me. The Lilliputians had names, like Steinbeck, Hemingway, Pamuk, Pinter, Naipaul, Golding, Bellow, Lessing. Some of them rang bells—the names, that is, not the little figures. Hemingway, or was it Hemmingway, reminded me of a writer I'd heard about. They nicknamed him Earnest because his writing was so serious, and there was a theory that his books were like icebergs because you could skip nine tenths of them and still understand the plot.

I looked inside and found a two-page spread with the title 'Wither now Ocram?' which seemed weird. Even weirder was that there were no pictures of me with my pants downs in the Tom Cruise mask trying to cover my embarrassment on the pavement in Panama. I started to read the article, and my blood pressure rose as I got further through it.

Those of you who have read *The Awful Truth about the Herbert Quarry Affair*—which I suppose means all of you—will remember the blinding moment of inspiration near the start when I realised that my destiny was to become the first person ever to win all the categories of Nobel Prize—the Nobel Grand Slam. I would start with the prize for literature by writing the story of how I was clearing Herbert Quarry of the charge of murdering Lola Kellog. By the time the story was published and the prize for literature was under my belt, leading theoretical physicists would have had the chance to explain the significance of my work on tau muons to their less-gifted colleagues, and from there it would be a short step to the Nobel Prize for physics. And doubtless by then I'd have found out what the other Nobel Prizes were for and figured out a plan to win them, too. Well, I can reveal to my affronted readers that the article in the *Times Literary Supplement* referred to my published ambition in what can only be described as mocking tones.

About halfway through, there was a quote where I was supposed to have said that the biggest barrier to my winning the Prize for literature was the precedent set by former winners which blinkered the judges to the merits of more innovative fiction. God knows what that was meant to mean—I suppose it was something Barney had made up. The article got worse as it went on, dismissing my book as 'meta-fiction.' Not even fiction, only meta-fiction! I was incandescent. I'd never written, sorry read, anything so insulting in my life.

I was so angry, I missed the call for my flight, and a stewardess had to come and find me. All the other passengers were tutting about the delay until they realised that the Ocram whose name was being called over the PA system was the literary megastar and physicist Marco Ocram; then they all started asking me to sign their copies of *The Awful Truth* and answer their questions about tau muons.

Once we were well into the flight, I stared through the window at the fluffy clouds below. These moments of inactivity, which would be a welcome rest for some people, were the most dangerous for me as a writer. They always tempted me to break Herbert's golden rule and think about the plot. To stop myself from thinking about what might happen when I got to Pasadena, I refocused my mind on my noble Nobel ambitions. It was true that the call from Stockholm still hadn't come. Barney said not to let it bother me. "Hey, what do Swedes know?" was the kind of thing he kept telling me, but I wasn't convinced. The Swedes did seem to know about some things, like . . . like flat-pack furniture and . . . and popular music, don't forget, with Abba. I always liked the fair-haired one—what was the name? . . . Benny. And it was no wonder they had a Nobel Prize for literature, because they had some very sophisticated writers, like the guy who wrote the Wallander books, and the one who did the books about the girl who played with the fire ant's nest. Although it can't have been much of a nest if a fire ant built it. That said, my book had sold faster than all theirs put together, so if there was any justice, and if the Stockholm judges weren't all taking back-handers from the Swedish equivalents of Barney, then I should be the next winner.

Bing. The pilot switched on the warning lights that said you had to fasten your seat belt, switch off your iPad, and stop thinking about the corruption of the judging panels for Nobel Prizes. Just in time, too, otherwise who knows whom I might have libelled.

I decided to skip the description of the plane landing and me getting my baggage and going through customs, because I'd already done that at Panama City and I couldn't face writing it all over again.

I went to the taxi rank and asked the taxi driver to take me to the Christian Brothers' place where Herbert was living. When we got there, we drove through the ornate gates and down the two miles of private drive. At either side were Christian Brothers in their traditional black dress attending to their daily devotions—golf, bowling, fishing, and so on.

I'd phoned ahead and agreed with Herbert that I would meet him at the thalassotherapy complex, where the bodily health of the brothers was maintained through a strict regimen of briny treatments using sea-water pumped from the far ocean. I saw him waiting for me at its main entrance, which was overarched by a huge concrete sea-shell in the manner of a Busby Berkeley film set. I felt suffused with literary energy, and prepared my mind for switching into the woodenly interrogative style—with frequent use of first names—that characterised my dialogues with my best friend and mentor.

"Marco, it is good to see you again, my friend." Herbert grasped my upper arms and looked intently at me. "But I see some pain on your face—some inner stress. You must tell me what is wrong."

It might well have been pain, after writing fifty thousand words of this rubbish, but I wouldn't rule-out the after-effects of the Tom Cruise mask—I was still finding bits of glue around my face.

"Herbert, it is good to see you, too."

So far, the wooden and corny quality of the dialogue was spot-on. I hadn't written a conversation with Herbert for over two years, but it was coming back to me like riding a bike. I began to feel some of my inner stress abate a tad.

"Come, Marco. Let me take your luggage."

Herbert smoothly shouldered my steamer trunk, hatbox and specimen case, which surprised me, partly because I thought I had only a satchel, and partly because he had been frail when I had last seen him in New York. His next statement went some way to explaining my surprise.

"I must tell you, Marco, that the Christian Brothers' regime is conducive to excellent health—mental and physical. I have booked a guest room for you here at the complex—it is simple and austere, but you will find it provides for your essential needs. Here."

He opened the door to the guest room and I looked inside. The last time I'd seen anything like it was when I was inspecting *Awful Truth* tattoos in the holding cell at Clarkesville County Jail, although at least the holding cell didn't have a bucket in place of a flushing toilet.

"Herbert, that's very good of you, but I would hate to put you to any trouble—a local hotel would be . . ."

"No, Marco, my friend. It is no trouble. Now, let us go to the sea-spa and catch up on old times. I want to hear everything about your new book."

Half an hour later we were relaxing in the main sea-pool, a giant cruciform hot-tub—or Jacuzzi if you prefer the term coined by Zola in his famous protest against the closure of public bathing facilities by a regressive French government in

1903. We leant against the side of the pool and gently kicked the bubbling waters while I told Herbert about the developments in the mysterious case at Clarkesville.

"What puzzles me, Herbert, is the question of motive. Why would anybody conspire to buy ten point four million copies of a book they already own?"

"There is one obvious explanation, Marco."

"There is, Herbert?"

"If I remember correctly, there was a certificate from the Guinness people in Barney's penthouse that officially recognised your status as the world fastest selling author, which stated that your last book had sold ten point three nine million copies in its first year."

"That's right, Herbert!" I ejaculated, amazed that a detail I'd written at random seventeen chapters ago should reappear now as a crucial plot pivot.

"Then it is plain, Marco, that someone has been trying to break your record."

For a moment I was too stunned by the audacity of the concept to write another word. I trod water, literally and metaphorically, then spun round to face my sagely mentor.

"But Herbert, who would do such a thing? And why would they do it?" I was going to add, and when would they do it, and how would they do it, but I remembered we'd already dealt with that.

"For all my teaching, Marco, you still have much to learn of the world of literature. Jealousy is the single most powerful motive for the author. You will remember it was the theme of my first novel, *The X and Y Coordinates of Evil*. In that seminal work the jealousy of a spurned lover was the motive for a huge crime. If sexual jealousy can produce such results, imagine, then, the motivational power of the professional jealousy of a writer."

"You mean . . ."

"Yes, Marco. With notable exceptions—among whom I would include you, my friend—writers are the most egotistical of all humans. The desire to be published is a desire for attention. When one writer draws less attention than another they suffer a humiliating insult to their psychological ego centres."

"You mean . . ."

"Yes, Marco. The mastermind behind your crime will be a rich writer with a chip on his or her shoulder, a chip of enormous proportions."

I struggled to decide whether the idea of a chip of enormous proportions made any sense, but then I remembered that none of the rest of the book did either, so what did it matter?

"So, Herbert, all I need to do is to find a writer who has sold fewer books in a year than I."

"Correct, Marco."

"But, Herbert."

"Yes, Marco?"

"Every writer has sold fewer books in a year than I—that's why Barney has my certificate from the Guinness people."

"Hmmm . . . I see your point, Marco." Herbert kicked the waters lazily to keep his body afloat, and I waited for his next words of sagely advice. "Then you must look for a writer with an exceptional ego, Marco."

"But, Herbert."

"Yes, Marco?"

"Every writer has an exceptional ego—that's why they write."

"Hmmm . . . I see your point, Marco." Herbert continued to kick the waters lazily to keep his body afloat, and I waited for his next words of sagely advice. "Then you must look for a writer with the means and the opportunity to mastermind the crime, and with a special motive to topple you in particular from your lofty position of pre-eminence."

I kicked the water lazily myself for a while and considered the implications of Herbert's words. The only person I could think of who would want to topple me from any position of pre-eminence was Como, and a) he wasn't a writer, and b) he didn't have enough money to fund such a big crime, and c) he didn't have powerful contacts in Panama and North Korea, and d) I wrote everything he did, so I would have known about it.

So there we were, after six hundred wasted words on the question of motive. I changed tack.

"Tell me, Herbert."

"Yes, Marco?"

"What do you know about Professor Sushing?"

I went on to tell Herbert about my meeting with the Professor in Panama, and his promise to let me know if he could think of any other extremely rich people with powerful connections in Panama and North Korea.

"He is a ruthless and capable man, Marco—a man with as many powerful friends as he has powerful enemies. You know, of course, that he and I have had a long-standing feud."

"I certainly do, Herbert. Only a few chapters ago, I reminded the readers of the scene from my last book in which Professor Sushing was found guilty of libelling you. I'm glad you've raised the point again, as the readers might have forgotten the reference to his abiding resentment at your success."

A thoughtful look made nuanced rearrangements to Herbert's face. "Might it be possible, Marco, that Sushing has transferred the focus of his resentment from me to you? After all, you are widely seen as my spiritual successor, and your success has overshadowed even my spectacular achievements. It was you who brought his paranoid jealousy to the attention of the world in your book, so it would be natural for him to want revenge. Perhaps Sushing is the mastermind behind the conspiracy. Marco! Marco! Are you alright?"

I had been so struck by Herbert's suggestion that I'd forgotten to kick water and swallowed what felt like a gallon of the stuff as I went under. I clutched at the folds of his horsehair bathing habit and dragged my face clear of the surface.

"Sushing!" I spluttered. "Sushing the baddie? But he can't be."

"Why not, Marco?" Herbert patted my back to help me cough up my watery cargo. "He meets all the criteria. He has the resources, the motive, the connections in North Korea."

"Why not?" I stared at Herbert's perplexed face, as I struggled to formulate a logical answer. "I've just been to see him. If I make him the baddie now, only a chapter later, the readers will think I'm a complete idiot for not having twigged it when I was in Panama." And it wasn't just the readers I was worried about. I could just imagine how Como and Barney would react—Como because I'd screwed up the chance to quiz Sushing in Panama, and Barney because it would mean we'd never win the big prize.

"I see your point, Marco. If Sushing proved to be the mastermind after you had wasted the opportunity to question him in Panama, you would indeed appear a most incompetent writer. Laughably so. Ha ha ha ha ha ha splt ha splt splt glck . . ."

It was now my turn to pat Herbert's back as he started to choke on his own laughter at my predicament.

"For a mentor, Herbert, you can be very unsympathetic at times."

"I'm sorry Marco, truly I am, but you have written what you have written, and now you must make the most of it. I'm sure that all will become clear in good time. Remember what Sherlock Holmes always said about the futility of hypothesising in the absence of conclusive data."

"You're right, Herbert. I must stop agonising pointlessly about the Professor's role until I find some conclusive data to agonise pointlessly about."

"Exactly, Marco."

"But Herbert . . ."

"Yes, Marco?"

"How am I going to find any conclusive data about the Professor after missing the opportunity to quiz him in Panama?"

"Don't worry, Marco. The Professor is a man with interests in every corner of the globe. I doubt it will be long before your paths re-cross."

I looked glumly across the sea-spa at the hundreds of Brothers loitering around the edge of the pool in a variety of attitudes. I was so tired after my rush from Panama and my emotional reunion with Herbert, that I couldn't even spot the opportunity of making a joke about a globe having corners. I decided to start a new chapter.

CHAPTER FORTY ONE

*In which Marco contemplates the disgraceful
gender bias prevalent in publishing.*

I HELD MY IPHONE ABOVE my head so Como couldn't see the Spartan shabbiness of my guest-cell while we had a video call about latest developments. Without mentioning the Professor, I told him Herbert's theory about the purpose of the conspiracy.

"Herbert thinks it's someone trying to break my record for selling the most books in a year."

"Who'd want to do that?"

"Who wouldn't? Every author would want to do it, according to Herbert."

"That's a big help. If everyone wants to do it, it doesn't help us identify the perp."

"No, but Herbert thinks it could be someone who's trying to break the record to get at me somehow."

"That's an even bigger help. The whole world would want to get at you somehow, if they had any sense."

"Como!"

"Don't 'Como!' me. You've been away three days in Panama and Pasadena, and all you've got is that some Professor promises to let you know if he thinks of anything, and Herbert Quarry thinks of a motive that pins the crime on everyone."

"That's not all I got. Listen . . ."

I told Como the story about Donna Maria Triabla De Medici and Steve McGee.

"I see. So in addition to the complete lack of conclusive information you dug-up from the Quarry and Sushing meetings, you discover a witness and lose her again just as she's about to reveal material facts. Nice work. I can see why you specialise in crime fiction. Aren't you gonna ask about my wounds?"

"How are your wounds?"

"They're great. Doc says I'll be out tomorrow, provided I don't do anything too strenuous, and I don't see how I'm going to be doing anything too strenuous, since I'll be stuck at a desk filing paperwork on every damn disaster that's happened since you came to Clarkesville. Speaking of disasters, when are you coming back to Clarkesville?"

"Tomorrow. The life here doesn't suit me. Too luxurious."

We agreed on a plan for getting together back at Clarkesville, said our goodnights, and killed the call. I sat on my slop-bucket—but not for long, as the rim cut painfully into one's buttocks—then washed with the ewer of cold water I forgot to mention earlier. I climbed into my horsehair bed. I didn't feel like writing, and I wasn't ready for sleep, so I flicked through the TV channels on my iPad, and blow-me-down wasn't there a current-affairs programme discussing Marco Ocram.

Actually, it was discussing the sensational news about the Sushing Prize, and the fact that I was the clear favourite to win it. One of the participants was a lady called Germaine Greer. I seemed to remember she was a eunuch. Quite how they make lady eunuchs has never been clear to me, but the process evidently leaves its subject with a grievance, because this Greer seemed a right grouch. According to her, my works typified the male-oriented themes sadly still prevalent in mainstream publishing.

I clutched my iPad with outraged hands. How could she sit there and accuse me of typifying male-orientation in mainstream publishing? *The Awful Truth about the Herbert Quarry Affair* had been bursting its bindings with strong female characters.

I went through the roll-call of memorable females who graced its pages. There was the absent star of the book—Lola Kellog—the underage girl who became Herbert's secret mistress and who was gruesomely murdered by Chief and Scoobie McGee. There was Marcia Delgardo, the psychotic sister of the beautiful waitress at the coffee-shop, who painted 3,820 pictures of Herbert Quarry, and who tried to incinerate me when she torched Herbert's house. There was Quimara Tann, the social climber who tried to marry her beautiful daughter Esmerelda to Herbert to become a celebrity mother. There was Flora Moron—sorry, Moran, and my Bronx mom. There was Marge Downberry, the former head of midwifery at the Clarkesville County Hospital who had switched babies after the freak fire. There was the whole raft of un-named female extras who gossiped inanely at the nail-bar. And to crown it all, the main villain—Elijah Bow—was a cross-dressing prom queen! How could anyone say that I didn't give women a fair crack in my previous book?

And as for this book—virtually all of the good new characters are women—Harbour Master McBeany, Timo Tsatarin's neighbour, the judge at my trial, and the beautiful Panamanian woman. Detective Fovantski was usually a woman, except when I made continuity errors and wrote him as a man called Fovinski. And don't forget the receptionist at the gym—and the lady sat-nav voice. I admit freely that they are all somewhat incidental, but then all the characters are except me and Como.

I stared at the door of my cell, wondering about the possibility of gender reassignment for Como, and all the puns I could make on the name Coma. No, tempting though it might be, the idea of a giant female ex-American-football-playing police chief lacked the authenticity that characterised my work. Which left only me, and a gender reassignment for me would be a rather contrived development at this stage in the book. Frankly—leaving my own feelings aside—I didn't see why my readers should have to suffer bizarre and improbable plot twists just to appease Germaine Greer.

Having satisfied myself that Greer's criticisms were entirely groundless, I returned my attention to the programme, which was now profiling the Professor. Overall, he came across as an austere but benevolent philanthropist, the only blots on his copybook being his undignified feud with Herbert Quarry and the suspicion that he was helping North Korea launch nukes. Since it was I who had authored both of those outstanding shortcomings, I could see why he might bear me a grudge, or two. That said, his remarks in Chapter 39 suggested I could yet bag the big prize. All I needed to do was avoid writing anything else that might upset him—which could be tricky for an author committed to the principle of typing whatever came into his head. Speaking of which . . .

Once again the strains of *Que Sera Sera* caressed the Ocram eardrums. It was my Bronx mom.

"Markie! So you've decided to answer your phone at last. I've been calling and calling. Where are you?"

"I'm in Pasadena, mom."

"Pasadena? I thought you said Panama."

"I was in Panama, mom, but I'm in Pasadena now."

"What's wrong with you Markie? Is the Bronx no good? Don't you want to be by your mom any more?"

"Mom! No, honest. I'll be home when I can. I'm just on a flying visit to see Herbert Quarry."

"Herbert Quarry! But he's a dirty old man, Marco. What are you doing with a dirty old man like Herbert Quarry?"

"He's not a dirty old man, mom. That was just what the papers said when bad guys were trying to frame him. Anyway, he's down here now in the . . ." I managed to stop myself mentioning the Christian Brothers' place—my Bronx mom can get odd ideas about things like that— ". . . in the place where I'm staying."

"Well you just mind what he gets up to. Now Markie, did you see the news? Everybody's talking about you winning the new prize. Everyone in the salon says you deserve to win it. Oh Markie, it's so exciting. You make your poor mom so proud. Tell your poor mom you're going to win the prize. Tell her, Markie."

"I can't guarantee it, mom. There are other authors and . . ."

My Bronx mom said what she'd like to do with other authors who tried to stop her Markie winning the big prize.

"It's not just that, mom."

I told my mom that all the facts pointed to Sushing as the brains behind the Dragon's Claw conspiracy, and if that news broke I'd have no chance of winning his prize.

"Markie, you gotta do something about that. Markie, what will your poor mom do if you don't win the prize? She'll have to cover her head in shame. Close the salon. Markie, don't tell your poor old mom such things. And I saw the Professor on tee vee. Such a sweet old man. You can't, Markie. You can't make the Professor the bad man. Think what it will do to your poor mom. Markie!"

CHAPTER FORTY TWO

In which Como catches Marco delaying progress.

HAVING PRESSED CONTROL+ALT+SHIFT+ asterisk+ hash+close parenthesis, which was the new easier way to get a page break in Microsoft Word, I wondered about the best way to start my next chapter. The call from my Bronx mom had really raised the stakes. Before that I just had a ten million dollar prize to lose by making the Professor the bad guy—now it could mean upsetting my mom too. Unable to make a logical decision about next steps, I waited for the next thing to come into my head. It was a reunion with Como, so I shifted the plot forward to his office, sacrificing the chance for pages of padding about my breakfast with Herbert and the journey from Pasadena to Clarkesville.

Como rose stiffly from his desk upon my appearance.

"Hey, Writer."

We fist-bumped then had a man-hug that Como rather tetchily cut short.

"Hey, don't squeeze, Writer. I've still got bullet holes, don't forget. What's the latest? Your friend Herbert got any new theories to narrow down the list of suspects to less than half the population of the USA?"

"Not yet," I said, somewhat defensively. "Though in fairness to my friend Herbert we were speculating in something of a vacuum as far as concrete evidence was concerned. And who is responsible for gathering concrete evidence, Como? Let me guess—is it the fire brigade? Is it the ambulance service? Is it the coastguards? Remind me."

"For your information, wise guy, my team has been working its butt off investigating the case while you've been swanning around and getting yourself in the papers."

He threw me a copy of the *Clarkesville County Gazette*, the front page of which bore a syndicated close-up of the parts of the Ocram anatomy that I had been trying to shield when I was thrown onto the street with my pants down. The tasteless headline read 'Ocram to have small part in new Cruise movie?' I hoped my Bronx mom hadn't shown it to Mrs. Angelman's daughters.

"Como, may I say that for a police chief who claims to be overwhelmed with form-filling, you seem to have a lot of time on your hands to read scandalous tabloid scuttlebutt."

"What else can I read? It's the same in every paper."

"Not true, Como. You shouldn't make sweeping generalisations unsupported by the evidence—it does no credit to your role as the Clarkesville County Police Chief. Here." It was my turn to throw something at him, namely the copy of *The Times Literary Supplement* I'd taken from the VIP lounge in Panama. "Perhaps, Como, you might find it edifying to sample highbrow reading matter for a change. Now, if your team really has worked itself buttless, perhaps you will be good enough to let me know what has been discovered."

There was a silent pause while Como allowed himself to be distracted by *The Times Literary Supplement*, presumably looking for the sports section. He was blatantly undermining my efforts at fast-paced dialogue, so I ahemed to bring him back to the matter at hand.

"Ahem," I said.

"What?"

"I said perhaps you will be good enough to let me know what your buttless team has discovered while I have been pursuing leads elsewhere."

"There's some good stuff in here, Writer."

I assumed he meant the photographs of lady novelists. "Yes, well, you can look at the pictures later. Let's get back to police procedure, please."

He tossed the *TLS* aside and picked up a sheaf of police notes. "Fact One: the DNA and fingerprints of Olmev Kamogin—the guy you killed, remember?" He looked at me in a way that I think is called censoriously, but feel free to check it.

"Never mind whom I remember or don't remember killing—get on with the facts."

"His DNA and fingerprints were found in the straddle that dropped the container that crushed Tsatarin. He was a qualified straddle driver, and his records were at the straddle driver agency. So it looks pretty certain that Kamogin killed Tsatarin."

"Ha."

I ha'ed because if it hadn't been for Como's psychotic stapling tendencies, we might have discovered the Kamogin connection a hundred pages ago when we had to leave the straddle driver agency in a hurry, to avoid allegations of police brutality.

"Fact Two: the black hold-all in Steve McGee's garage exactly matched hold-alls found at the apartments of the other Bulgarian suspects, and bore the fingerprints of the other Bulgarian suspects, and contained chemical residues consistent with large amounts of paper currency having been stored therein."

"Ha."

I ha'ed again because Como had poo-pooed my suggestion that the black hold-alls were a common thread.

"Fact Three: Steve McGee's silver Audi was found outside town, with six bullet holes in a tight cluster in the driver's door." He handed me a photo of the bullet holes.

"Ha."

I ha'ed even more loudly this time, since Como had made a cruel joke about my inability to hit a barn door, and here we were with a tight cluster of bullet holes, a la Jack Reacher, after I'd shot at the perp from the window of the evidence suite.

"Fact Four: Inside Steve McGee's silver Audi was the third Bulgarian guy from the photofit you got from Tsatarin's neighbour. All six bullets had got him." He handed me a photo of a dead person slumped in the seat of an Audi, with blood everywhere.

My fourth ha died on my lips. How could he have driven away from the police car park with my six tightly clustered bullets inside him?

"Fact Five . . ."

I interrupted Como with a wave of the photo of the dead Audi driver. "Just a minute. How did he get to drive the Audi from the car park at Police HQ to a place outside town if he had six bullet holes in him?"

"If ever I redo this list, Writer, Fact One is going to be you sure are a dumbass. He didn't drive anywhere with the six bullets in him. You're crazy if you think anyone could drive with one bullet, let alone six. He was shot where the car was found. Fact Five: the shell cases were on the ground right alongside the car."

"But . . . but . . . I shot him from the window of the evidence suite—how can the shell cases be on the ground next to the car outside town?" I was beginning to lose the plot.

"You! You think you made those bullet holes?" Como's deep belly-laughs morphed into groans of agony as they re-opened his gunshot wounds. Doubling over with the pain, he took the next few papers from his sheaf of notes and threw them at me.

I scanned the papers. Facts Six to Ten were about the bullets I'd fired from Como's gun having been found in various places around the Clarkesville Police HQ, viz in the big maple tree (x2), in a sand bin, in a City Council notice board, and in the flower-bed just under the window. Fact Eleven was that one of the bullets from Como's gun had gone through the rear window of the silver Audi, which was something positive at least. Fact Twelve was a letter from the Clarkesville City Council Maintenance Department reporting a crime of firearms damage to one of its notice boards. So only one of my shots had been anywhere near the target.

"Fact Thirteen," said Como with another loaded look: "The money in Steve McGee's freezer can be traced back to Timo Tsatarin's bank account."

I'd lost the will to ha, so I made Como continue.

"Fact Fourteen: Timo Tsatarin was a computer-science PhD from Sofia Computer Science Institute, one of the most advanced computer science teaching institutions in the world.

Fact Fifteen: Timo Tsatarin's DNA and fingerprints were found on keyboards at the datacentre. Fact . . ."

"No, Como, wait," I said. I looked at the bottom left of my screen where my iPad told me I'd written sixty one thousand words. Barney said my overriding artistic objective should be to make my books about seventy five thousand words, otherwise he'd be in breach of some contract or other. Allowing five thousand words for an epic ending, I still needed nine thousand words of plot development. If Como spilled the rest of his boastful beans now, I might climax prematurely and have Barney on my back. With that appalling image in my mind, I decided to write a convincing excuse to shut Como up and stop him revealing key facts too soon . . .

"I've just remembered, I've got an appointment at the hairdresser's, so I can't go through any more of the facts just now."

Como gave me an odd look. "No problem," he said. "You got a stylist booked? I can recommend mine if you want. I got his card somewhere."

Como went rooting in his drawers for his stylist's card while I swivelled my eyeballs to the top left to denote a moment of confused introspection about why Como would suddenly start recommending hair stylists. I admit I'd written it, but I couldn't quite believe that I had.

"It's OK, Como, I've got a stylist already. I've booked an appointment."

"In Clarkesville?"

"Yes."

"That's interesting. Which stylist have you picked?"

I was even more confused now. Why would he want to know which stylist I'd picked? I didn't know any stylists in

Clarkesville, but I was too smart to be caught out by Como. Instinctively I adopted clever tactics of evasion . . .

"I can't remember. It's on my iPad somewhere. I'll look it up as I walk to the car."

"Hey, let me give you a lift." He stood and started to put on his Police Chief overcoat. "I could do with the fresh air."

"No, it's kind of you, Como, but I need to move my car anyway or I'll get a parking ticket."

"Are you kidding, Writer? Who d'you think runs parking enforcement? You get a ticket—you give it to me. We don't ticket our buddies in this town."

"No, really, Como, I can drive myself."

"You saying my car's not good enough for Mister Fancy Pants, or my company?"

"No, honest, Como. The car's fine. And the company, honest."

"Good, so that's settled. I'll give you a lift. So you just need to look up the name and address of your stylist on your iPad right now, so I can let the dispatchers know where their chief's gonna be."

I gave him a steely stare.

"Well, would you look at that. Typical. My iPad's flat. I'll just have to forget about the appointment, I suppose."

He gave me a steely stare right back.

"No, don't do that Writer. Use my charger. Here you go."

He tossed his charger across the desk with a defiant gleam in his eye.

"Oh, silly me. I forgot. I cancelled the appointment while I was in Panama."

"You cancelled the appointment while you were in Panama. Yeah, right. You know, Writer, you are so full of bullshit. You never had no appointment. You just made it up. I'm getting wise to your tricks, Mister Smarty Pants."

"OK, clever dick. So I made it up. So what?"

"So what? I'll tell you so what. You're a fancy pants writer who gets money for making up shit. You wannna drag-out this case to make a story of it, that's up to you. But let me tell you something, I've got a police department to run, and that means meeting targets set by the Mayor. And if Chief Galahad doesn't hit his targets Chief Galahad isn't gonna be Chief Galahad much longer. You think I can just let this crazy case go on and on and on just to give you stuff to write about, you've got another thing coming—not unless I get cover from the Mayor. You understand me?"

I gave him a look that blended resentment with resignation in equal measure. I switched on my iPad in a haughty manner and started to type. There was a tap on the door and the Mayor came in.

CHAPTER FORTY THREE

In which the boys catch some perps.

"MISTER OCRAM, WHAT A DELIGHTFUL surprise to find you here working hand in glove with Chief Galahad. I wouldn't want to be in the shoes of the local villains knowing that you two boys are on the case. No sir."

I gave Como a look. The Mayor continued . . .

"Now, Chief Galahad, about those wounds of yours. I'm very concerned, and the City Council's very concerned, that we shouldn't be risking the health of our best ever Police Chief by putting him under too much pressure while he's still got bullet-holes in him, so we've agreed that all your targets for the year are scrapped with immediate effect. I want you two boys to focus on nailing those bastards that are trying to turn our town into a major centre for organised crime, and I don't care what it takes as long as you nail 'em. Do I make myself clear?"

"Yes, Mayor," we both said at the same time.

"Good. Now I'll leave you boys to get back to your crime fighting, or whatever it was you were doing before I interrupted. And remember, nail those bastards."

We promised to nail those bastards, and Como showed the Mayor out.

"Satisfied?" I said.

"I don't know why you didn't do that in the first place. You know what your trouble is, Writer?"

It was a rhetorical question, so I said nothing and waited for him to tell me what my trouble was.

"Your trouble is, you don't plan enough. Sometimes I swear you just write the first shit that comes into your head."

I slumped in one of Como's conference table chairs. He was right, of course. I did always write the first thing that came into my head, and sometimes it wasn't that clever. But, I reminded myself, that was the way of the artist. That was commitment to an artistic principle. Other writers wouldn't take the risk. Other writers would be too concerned about their image and reputation to allow their spontaneously created words to be exposed to a harsh and judgemental public. Like Tom Cruise with his rubber face and his makeup and his retakes and his stuntmen and his airbrushed close-ups, most writers used artificial tricks like editing and rewrites to prop up their reputations. Where's the integrity in that? And besides, it would take you weeks to finish a book if you kept having to perfect everything. No, Herbert's philosophy of literature might not be ideal, but writing the first thing that came into your head was pure and honest, and I wasn't going to start compromising my principles now.

"Como, you're right. Sometimes it is shit. But do you know what?" It was my turn to ask the rhetorical question. "I'd rather write fresh shit than the stale shit everyone else writes, so stop complaining and let's get on with the case."

"That's easy for you to say, Writer. You're not a police chief. You can dick around with a case any way you like, but I've got rules to follow. I've been to police college. I've taken an oath to fight crime in the right way. An *oath*. You know what an oath is?"

I was about to show Como that not only did I know what an oath was, but I also knew several choice examples, when his phone rang. He put up his hand to shush me while he listened to the caller, his expression growing more intense as the call progressed.

"They've got the perps who killed Steve McGee," he said when he'd finished the call. "Holed up in a motel at Barton Hills. Get your coat, Writer—you're gonna see how we deal with bad guys who torture cops."

We got into the red Gran Torino with sober purposefulness, and only one thing on our minds—retribution. Well, not quite only one thing, as I was starving. Como, however, selfishly rebuffed my proposal that we should stop for burgers and fries and seemed blind to my perfectly rational argument that dealing with torturers on an empty stomach was a sure-fire recipe for grouchiness.

The motel was just off the N66 by the Barton Hills interchange—the only interchange I ever mention in my books. The entire fleet of Clarkesville prowlers was there, along with its usual entourage of outside broadcast vans and rubbernecking locals. When the reporters saw us, they raced over with their cameras and outstretched microphones.

"Mister Ocram, are you on the verge of solving the container port mystery?"

"Mister Ocram, did you really fight off armed criminals trying to steal money from Officer McGee's garage?"

"Mister Ocram, is it true that you are suing J.K. Rowling for plagiarism?"

I made a sign to signify that I was prepared to give a statement if they would all just shut up for a minute, and I composed my thoughts as I waited for the cameramen to get into position around me. Finally I was ready to speak.

"People of Clarkesville, people of America, and people of the world. We face a grave and difficult crisis. However, you can rest assured that I will . . ."

I never got round to assuring the peoples of Clarkesville, America, and the world, because Como yanked me away from the cameras to follow him to the front of the clustered prowlers where the cream of the Clarkesville County PD were crouching behind car doors. Como took a loud-hailer from one of the prowlers and loud-hailed the perps.

"This is Police Chief Galahad. You are surrounded and have no chance of escape. Either come out now with your hands high or you will be killed by gunfire."

There was a moment of intensely dramatic silence, while I waited to see whether we were going to be in for a long siege. No. The door to the room opened a crack, and a white handkerchief fluttered through it; following which the swarthy perps perped out with their hands in the air. Phew! That was a relief. Spared thousands of words of boring padding. Como nodded at his team to collar the perps, then loud-hailed in the direction of our media retinue.

"People of Clarkesville, people of America, and people of the world. Through strong and decisive action by its Chief, the Clarkesville County PD has . . ."

I yanked the power cord of the loud-hailer out of its socket. This was no time for pompous, self-congratulating speeches. I was on the brink of writing something I'd never written before— one of those scenes where the police interview perps in a room with a two-way mirror. We needed to get back to police HQ at the double.

CHAPTER FORTY FOUR

In which a confession is extracted.

BACK AT POLICE HQ, THE two swarthy perps had been read their rights, booked in, photographed, and printed. In the process, they'd also had various accidents, which made them look as if they had been maliciously beaten in memory of their tortured victim, although I'm sure that was just a coincidence. They had each been taken into a separate interview room, where they had been subjected to relentless questioning. I had decided to spare my fans the tedium of a full transcription of the interviews, as we couldn't spare the word count for that. Instead, I started the action *in media res* at the point where Como and I were pacing about in the dimly-lit observation room that had the two-way mirrors overlooking the interview suites . . .

Our patience had been stretched to breaking point by the blatant smug evasiveness of the perps, who had answered 'no comment' to every one of the many questions that had been put to them so far. The observation room would have been thick with the smoke from our cigarettes, and littered with their butts, were it not for the law that banned smoking in workplaces, and the fact that I never smoked because it gave me a bad cough. Como and I each ran our hands through our respective hair in a clichéd gesture denoting extreme impatience with dissembling perps.

"How long are we going to let this pathetic charade continue?" I said. I meant the interviews, of course, not the book, which still had twelve thousand words to run.

Como paced back and forth like a caged tiger in a cage.

"OK, we've seen enough, Writer. Let's have a little talk with these guys off the record."

"Ooooof." The swarthy perp groaned as Como slammed him into the wall of the interview room, and I squeezed my eyes shut to avoid the moment of contact. I knew it was a bad idea to do this on an empty stomach—Como was grouchy as hell.

"You know what 'no comment' means in my language, buster? 'No comment' in my language means this." Como gripped the perp's wrist, put the perp's fingertips on the edge of the table, then pressed down so the perp's fingers were bent backwards until one of them snapped at a knuckle. "And sometimes it means this . . ." Ignoring the perp's screams he took out his gun and hammered the butt down on the perp's thumb, leaving a squidgy mess like a miniature version of the body on the container roof. The perp screamed again. "And sometimes it means . . ."

"Como, no!" I couldn't take any more, so heaven knows how the perp felt about it. "He's going to speak."

"I tell you, I tell you," said the tortured perp, looking from his mangled hand to Como as if he wasn't sure which was the more horrific.

"OK, buster, spill it. Why did you kill McGee?"

"He was blackmailing us."

"Us? Who is us?"

"He was blackmailing Tsatarin. Tsatarin was weak. Tsatarin gave money to McGee. Our money. He gave our money to McGee. We work hard for that money, and McGee he take it."

"What was he blackmailing you about?"

"What you think? The job. Our job. Our job to sell all the books. All those stupid books. I wish I never seen those stupid books."

"Who was the job for?"

"Huh?"

"Who was the job for? Who was paying you to do the job?"

"I don't know."

"In my language I don't know means the same as no comment." Como grabbed the perp's hand and went to smash another digit with the butt of his gun.

"I swear it! I swear it! I swear I don't know," sobbed the feckless perp.

"How d'you get your instructions then, if you don't know who you're workin' for?"

"Whom, Como, whom," I chipped in, to help the interview along and raise the tone somewhat.

"The lawyers. The lawyer men, they give us all the instructions."

"You have the names of the lawyers?"

"Yes yes. We have names and phone numbers and everything. I give them to you. Please."

"And why did Tsatarin die?"

"I tell you, he was weak. He gave away our money. We drug him to get rid of him, to take him away, but he climb out of the datacentre into the port, over the fence. And he collapse on roof of container. And we can't leave him there and we can't carry him out of port, so Kamogin has idea to squeeze him under container like an accident."

"Hmmf."

It was me hmmfing at the flimsy plausibility of the explanation. I had hoped for something far more inventive and convincing, but as I always said—that was the difference between true crime and fiction.

Como walked to the door and called to one of the officers outside. "OK, get this clown cleaned up."

The officer came in and went to grab me.

"No, not that clown, the other clown."

"Sorry, Chief."

I walked out of the room with all the dignity I could muster, while the officer assessed the perp's wounds.

CHAPTER FORTY FIVE

In which the reader had best pay close attention.

"SO, COMO," I SAID. "I suppose you're feeling pretty pleased with yourself, now that you've extracted a confession and cleared up the murder."

"Maybe, Writer, but not as pleased as I would have been if I'd been left alone to clear up the case the proper police way from the start."

"Yes, Como, but in those circumstances, you wouldn't have become the second most important character in the next bestseller by a world-famous publishing phenomenon. In this life, Como, one can become famous or one can adhere slavishly to proper police procedure: one cannot do both."

"True," said Como, much to my surprise—I was expecting his usual uncivil comeback. "Where d'you think all this fame is gonna get me?"

"Get you? What d'you mean, get you? Is fame not a reward in itself?"

"It seems to me there's two types of fame in your book, Writer. There's the keep-on-doing-your-lowly-menial-police-chief-job fame, and there's make-a-fortune fame, and I don't see why you get the make-a-fortune fame and I get the keep-on-being-a-police-chief kind."

"That, Como, is the way of things. It is called fate, or karma, or destiny, or fortune, or providence, et cetera. You must have done something bad in a former life."

"I don't see how it could be any worse than what I'm doing in this life. Seems to me that I do all the work, I get you out of all the scrapes, I save your life—twice—I clean up all your mess, and you write about it and you get millions of dollars and fame, and I get just fame. Where's the fairness in that?"

"No one said it was fair. Remember, Como, life can't always be a bowl of cherries. Anyway, there might be a remunerative aspect to your fame."

"Such as?"

"Well . . . you know that Tom Cruise has bought the film rights to my last book."

"Our last book, you mean."

I ignored his provocative remark.

"When he gets round to making the film, it will have to have a police procedure advisor, to ensure that the film is every bit as authentic as the book—it's a stipulation of the contract. You could be the police procedure advisor if you play your cards right, and police procedure advisors can earn a pretty penny."

Como considered my words for a moment. "Would I get to work with Tom Cruise?"

"Very possibly—and with Steven Spielberg."

"And would I get to go to Hollywood?"

"I expect so. Some of the work would be on location, but some would indeed be in the studio."

Como twiddled with his handcuffs in a ruminative sort of way, then leant back and looked at me with hooded eyes. "You able to pull any strings to make me the police procedure advisor?"

"Possibly, but only within my strict ethical code."

"Your strict ethical code. OK, Writer, tell me about this strict ethical code of yours that's so strict I haven't been able to notice it in the three years since we first met. Which, incidentally, was the day I found you skulking in Herbert Quarry's house. I should have shot you then if I'd had any sense."

"I concede, Como, that it's probably more of an artistic code than an ethical one. I have to be true to my artistic principles. If someone asks me to write a reference for you, it must be convincing and authentic. Obviously, I can't just write the first thing that comes into my head."

And with that my phone rang.

"Marco Ocram speaking. How may I help you caller?"

"Markeeeee!" It was Barney. "How ya doin', Marky baby. No don't tell me now—save it. I got some news, Marky. Listen. You're going to love this. You must have made a big impression on your professor friend down in Panama. His people got on to my people this morning to say that he'd be pleased if you'd accept his offer of a lift to the Games. You know what that means? Sushing chairs the prize committee, and he's giving you a lift to the show in his jet. Nobody gives anybody a lift to the show in their jet if they're not going to give them the prize. I tell you, Marky, you're in for a cool mill or my dick's not got a hole in it."

Wow. I know Barney exaggerates but it did seem plausible. I could be in for ten percent of a ten million dollar prize. Wow.

I exchanged a few other words with Barney and killed the call.

"You look excited, for a change," said Como. "Your mom got you engaged to one of those girls at last?"

"No. Barney's just said that Sushing's offered me a lift to the Literary Games. He thinks I might be in with a chance to win a prize or something." I decided not to mention the size of the prize—that might just fuel the fire of Como's financial envy.

"The Literary Games, huh? Are they on already?"

"Yeah. Opening ceremony's the day after tomorrow. Barney says Professor Sushing is going to fly me there in his jet. I wonder what all that's about."

"Well, you give Professor Sushi my very best regards. Say Police Chief Como Galahad wants to thank him from the bottom of his heart for helping say who's behind this *Dragon's Claw* business. Which reminds me, Writer."

"What?"

"Perp says he gets instructions from the lawyers in Panama. All the leases for the warehouses and the datacentre are held by the lawyers in Panama. All the money that's been floating around has come from the lawyers in Panama. All the freight consignments for the books have been triggered by the lawyers in Panama. According to you, your beautiful woman in Panama says she gets her instructions and money from the lawyers in Panama. Did you look up those lawyers in Panama, you know, when you were in Panama?"

"Not exactly."

"Not exactly, huh? You were in the place where everything leads to, and you never thought to look up the lawyers in Panama while you were right there. In Panama." He waggled his head in a manner conveying disbelief. "I hope there's a category at those Literary Games for stories about complete dumbasses. You'd win gold medal in that one, that's for sure."

"OK. OK, I admit I should have looked up the lawyers in Panama when I was in Panama. But can't you get the FBI or the CIA or someone to do it?"

"You know, Writer, that's the second sensible thing you've said in this entire book. I forget what the first sensible thing was, but I remember pointing it out. Let me see."

Como flicked through the Rolodex on his desk to find the Cs and then found the tab for the CIA in Panama. I wondered whether I was up to the task of writing a realistic dialogue between a US Police Chief and a CIA field office in Panama. I decided I wasn't up to it, so I'd write an entirely unrealistic one instead and see if anyone noticed. Actually, I'd write half an entirely unrealistic one—Como's half. He rang the number . . .

"Is that the CIA field office in Panama? Police Chief Como Galahad here, Clarkesville County PD. Yeah, that Clarkesville County PD. Yeah, the one with the books on fire in the warehouses. I need your help with a little matter. We've been investigating this little ol' case and all the leads point to a firm of lawyers registered in Panama as being responsible for funding and facilitating every aspect of the crime. We don't think they'd be doing it off their own ticket, so they're probably working for a client. We need to know who that client is, you get me? Right. And to get to know who their client is we need to know who these lawyers are. Right. OK, I'll fax you the names and details we got here, and I'll wait for a fax back. You betcha."

He put down the phone.

Actually, Como's half of the dialogue hadn't been as unconvincing as I'd feared. Except that Como got through to the right person first time, which with hindsight was a bit unrealistic. And they didn't check Como's credentials in any way after he'd called them out of the blue, which was obviously wrong. And he said he'd send them a fax without asking for their fax number, which was a major continuity error. And probably no one uses faxes any more. But apart from those things, it wasn't too bad.

"So they couldn't give you an answer over the phone?" I said.

"Are you kidding? I didn't even get through to the right guy. Besides, they're not gonna give information to someone who just rings up out of the blue—they gotta check my credentials. Damn, I forget to get their fax number."

CHAPTER FORTY SIX

*In which a dead end is reached after
a digression upon the topic of respect.*

COMO CALLED THE CIA PANAMA field office to get their fax number, then faxed the details of the Panamanian lawyers while I wondered if I could write a joke about the CIA always having offices in fields. We decided to wait in Como's office so we could have a scene where the tension slowly builds to an unbearable level until the fax machine beeps and we snatch out the paper to learn something about the Panamanian lawyers that allows us to nail the sick mastermind behind the plot to topple me from my pinnacle in the sphere of literature.

Well, now that I think about it, I'm not sure spheres have pinnacles, but you know what I mean.

While we waited for the fax, the tension rose unbearably until about seven o'clock, when we decided to pop next door to get takeaway pizzas. Back in Como's office, we ate the pizzas and talked of this and that to take our minds off the unbearable tension.

"So what are you trying to get out of life, Writer?"

I raised a hand to ask Como to wait while I swallowed enough of the pizza in my mouth to be able to talk. "Gee, that's a hard question, Como. I never really think about it."

"I don't suppose you need to think about it when you just swan around making millions from writing crap."

"That's true." I stuffed another slice into my mouth for a spot of reflective mastication. From reading *The Times Literary Supplement,* you would think writing was some high artistic achievement. Writing was like eating pizza—it was something you did to satisfy an animal need.

"You gonna ask what I want to get out of life, Writer?"

"Sorry, Como." I asked him what he was trying to get out of life.

"There's only one thing a man or woman needs to get out of life, Writer—respect."

I pondered the wisdom of his words. I certainly agreed that lack of respect was a bad thing, as was recently proved by the painful episode I spent with my pants down surrounded by paparazzi in Panama. But I wasn't sure that respect was everything.

"Are you sure respect is everything, Como? What about health and wealth and comfort?" I thought a bit more about it. "What about mixing with celebrities, and being on TV, and driving the latest black Range Rover with tinted windows, and having a Rolex, and being recognised by everyone, and winning Nobel prizes, and all that kind of stuff?"

"You sure are mixed up, Writer, when it comes to thinking about respect. All those are just things that make it easier to get respect in this twisted world. Now," he waved some pizza crust at me, "you take some complete asshole no one likes. Give him lots of dough, a Rolex, a black Range Rover with tinted windows. Then put him in those trashy celebrity magazines a lot. The asshole is still an asshole but now people are 'respecting' him. And he might even respect himself for it, but you wanna know something?"

I was still champing, which Como took as a sign of intense interest in his forthcoming words.

"He won't be respecting himself for long. You know why so many celebrities and rich people top themselves? I'll tell you why—they don't have real respect. Real respect comes from here." He tapped his massive Police Chief chest, then carefully separated a slice from the rest of his pizza and lowered it into his mouth.

I thought it was easy for Como to trot out his philosophy over a pizza, but I suspected real life was more complicated.

"Any more of that four seasons pizza left?" I said.

"No. I told you we should have got two of them."

We finished the other pizzas and sat around waiting for the fax in an unbearable state of tension—Como reading the *TLS* while I looked up the latest news about the Literary Games on my iPad.

"I don't know who writes the most crap," said Como, looking at the *TLS*, "writers of books or the writers who write about writers of books. Sure is a load of crap in here. The only good bit I've found is someone going on about something they call the death of the author. Now *that* sounds like a good idea."

I just waved my hand at him. I couldn't be bothered arguing.

It was about half seven the next morning when I woke with my head on Como's conference table. Como was in his Police Chief chair with his head lolled back, snoring like the V8 in the

Gran Torino. The unbearable state of tension had knocked us out. I yawned, eased my stiff back, and walked to the fax machine. It had a blinking light to show that a fax was waiting, but someone needed to enter a security code to make the fax print. So much for my idea of dramatically ripping the paper from the machine. I nudged Como's beefy arm.

"What?"

"There's a fax waiting. You need to enter your code to get it to print."

"What? Let me see."

I let him see.

"I ain't got no motherfucking code. Shit."

In the end it was about nine when we dramatically found someone who knew what the code was, and dramatically waited for them to come over to Como's office, and dramatically watched as they dramatically keyed the code then dramatically found some more paper after another light blinked to say that the machine had dramatically run out. Finally, breathless with all the drama, I looked over Como's shoulder as he read the fax. He muttered its contents under his breath.

"Panamanian law firm is shell company. Registered owner of firm is privately owned company—Evestmente EDX—registered in Pyongyang Democratic People's Republic of Korea."

"Wow," I said, in a dejected, ironic sort of way.

"Wow's the word, Writer." Como let the fax slip from his hand onto his desk and looked at the oil painting of President Lincoln above the splendid fireplace on the opposite wall. "We've got exactly one lead left and it's the name of a private company in North Korea. And I bet that's a shell company, too."

"I don't suppose there's a CIA field office in Pyongyang?"

"You think I'm going to sit round waiting for another fax?"

So that was it. We'd more or less solved every mystery about the case except for the most important one—who had been behind it. The trail of evidence led to the least transparent society on the planet, and the obvious suspect was someone I couldn't implicate for fear of losing a ten million dollar prize. A surge of anger ran through me. I wasn't going to be beaten. I voiced my thoughts.

"Surely there's some other way to trace the person behind this heinous crime?"

"Think so?" Como didn't sound convinced.

"But . . . surely there must be."

"You can say 'surely' as much as you like, Writer, but the way I see it, whoever's behind this is cleverer than you and me put together, and is richer than you and me put together a thousand times. And when you get someone that rich and that clever, there's no surely about anything. If he's organised everything here through a Panama law firm, and if that law firm has just been acting on instructions from a North Korean law firm, and God knows how many other law firms are in a chain behind them, then the chances of you tracing the evidence that far is zip. The only hope left now is that your new best friend Professor Sushi knows someone who knows someone who knows someone, if you get my meaning."

"You're right."

Como was right. Just spelling the name of a Korean law firm would be hard enough. Forcing them to reveal details of a client was unthinkable—even for me. I had an idea. What if I made Professor Sushing the perp *after* he'd awarded me the prize?

Yes!

A surge of excitement ran through me, purging the surge of anger from just a few paragraphs ago. My fingers felt on fire as

I typed my evolving vision. Imagine the big night of the prize ceremony. The huge conference hall is filled with excited A-list celebrities. Three lines of arms-linked police struggle to hold back the crowds outside. A thousand cameras click as Oprah reads the names of the shortlisted authors from a gilt-edged card—four names in all, but only one on everyone's lips. Huge applause explodes as that name is read out. Bashful, modest, publishing legend, Marco Ocram, rises from his table, straightening the creases in his black corduroy tuxedo. He nudges an unruly lock of his famous auburn afro as he threads past the cheering VIPs to take the stage. The four-minute standing ovation over, he begins his warm, witty acceptance speech. Greatly honoured. Others more worthy of the prize. Huge debt of thanks to mentor Herbert Quarry. Bronx mom will be so proud. Etc etc. Then, unexpectedly, the darker note. Sombrely, Marco reminds audience of recent outrages in Clarkesville County. The deaths of brave Lieutenant McGee and miscellaneous Bulgarians. The arson at the warehouses. The near-fatal injuries sustained by heroic Police Chief, Como Galahad. What embodiment of evil could be responsible? Then the out-flung hand. The finger pointed at Sushing. The shocking revelation. The thousand gasps from assembled VIPs. Sushing grabbed by police and led away in cuffs. The world's TV presenters gabbling in fifty languages to report the unfolding drama. The incredible denouement goes viral. *The Awful Truth about The Sushing Prize* is published to a world gagging to read the full story . . .

Phew!

But then a surge of fear ran through me, purging the surge of excitement. The big night was almost two weeks away. What if Como twigged the Professor's guilt in the meantime? The big prize cancelled. No moment of glory. Endless recriminations from Barney . . .

What was I to do?

But then a surge of relief flooded through me, purging the surge of fear. I could take Como to the Games as my bodyguard, keeping him at my side and too busy to think about Sushing. Better still, Sushing could pull a gun on me at the award ceremony, and Como bravely knock it from the villain's hand just as the trigger is pulled, saving my life—beautiful women fainting as the diverted bullet grazes my cheek.

Yes!

Thankfully, before I could suffer any more purging surges, Como waved his big hand in front of my eyes. "Is there anybody in?"

"Sorry, Como, I was distracted by some thoughts. Listen, Professor Sushing is going to fly me to Nassau to the Literary Games. Why don't you come along? We might get him to spill some beans on the flight. Even if we don't, we'd have fun in Nassau. What d'you think?"

Como scratched his sternum.

"I'm not sure, Writer. The Clarkesville PD's not loaded. I'm always going hard on the guys not to waste the tax-payers' money. Won't seem right to be living the high life in the Bahamas."

"Christ, Como—don't worry about the money. You can be my security. Barney can pay for your time, so you'll end up earning the PD money not spending it. Come on. It'll be a laugh."

CHAPTER FORTY SEVEN

In which Marco imagines a fabulous air conveyance.

AFTER ITS FOURTH RUNWAY WAS built, the Clarkesville County International Airport burgeoned into a major hub, and its VIP lounge was upgraded and extended to become a go-to destination for top businesspeople and celebrities. As a result, when Como and I were waiting for the arrival of Sushing's private jet, I was relaxed and at-home, while Como walked around with his mouth open, gawping at the famous people and eating as much of the free food as he could. With a huge nudge to my ribs he asked if that was really Beyoncé over there.

"Where?" My gaze followed his rudely pointing finger. "Yes indeed, Como. As you see, when you hang around with a publishing legend, you are likely to meet the rich and almost-as-famous from other spheres of achievement."

"You know her?"

"Of course, Como. Of course. Is the Pope a Catholic? Does he write books?"

"Can you, like, introduce me?"

"If, Como, you promise to behave yourself, with no mauling or attempts at French kissing. Follow me."

Folding the latest TLS under my arm, I padded across the deep-pile carpet to where a circle of cameras focussed on the beautiful celebrity chanteuse.

"Marco!" She leapt to her talented feet. "Mmmmmmwaaah. How are you, baby? Amazing to see you."

I reciprocated her sentiments, and we stood for a few moments in various poses to satisfy the demands of the photographers. Then I introduced Como.

"Oh you're Chief Galahad! A real knight in shining armour. I read about you in Marco's book."

Como beamed in an embarrassed, Oliver Hardy sort of way.

"Yes ma'am."

"And you were shot, weren't you?"

"Yes ma'am."

"And you've been on TV rescuing Marco from the river!"

"Yes ma'am."

"You must be awfully brave."

"Yes ma'am."

"He's coming with me to the Literary Games," I said. "My bodyguard."

"A bodyguard! You can guard my body any day, baby."

"Yes ma'am."

Well that was enough of that. "Anyway, Bee, lovely seeing you. Gotta dash. Mmmwaaah."

"You too Marco. Mmmwaaah. Bye bye Chief Galahad. Pleasure meeting you."

"Yes, ma'am."

We walked back to our table. "There, Como. See what happens when you accompany me on important business? Was that, or was that not, better than eating pizza at the Clarkesville County Police HQ?"

"Yes ma'am."

I rolled my eyes and went back to the TLS. There was an article about someone called Roland Barthes who seemed to be one of those writers who wrote things no one was meant to read or understand. This kind of thing: *"writerly text is ourselves writing, before the infinite play of the world is traversed, intersected, stopped, plasticized by some singular system (Ideology, Genus, Criticism) which reduces the plurality of entrances, the opening of networks, the infinity of languages."* And I thought I was the only one who wrote made-up crap. God knows how people like Barthes's agents made any money. I'd have to ask Barney about that. Maybe there was a . . .

Bing bong.

My literary deliberations were interrupted by an announcement that Police Chief Galahad and Doctor Ocram should please make their way to Gate 206.

"I didn't know you were a doctor, Writer."

"You don't seem to know much, Como. How did you think I discovered tau muons? I have a PhD in particle physics."

"That come in handy for anything?"

"Yes, if you need to know about the physics of fundamental particles."

"But does it come in handy for anything real?"

"If you mean breaking into warehouses and shooting perps, then possibly not. But breaking into warehouses and shooting perps isn't everything, Como. Now remember. Be polite to Professor Sushing, and keep your ears open for any clues he might drop, but don't go upsetting him with accusations. If we have any suspicions, let's keep them to ourselves. We'll be on a plane, after all, so Sushing can hardly get up to any funny business."

We had our ID checked and were driven in a VIP stretch buggy across the vast concrete apron of the huge airport towards a sleek private jet. I recognised it as a JetStar Galaxy Stealth Voyager Turbo, one of the most exclusive models, in black with tinted windows. As we left the stretch buggy, the Professor came down the stairs from his jet, reminding me of a non-aquatic Captain Nemo in his bearing and mien.

"Doctor Ocram, I'm delighted you are here. And this must be Police Chief Galahad."

"Yes, sir," said Como, which was a nice change from 'Yes, ma'am.'

"Welcome." He gestured for us to climb the stairs ahead of him. "Please accept my apologies, gentlemen, for having to climb the stairs, but the Clarkesville County Airport Authority has been slow to act upon my request for escalators."

Como and I tut-tutted sympathetically at the slowness of the Clarkesville County Airport Authority, as if we thought it an outrage that billionaires should have to climb stairs to their private jets.

"Wow!"

My affected nonchalance vanished as we entered the spectacular aeroplane. I had never written, sorry, seen, anything like it. To waist-height, the walls of the immense cabin were clad in book-matched panels of polychromic marble from the most prestigious Etruscan quarries. The upper walls and the sides of the ceiling were finished in glittering mosaics, each depicting a branch of human intellectual endeavour, with the renowned thinkers, writers, scientists, artists and statesmen of the last fifty years recognisably picked out in tiny hand-knapped tesserae. The floor was paved with the most exquisite Tsumalti limestone, each piece selected for the rarity of its fossils. The fine gaps between the slabs were grouted with powdered sapphire. Rugs of inestimable value scattered the floor, with pile of downiest angora, knotted by virgins in Hakrishni temples. The TVs in the backs of the seats had only the finest liquid crystals, made on a dedicated production-run by Samsung's most experienced technicians. And no words could describe the sophisticated detailing around the air-vent nozzles below the luggage lockers. The splendid whole was illuminated by a sunroof the length of the plane, machined from a single billet of peerless Minnesotan Perspex. It was, quite literally, unbelievable.

The Professor locked the cabin door behind us and pocketed the key.

CHAPTER FORTY EIGHT

In which there is an unveiling.

"MAKE YOURSELVES COMFORTABLE, GENTLEMEN. I shall just attend to our departure."

While the Professor attended to our departure—whatever that meant—Como and I wandered round the luxuriously appointed cabin, I taking in its many unique and priceless works of art, Como taking in its many miniatures of spirits on the drinks trolley.

Bing. The small display panels beneath the luggage lockers showed the internationally recognised symbols that instruct the passenger to take their seat, fasten their seat-belt, and extinguish their welding torch—at least, that's what it looked like to me, but it might have meant something else. We strapped ourselves in, and the Professor returned from the cockpit.

"I am sorry, gentlemen, but even in my private jet certain safety rules must be observed. Please give me your full attention."

While an actor's recorded voice explained the safety features of the sophisticated plane, the Professor stood in the aisle to indicate the escape hatches and demonstrate the correct way to fit and inflate the life jackets. I watched attentively, while Como flicked through the in-flight magazine in an irresponsible manner entirely inappropriate to his role as Police Chief. I would have words to say about that later.

"Thank you, gentlemen," said the Professor, neatly stowing his life-jacket in a rare Japanese cabinet with lapis lazuli inserts. "I will join you for the take-off."

He strapped himself in a seat facing ours.

"How many are the crew?" I asked.

"Oh there are no crew, Doctor Ocram. I am a licenced pilot, although the plane is perfectly capable of flying itself, as we shall now see."

His sentence was hardly finished when the powerful engines spun up to maximum revs and we hurtled down the runway and into the air, climbing at a stupendous rate.

"I am amazed, Professor, by the plane's speed, given the weight of the ornate stonework and mosaics."

"They are no weight at all, Doctor Ocram, I assure you. All of the ornamental surfaces are the product of nano-veneering— a straightforward elaboration of the ion-deposition process I invented for the manufacture of integrated circuits. The decorative veneers are only a few atoms thick, and deposited on bearers of carbon-fibre, so the plane is actually the lightest in its class, with an unprecedented power-to-weight ratio."

"Indeed." I said, desperately trying to restore my air of nonchalance, and wondering what might be coming next.

"Yeah, I got some of that carbon fibre stuff in the dashboard of my police car. Real cool."

"It is becoming ubiquitous, Chief Galahad. That is why my charitable research foundation has invested in facilities for manufacturing the fibre. I expect world demand to soar in the next seven years, generating a sustainable income for my other charitable works."

Bing. The various warning lights went out as we reached cruising altitude.

"Ah, gentlemen. We can now relax. Make yourselves entirely at home. Use the facilities of my modest craft in any way you wish."

"Great," said Como, saluting the Professor with a huge glass of bourbon he'd plundered before take-off.

"Am I correct in believing, Doctor Ocram, that you have never piloted a plane?"

"No, never. Not really got a head for heights. Never fancied having my own plane, even if I could afford one."

"Really? I would have thought a plane would have been well within the budget of the world's fastest-selling author."

"Writing isn't as lucrative as you might think—not for the writer, anyway."

"How do you mean?"

I leant forward confidentially. "Just between the two of us, it's the agents that make all the money."

"Really, Doctor Ocram."

"And I mean, *all* the money. My agent Barney says the ten percent he gives me is a special deal because I'm such a great writer, and everyone else just gets one percent."

"Really, Doctor Ocram. I never imagined your financial acumen would be so acute. And you, Chief Galahad—have you ever flown a plane?"

"Ha. I can just about drive my police car, Professor."

"I see. Excellent, excellent. Now tell me, did you achieve any break-through in your investigation of that rather strange case you were telling me about?"

"Funny you should ask," I said, with a wink at Como to tell him to pay attention. "We've pretty much cracked everything, but we've reached a dead-end tracking down the mastermind behind it."

"Perhaps you could give me a summary of what you know."

I wasn't sure where to start. Should I go all the way back to the big let-down I suffered at Como's hands on Page 2, where I had to invent the squidged body, or should I skip all that stupid padding? To protect what sanity my readers might have left, I decided to skip it, and start about halfway through the book . . .

"We found there was a plan by someone to break my record for being the fastest-selling author. They'd filled warehouses with millions of copies of a book, and they'd written a computer program that was going to order the book from Amazon and people like that using stolen credit card details."

"Ingenious."

"But what really confuses me," said Como, acknowledging one of the dodgier parts of the plot, "is how those jokers expected to get away with it. When the books were delivered to the people whose credit card details had been stolen, wouldn't they send the books back?"

"I would imagine, Chief Galahad, that the mastermind will have anticipated the difficulty. The delivery addresses might have been those of institutions such as charities, where books would be welcomed as anonymous gifts."

Wow, that was clever. I wish I'd thought of it. There was one other snag bugging me which the Professor might be able to iron out . . .

"But wouldn't the owners of the credit cards spot the bogus transactions?"

"Statistics show, Doctor Ocram, that only one person in a hundred thousand will check their credit card statement to query unrecognised transactions below ten dollars. For every million books ordered by your plotters, perhaps ten transactions will be queried, and refunds for small amounts are never analysed. No, Doctor Ocram, it seems to me to be a perfect plan. Only luck has caused it to go awry. Good luck for you, and bad luck for the plotters."

That gave me a cue for a line I'd read in a book. Or maybe I heard it in a film. Or was it on TV? Anyway, it doesn't really matter which.

"People make their own luck, Professor."

"Very true, Doctor Ocram. And tell me, what luck have you had in tracing your mastermind?"

I nudged Como to remind him not to give anything away. "That's something you might be able to help us with, Professor. We're pretty sure the mastermind's an extremely wealthy person with powerful connections in Panama and North Korea, with an interest in literature and a special reason to topple me from the pinnacle of the sphere of literary achievement. Since you are an extremely wealthy person, with powerful connections in Panama and North Korea, and an interest in literature, we wondered if you could suggest why someone else in your position would mastermind such a bizarre plot."

Como nudged me back. "Would you excuse us a minute Professor?" he said. "I've just remembered a bit of police admin that I didn't finish with Doctor Ocram before we left Clarkesville."

"Of course, gentlemen. I have some work of my own to do, so please use the jet as you wish and let me know when you are ready to talk about your case."

Como dragged me by the sleeve to the end of the cabin. "You never told me this guy has powerful connections in North Korea."

"You never asked."

"So spill. What kind of connections?"

"He's helping them build an inter-continental ballistic satellite launcher."

"What? Are you fucking mental?"

"Como, calm down. What's the big issue?"

"If he's helping the North Koreans do that then he'll be best-ever-mates with the head honcho that runs the whole mothering country."

"So?"

"So? Are you really that dumb? With his connections he could find out who's behind the plot like that." He snapped his fingers.

"So?"

"So? I'll tell you so. One, this guy's rich—mega, mega rich. Two, he's got powerful connections in Panama—he probably makes half their GDP. Three, he hates Herbert Quarry—in that last stupid book of yours there was the court case when Quarry sued him, for Christ-sakes. And now, four, you say he's got the most powerful connections anyone could ever have in North Korea."

I could see where this was going. I wondered whether to come clean to Como about wanting to keep the Professor's guilt un-proven until after the big prize ceremony, or whether I should just play dumb. Sticking in my comfort zone, I decided to play dumb.

"What are you getting at, Como?"

"Let me ask you this, Writer. If he's got that much pull in North Korea why hasn't he offered to use it to find out who's behind the plot?"

"Don't ask me. Maybe he just didn't think about it."

"Oh yeah, that's believable. The guy with the biggest brain in the world didn't think about something that's so obvious even dumbass Como thought about it. I'll tell you why—because *he's* the guy behind the plot. *He's* the guy we're looking for."

I looked behind to check the Professor wasn't close enough to overhear. I would have to talk Como out of his suspicions or kiss goodbye to the prize. "How much of that bourbon have you had, Galahad? You're talking through your a-hole. Why would the world's richest man want to sell ten point four million copies of a book by a nobody?"

"You already said it—to get at you."

"Me? Why would he want to get at me? What have I ever done?"

"You're Quarry's protégé. By getting at you he gets at Quarry."

"I'm not so sure about that, Como." I wasn't sure that Como would use a word like protégé either, but I couldn't think of a different way to handle his lines. "Besides, if he hated me why would he fly me to the Literary Games in his jet?"

"I don't know, Writer, but I'm telling you—he's our man, and I ain't happy."

"Exactly—you don't know. I suggest, Como, that you keep your wild surmises to yourself. The Professor chairs the judging panel for the big prize at the Games, and fat-chance I'll have of winning that if you go accusing him of things. Now, let's not say a word more about it. Come on."

We returned to the forward part of the cabin, where the Professor was scratching with a razor-blade at a large inked sketch to erase some of the lines on it. "Ah, gentlemen. Have you finished your work? Good, good. Forgive me, I was just making revisions to this diagram—a sketch of a new chip for Intel. But you have my full attention now. I believe we were talking about the question of motive, Doctor Ocram."

"Where we? Sorry, were we?"

"Specifically, the motive of a person who might try to topple you, Doctor Ocram."

"Ah, yes. From my pinnacle of the sphere of literature."

"Correct, Doctor Ocram. Tell me, are you familiar with literary spectroscopy?"

Having no idea what he meant, I replied with suitable evasiveness. "It's not a field I have studied, particularly."

"But, as a physicist, you must know of spectroscopy."

"Specwhatscopy?" said Como.

"Spectroscopy, Chief Galahad—the study of colours emitted or absorbed by matter. Sodium emits a characteristic orange light—copper a blueish green. The relative intensities of those colours show the proportions of copper and sodium in a substance. That is a trivial example, you understand—spectroscopes can distinguish hundreds of shades to identify the most complex compounds."

"Right," said Como, looking as confused as I was about where this was leading.

"As a giant of post-modernism, and an expert in conventional spectroscopy, it was natural that I should extend the concept to literature. With literary spectroscopy I analyse the frequencies with which certain markers occur in works of fiction. Paragraph lengths. Sentence lengths. Figures of speech. The various stops, and other punctuation marks. Specific words.

The mix of these markers is unique to each writer. Given a sample of any novel, literary spectrometry can identify its author."

"Forgive me, Professor. I might have missed something, but I can see who wrote a novel by looking at the cover."

"Very true, Doctor Ocram. Ten out of ten. But the spectra can be used to compare and evaluate. You show me one book you enjoyed, and through literary spectroscopy I will show you hundreds you will enjoy just as well. Proverbially, you cannot do that by looking at covers."

"That's true," I said.

"That's true," Como said.

"Imagine the power of literary spectroscopy as a marketing tool," said the Professor. "What have we today to help us choose books? We can see what books other people bought. Pah! Why should we repeat their mistakes?"

"Good point," I said.

"Good point," Como said.

"Literary spectroscopy can uniquely assess and categorise the worth of any work of literature. It has been a secret until now, gentlemen, but I am happy to confide that for the last three years I have correctly predicted the winners of all the major literary prizes by comparing the spectra of their shortlisted novels."

I saw an opportunity to raise a question close to my heart, and even closer to Barney's—nine times closer to be precise. "That's interesting, Professor. Coincidentally, one of my books has been shortlisted for a prize recently. I don't suppose you have analysed that by any chance?"

"I have indeed, Doctor Ocram. Your spectra are quite distinct. You might like to know that amongst its other idiosyncrasies, your work is characterised by excessive use of anaphora, aposiopesis, and epizeuxis."

"Drugs!" said Como. "That explains those crazy books."

"No, Chief Galahad. They are not drugs. They are figures of speech. They are the herbs and spices of literature. Used sparingly and with skill, they can add flavour and piquancy. Used heavily, they render literature unpalatable. Anaphora is the repetition of a phrase at the start of successive sentences. Aposiopesis the cutting short of speech. Epizuexis the consecutive repetition of a word or phrase."

I started to smell a rat. "Does literary spectroscopy have any other uses?"

"Since you ask, yes. The technique can be used to identify dreadful books. For my own entertainment, I refer to such use as crapometry. I can tune my software to count the occurrence of cliché, pleonasm, solecisms, and so on. The frequency with which these occur is an objective measure of a work's lack of merit. At last it is possible to rank books according to how badly they are written."

The rat smell was getting smellier. "And have you ranked many books in that way?"

"Oh yes, Doctor Ocram. But a more meaningful ranking is achieved when one takes into account the sales of a book. After all, an awful book that never sells does no harm. An awful book with few sales does little harm. But an awful mega-seller does mega harm."

The rat smell was now overpowering. I wondered if my readers would have noticed that the Professor had used the word awful from the title of my books and had repeated 'an awful book' three times at the start of three successive statements, fiendishly compounding the excessive use of anaphora which characterised my work. I realised I was dealing with a foe of exceptional cunning.

"So tell me, Professor, what does one find when one factors the sales of a book into a crapometric assessment of it?"

"One finds, Doctor Ocram, that the worst book in the world is *The Awful Truth about the Herbert Quarry Affair.*"

"Ha!" said Como. "I could have told you that without any crapofactoring, Professor Sushi."

"Most probably," said the Professor. "Now, Doctor Ocram, since you appear entirely lost for words, can I suggest that you open the left hand draw in the desk next to you and remove what you find within it."

I did as he said, and extracted two intensely thought-provoking objects—a pair of hand-cuffs and a copy of *Dragon's Claw.*

"Hey," said Como.

"Don't either of you move," said the Professor, a gun suddenly in his hand. "Doctor Ocram, cuff Chief Galahad to the arm of his seat."

"You ain't gonna cuff . . ."

Como's words were cut short as the Professor fired a warning shot into the seat an inch from my friend's arm, cleverly creating another instance of the excessive use of aposiopesis that marred my work. The cunning fiend was playing games with us.

"Cuff Chief Galahad, quickly," ordered the Professor.

"Sorreee," I said to a wincing Como as I nipped the skin of his wrist with the cuff.

"Now Doctor Ocram. It is time for the dénouement. Time for the villain to reveal his hand. You might wonder why I should waste ten million dollars on a prize for the 'best' writer of commercial fiction."

I was too bewildered to wonder about anything, other than how I'd written myself into this mess, so I said nothing. He continued . . .

"I know of your avaricious agent, Doctor Ocram. I knew the lure of a large prize would have him drooling. I knew he would make you accept my offer of a lift to Nassau so you could schmooze with the chair of the prize committee. And here you are, just where I planned you to be."

"But why . . ."

"Shall I tell you about *Dragon's Claw*, Doctor Ocram?"

I was glad he asked—I'd been wondering how to work the story round to it, and he'd just done it for me.

"*Dragon's Claw* is the first book written by computer using the techniques of literary spectroscopy. Its plot is an amalgam of the ten best-selling thrillers of the last thirty years. Its style reflects the literary spectra of the winners of the last ten Nobel Prizes for Literature. By any objective measure it is an excellent book. I sent it—under a pseudonym, you understand—to fifty leading literary agents, your own included. From everyone, I received a standard rejection letter, the unanimous opinion of that body of charlatans being that the work had insufficient commercial potential."

"I see," I said, not really seeing.

"My little entertainment in Clarkesville was designed to prove a point. I would create the fastest selling book ever, then publish the rejection letters. It would have been a sweet moment of victory, Doctor Ocram, except that you stumbled into my story.

"I am a man of immense intellectual integrity, Doctor Ocram. I cannot bear to see dross passed off as art. The critical acclaim given to the works of your so-called mentor—Herbert Quarry—made me sick. And then you—a complete buffoon entirely bereft of literary sensibility—you are feted as his spiritual successor. You write the first things that come into your vacuous head, and you become a celebrity, famous for your inanity. I hate not you, Doctor Ocram, but everything your success represents—the twisted insincerity of a publishing industry that is incapable of distinguishing honestly between art and garbage. That, Doctor Ocram, is why you must now die."

My eyeballs were darting everywhere as I desperately tried to think. What would Bond have done? Taken a calm mouthful of Martini, most likely. I had no Martini to hand, however, and I didn't really like the taste of it anyway. It has that funny herby component that I find really off-putting. It reminds me of a type of sweet we used to get given by our gran when we were on holiday in the summer. She used to have this really big house with a massive garden, and . . .

Sorry, got distracted for a moment. Where was I? Oh yes . . .

"And how am I going to die?"

"Unpleasantly, Doctor Ocram. You are going to die when this plane crashes into the first mountain just beyond Runway Three of Nassau airport. I will have left you by then, and parachuted to safety."

"Hey, you just wait a minute, Sushi. You want to get rid of Ocram, that's no skin off my nose, but what am I supposed to do?"

"You are supposed to die, Chief Galahad. I am sorry. You were not part of my plan, but since you are here, you must share your friend's fate."

"Hey, he's no friend of mine. Hey." Como started trying to wrench the arm off his seat.

"You will struggle in vain, Chief Galahad. The frame of your seat is made of carbon fibre. You will not break it, in spite of your great strength."

"But wait. This won't work. It's madness," I said.

"Really, Doctor Ocram. Why?"

"You'll get arrested. They'll put you in prison."

"Oh no, Doctor Ocram. There is no danger of that. The only person who will have committed a crime is you, and you will be dead. I will tell them how you went mad with rage when I revealed that you were not to win the Sushing Prize. How you threatened to kill me with a knife. How I managed to escape to the cargo hold, and fled the plane in fear of my life."

"But they'll never believe you. They'll think you invented the story. What about when they find the crashed plane. They'll find Como cuffed to a chair with a bullet in it. How will you explain that? What about the black-box recorder?"

"Doctor Ocram, your ability to write awful books is matched only by your ability to underestimate my intelligence. The only fingerprints on your friend's cuffs are yours. If the authorities find the bullet-hole in the chair—which is unlikely, since the plane will be destroyed—they will assume that you fired the gun. The gun, understandably, will be lost in the crash. Why should the authorities suspect me? Why would I deliberately allow a billion dollar aeroplane to crash? And as for the black-box recorders—they contain a synthetic recording of myself pleading with you for my life, and of you ranting like a crazed megalomaniac that you were going to kill us both if you could not win the Sushing prize. It was a simple matter for me to create it by manipulating a recording I had made while you were my guest in Panama."

"You unspeakable fiend," I said, not having the energy to write anything longer after tiring myself on his villainous explanation.

"As for the ten million dollars, it won't be wasted. I will declare that none of the writers nominated for the prize had met the anticipated standards, and no award will be made. Now, we are approaching Nassau. It is time for me to leave before we lose more height. You needn't worry about flying the plane—it is programmed to crash all by itself. Enjoy the short remainder of your life."

Pointing the gun at me, he backed down the stairs to the cargo hold, locking the door behind him. I rushed to the window. Minutes later I saw a fast-moving blur as the Professor's parachute-clad body whipped out of the cargo bay door and into the wake of the plane.

Or was it the wash, I wondered, ruining another moment of suspense.

CHAPTER FORTY NINE

*In which, to escape death, Marco invents an
utterly bizarre and implausible denouement
of the sort that characterises his best work.*

"**W**HAT NOW, MISTER FANCY PANTS Writer? 'Come
with me to Nassau. It'll be a laugh.' Ha!"

Ignoring Como's sarcastic remark, I raced to the cockpit. One glance at its bewildering arrays of dials and knobs was enough to convince me of our miniscule chance of survival. I cursed my stupidity. Why had I written that I had no flying experience? Why had I allowed Como to make that fatuous crack about hardly being able to drive his car? Why hadn't I made at least one of us a pilot with thirty thousand hours at the controls of the widest range of civilian and military jets? If only I'd thought ahead, we could now be making our confident approach to Nassau Runway Three, instead of cruising into the face of Nassau Mountain One. Bloody Herbert Quarry. The next time he tells me to write the first thing that comes into my head I'll . . ."

"Writer," called Como from the cabin. I ran back to him. "Get me a knife or a fork or anything metal with a point."

I ran to the lavish galley at the rear of the plane and opened the top drawer next to the sink where the knives and forks are always kept. There was a twin-pronged fork of the type used when carving meat. It looked ideal for Como's purpose—and before you say it, I know that Como hasn't yet said what his purpose is, but this is a crisis, remember. You just try maintaining continuity next time you're in a huge private jet about to crash into the first mountain behind Runway Three, and you'll find that it's not the first thing on your mind.

"Give it to me, Writer." Using his free hand, Como inserted a tine of the fork where the curving part of the hand-cuff clicked into its retainer. He levered it up and the shackle sprang open. Como was now free, but aside from buying us three extra paragraphs, his escape seemed pointless.

"Ok, clever dick. What now?"

It was a good question.

"Let's try phoning for help."

We grabbed our respective phones—no signal.

"Ok, let's try radioing for help. There must be a radio."

We ran to the cockpit. Among the thousands of buttons was one bearing the legend 'Press Here to Radio Nearest Air Traffic Control.' Ha. I'd show Sushing that I wasn't as dumb as he thought. I pressed the button. A recording of the Professor's voice came from a loud-speaker.

"Congratulations Doctor Ocram. You have found the radio button. However, you must be dumber than I thought if you expected it to work. Goodbye."

"Damn damn damn damn damn damn damn," I said, in yet another instance of the excessive use of epizeuxis that marred my work. I felt so stupid.

"You said it, Writer. Looks like Professor Sushi's cooked our gooses good and proper."

"We can't let him get away with it, Como."

"Let him? There ain't no letting about it, Writer."

"It's a figure of speech Como, it's an example of . . ." I couldn't remember what figure of speech it was an example of. I stared at the banks of knobs, levers, buttons, and dials, trying to make sense of them. Some matched those in my black Range Rover with tinted windows. I could see the fuel gauge, the temperature gauge, the switch that stopped the courtesy light from coming on when the cockpit door was opened, the demister, the wipers, the horn, the hazard warning lights, and so on. But the crucial controls were unfamiliar. Which of the many levers changed the gears? Which pedal was the clutch? Experimenting at random could be fatal. What were we to do?

I wondered if I could reverse my back-story. What if I told the readers I was lying when I said I had no flying experience? No—they'd never believe it. As Herbert always said, credulity is like an elastic band—you can stretch it so far and then it breaks.

I stared at the mountains before us, the ancient immovable mountains against which our mighty jet would soon be smudged like a fly on a windshield. With Como's panicky recriminations in my ears, I had a moment of perplexed, embittered introspection about the lot of the writer and his reactionary readership. What was it with readers—why did they make these irrational demands for internal consistency of narrative frame? If this were one of the wizard books I used to write—the ones JKR copied—I could wave a wand to make fairies carry the plane to the ground, and the readers would all be saying 'good-oh, fantastic stuff, saved by magic, hurrah!' Or if it were one of the books I did for Rushdie, I'd just include a bit of magic realism about a time-shifting karma that placed us back at Clarkesville, and everyone would say how incredibly imaginative it all was. But just because I'd done the decent thing and tried to treat my readers to a fast-paced thriller, they expected me, in their prejudiced conservative philistinism, to die rather than stretch credulity beyond its breaking point with some bizarre plot twist. It wasn't that I was afraid to die. It made no difference one way or the other. I could always come back in another guise. But it would be tough on Como if we were to smash into the mountainside, leaving no one to write him into another book.

Another book . . .

Surely that was the justification. Surely that was the bargaining chip I could offer my readers. What did they want—a few last paragraphs that would satisfy their reactionary urge for a consistent narrative and see us die forever, or the blissful joys of yet another brilliantly inventive Ocram/Galahad adventure if we survived this one through a corny plot twist?

I knew my readers.

If credulity were like an elastic band, then perhaps in the hands of a skilful manipulator, it could be pinged unbroken into a waste-basket on the other side of the room.

"Quick, Como, look under the seats. Or the glove compartment. Quick. Somewhere there's got to be the manual. Quick."

He found it under the co-pilot's seat, with old burger wrappers and some of the Professor's CD collection. I paged through it frantically as the mountainous Bahamian terrain loomed ahead. Yes—there was the diagram showing the layout of the cockpit controls. Quickly but calmly, I worked through it to identify the crucial ones.

"Right, Como, it's now or never. Buckle up."

Reversing our usual roles, Como took the passenger seat while I took the driver's. I settled myself, adjusted the backrest and the rear-view mirror, and popped in one of the Professor's CDs.

"Right, Como, it's now or never. Buckle up."

"You already said that."

Oh yes, I had. Sorry—I was panicking. I grasped the tense-selector and wrenched it from 'Past' to 'Present' for a climax of greater immediacy.

With the mountainside only seconds away, I look across the instruments to my left. I see the knob that sets the flying mode, and I switch it from auto to manual. Immediately the plane drops sickeningly downwards. I'm so frightened I don't notice that the word downwards is entirely un-necessary in that sentence. I ram the gears into third, floor the gas, and heave back on the joystick. The jet clears the mountain like a thoroughbred jumping a fence. My confidence growing, I signal a right and bank around to the south.

"Good work, Writer," says Como, but whether he is referring to my writing or my pilotry, I cannot tell.

I wipe the sweat from my stressed brow. The runway is directly ahead. We've no radio, so I hit the mayday button and hope it will alert the air-traffic controllers to our plight. Then I think to try my phone again. Yes, there's a signal. With a token hint of realism, I don't have the number for the control tower, so I ring Barney, who's at the airport to meet our flight and schmooze Sushing. He answers on the third ring. I shush his 'Hey Marky', and tell him what's happening, my phone wedged between my ear and my shoulder. He says he'll sort the flight control people. I kill the call before he starts pestering me about how many words I've written today. I ease off the gas and hold the stick steady. The jet drops like a thoroughbred landing after a fence. Down, down, down, in yet more of the excessive use of epiwhatsis that mars my work. I can see the tyre-marks of other landings on the concrete ahead. Surely we are safe now. But what's this? Out of the sun to my right. I glimpse it only for a moment, a huge white shroud-like form, a man's body suspended below it. It is the Professor! His parachute has drifted across our path. He flashes past to starboard, his mouth distorted in a rictus of rage. There is an enormously loud *sslllooooorrrssccchhhhh*. The Professor is being sucked through the starboard engine! In my wing-mirror I see a growing plume behind us as the Professor's body is sprayed out in a foamy pink con-trail of evil. The plane lurches to the right. I fight the stick to correct the slew. Como's knuckles are metaphorically white on the arms of his seat. There is a screech and a bump as the tyres make contact and at last we're down, hurtling towards the end of the runway, the emergency vehicles already converging on our path. I yank hard on the lever, and bring the JetStar Galaxy Stealth Voyager Turbo through a tight handbrake-turn to skid neatly to a stop against the airport's fence, where it stands like a thoroughbred panting after a race.

Phew!

Safely back in the past-tense, Como let out a huge long whistle of relief.

"That, Writer, was the closest I've come to pooping my pants since Beyoncé."

"Me too," I said, figuratively of course, since the Ocram pants were in no danger of a pooping when I introduced Como to the delectable chanteuse. "Let's get out of here."

I turned off the ignition, ejected the CD, and scanned the manual to find the knob that unlocked the cockpit door and let down the steps. Around us was a semi-circle of emergency vehicles and outside-broadcast vans. All the world's media had been assembled at the airport to catch celebrities arriving for the Games, so when news broke of a plane about to land under mayday conditions, they had filmed every foot of our descent. Even now, video was being relayed around the world to show Professor Sushing's liquidation through the starboard engine of his own aircraft.

We were blinded by the camera flashes as we stepped wearily down the stairs to terra firma. A hugely fat man in a ten-thousand-dollar suit pushed through the gawping crowd and broke the ring of policemen holding it back. It was Barney. He jogged over to us as fast as he could, which was hardly more than a crawl, and hugged us both tight.

"Guys, did you see what happened? The Professor! He was sucked straight through the engine! You never saw anything like it. No one ever saw anything like it. The world's going crazy about it. This is gonna be huuuuuuuuuuuuuge."

EPILOGUE

I T WAS EXACTLY A YEAR since Como and I had narrowly missed death and sslllooooorrrssccchhhhhhed Professor Sushing through the starboard engine of his black JetStar Galaxy Stealth Voyager Turbo with tinted windows. Barney's prediction had proved exactly true—everything had been huge with eleven U's. The footage of the Professor's spectacular demise had gone viral. Everybody wanted the inside story, so when *The Awful Truth about The Sushing Prize* was published, it sold even more copies than *The Awful Truth about the Herbert Quarry Affair*. Ironically, the Professor had achieved his aim to have my record broken, although it was me who broke it. Barney had a new certificate from the Guinness people to put on his wall.

The other irony was that I won the prize that bore the Professor's name. The surviving members of the Awards Committee hated the Professor for his dismissive attitude towards the literary community and were grateful to me for bumping him off. Barney got his ten mil, and I got my ten percent. I donated it to the Clarkesville County Police Benevolence Fund, hoping some of the benevolence might rub off on the Clarkesville County Police Benevolence Fund's Chair of Trustees—Como Galahad.

To celebrate the anniversary, I invited Como to join me for a party in Nassau with my celebrity friends. There were lots of 'Yes ma'am's from Como as I introduced him to various stars of film and music, until Barney cornered us and started nagging me about getting to work on another book.

"Come-on Marky babes. We can't go resting on those big laurels of yours. Variety's already talking about the next big film. They reckon we could have a franchise bigger than Bond, but that ain't gonna happen if you spend every night partying, kid. We need words, words, words. You gotta come up with the next big idea. What about you, Como—got any great cases in the pipeline for you and the kid to solve? I was just saying . . . hey, Cruisey baby."

Tom Cruise had just patted Barney on the back. While he was distracted, I looked at Como and Como looked at me. Never had two minds so unitedly held the same thought. There was a long line of people near the entrance waiting for us to sign copies of my new book, so we made a plan to escape through the kitchens, Como flashing his badge to get us out the back way.

In a nostalgic mood, we drove to the airport and sat in the observation lounge overlooking the scene of our other miraculous escape a year earlier. Over a bourbon and water (the bourbon for Como, the water for me), we reflected on our part in revealing the awful truth about The Sushing Prize.

"So, Como, in hindsight, would you rather have stayed at home and watched the game?"

"Rather than what, Writer—kill three guys, write-off a police car, nearly die three times, and nearly lose my mind?"

"Rather than be a hero, meet Beyoncé, get a million for the benevolence fund, be famous, maybe start a new career as a celebrity cop, get to work with me again."

"That sentence was growing on me until you went and ruined it at the end, Writer."

I didn't mind him saying that. He criticised me out of habit.

"One thing I still don't understand, Como."

"What's that, Writer?"

"How did we come to suck the Professor through the engine?"

"*We* didn't. It just happened. We were just landing the plane and he fell in our way."

"Yes, but think about it. He must have dropped out of the plane minutes before we landed. If we were doing a couple of hundred miles an hour he'd have been at least ten miles away."

"Yeah but they already went through all that at the inquest."

They had. I remembered the formalities at the Clarkesville County Court-house, when, before hushed crowds of reporters, an expert in Caribbean meteorology testified that our landing had coincided with a freak Noutrana, the legendary onshore wind of the Bahamas, whose thermals had slowed the Professor's descent while blowing him into our path.

"I know, Como. But the thing is . . . the Professor was such a bright guy. I remember climatology was one of his research interests. I just can't see him overlooking the possibility of a freak Noutrana."

"Well, he overlooked the possibility of us finding the manual under the co-pilot's seat, and that's an even dumber mistake."

"True, but . . ."

"Writer, look at me." I looked at him. "If for one moment you're thinking that it wasn't the Professor we ssllllooooorrrssccchhhhhhed through the engine, and that somehow he fooled us, then you're an even crapper writer than I think you are. And if you're thinking about a big come-back, where the Professor turns out not to be dead after all . . . No one, and I mean *No One*, could be crazy enough to write that kind of shit."

"True . . ." I said.

Unless it was the first thing that came into his head.

THE END

But continue reading for an exclusive extract from
Marco's next mega-selling crime memoir . . .

THE AWFUL TRUTH ABOUT THE NAME OF THE ROSE

BY
MARCO OCRAM

CHAPTER ONE

*In which Marco receives the customary
first-chapter call from Como Galahad.*

"I'M AFRAID, MISTER OCRAM, YOU need a period of complete rest. Your physical health is perfect—apart from your haemorrhoids—but you have mental and emotional exhaustion. Unless you take a break from your duties as a mega-selling writer, you risk a complete mental breakdown."

I nodded my head to show that the distinguished medic's message had been received and understood. I wasn't surprised by her words.

I took my legs out of the stirrups.

"Can I get dressed now?"

Since I'd published my second mega-selling book—*The Awful Truth about the Sushing Prize*—my life had gone crazy. I had no time to myself. If I wasn't being interviewed for some arts programme on TV, I was being filmed in the White House where I received my Congressional Medal from the President, or he was speaking with me afterwards about how he was writing a novel and would I look at his first three chapters, or I was guest of honour at the opening night of the new film about my first book, or the opening night of the new play about it, or the new ballet about it, or at a trade conference in Beijing where a new range of Marco Ocram mobile phones was being launched by Huawei, or . . .

I hadn't driven my black Range Rover with tinted windows for weeks. Worse still, I missed my Bronx mom's birthday from being stuck with Piers Morgan at a charity event in East Timor. I didn't mind missing my Bronx mom's birthday, but being stuck with Piers Morgan was a nightmare. On top of all that, my agent Barney was on my back every day about my next book.

"Marky baby," he kept saying, "this is the most dangerous time for a writer. You know what it's called? I'll tell you what it's called—it's called third book syndrome. You get the second book published, you sit down to write the third, and wham—all the creative juices stop. You dry up like a . . ."

I won't say what Barney said I'd dry up like—it was too rude for my mass-market sales category.

I finished dressing and put on my anorak.

"That'll be five hundred bucks," said the doctor.

I peeled off the money, then walked into the corridor of the busy hospital. I was looking for the word 'exit' among the signs for the various departments—Liposuction, Facial Tucks, Breast Enlargements, Breast Reductions, Self-esteem Counselling—when the sound of Doris Day singing *Que Sera Sera* came thinly from my pocket. I put my phone to an exhausted ear.

"Publishing legend Marco Ocram speaking. How may I help you?"

"Writer, it's me."

Only one person calls me writer—Como Galahad, the giant black Chief of the Clarkesville County Police Department, who appears in all my books, sharing the unpredictable twists and turns of my plots, usually while whingeing about them.

"Como!" I said, typing an exclamation mark to denote surprise, even though my books always start with Como calling me in the eleventh paragraph.

"How are tricks, Writer?"

"Not so good, Como. I've just been told by the doctor that I'm on the edge of a mental breakdown and I need complete rest. So if you're ringing like you usually do, to tell me about some innocuous-sounding case in Clarkesville that ends up being one of the world's most spectacular crimes that I solve with your help, then maybe we better leave it a few weeks."

"That *you* solve? Ha!"

"I'm too tired to argue, Como. If you want to say that you solve the crimes while I just get in your way then that's fine." Which just went to show the psychological depths to which I had sunk.

"That's the first sensible thing you've ever written, Writer. When this book comes out, I'm gonna frame that bit and stick it on my wall. If it ever comes out—which it won't if you keep feeling sorry for yourself with all that nervous breakdown crap. Listen. Something's come up, and before you start bitching, it's something that's just right for a writer feeling sorry for himself, so get your sorry ass down here and I'll tell you what's what."

In a break with my well-established tradition, I didn't race down the N66 to Clarkesville in my black Range Rover with tinted windows; instead, I pootled down the N66 to Clarkesville in my black Range Rover with tinted windows, twiddling a listless steering wheel, my legs tucked into a plaid rug. For the first time in my life, I was approaching the start of a new

Ocram/Galahad book without any sense of excitement. Now I knew how my readers felt. Perhaps Barney was right—maybe I did have third book syndrome.

As I got close to Clarkesville, my phone beeped. It was a text from Como.

"Don't meet me at PD HQ. I need 2 tell U a secret. Meet me @ Kelly's Bar and Diner instead. B discreet. C"

At Kelly's, I threaded through the crowd of boisterous revellers, wishing that I could be infected by their energy. Como was in a corner booth, his police chief hoody raised to avoid recognition. I had my anorak hood raised likewise, which was a habit of mine. I wondered if my readers would spot the weak pun on the word habit without me having to point it out.

I squeezed into a seat next to Como's huge bulk. He surveyed the busy diner as if he suspected we were being watched. I caught his mood of caution and said nothing, waiting for him to talk. Which, it seems, was exactly what he was waiting for me to do, so we spent ten minutes without saying anything. Hardly a promising start for a mega-selling thriller. I broke the impasse.

"What gives?"

"Here."

Como passed me a torn fragment of vellum under the cover of the table. I looked at it in my lap. It showed the start of a typed Latin text:

Lorem ipsum dolor sit amet, consectetur adipiscing elit, sed do eiusmod tempor incididunt ut labore et dolore magna aliqua. Ut enim ad minim veniam, quis nostrud exercitation ullamco laboris nisi ut aliquip ex ea commodo consequat. Duis aute irure dolor in reprehenderit in voluptate velit esse cillum dolore eu fugiat nulla pariatur. Excepteur sint occaecat cupidatat non proident, sunt in culpa qui officia deserunt mollit anim id est laborum.

I recognised the font as fourteen-point Hensteeth, as rare as a semi-colon in a Jack Reacher book.

"Where did you get it?" I said.

"It was posted to police HQ. No covering letter."

"You know what it means?"

"No. We showed it to a translator. She said it was just crazy words all mixed up."

"So why did you think I'd be able to help?"

"I dunno. But when she said 'crazy words all mixed up' I thought of you."

CHAPTER TWO

*In which Marco impresses the brethren
with his powers of perspicacity.*

I SKIPPED TO A NEW chapter so I could stop looking at
Como's hurtful quip.

"So why are we looking at random Latin words in Kelly's
Bar and Diner?"

"You tell me. You're the writer. I don't make this shit up. All
I know is that forty years ago a commune opened just outside
town, near Barton Hills. It runs itself like a medevil monastery."

"Medieval, Como, medieval."

"That's what I said—medevil. They take in celebrities who
wanna retreat out of the limelight—which is a joke, since they
spend their whole lives wanting to get in the freakin' limelight
in the first place. Anyway, I been hearing rumours that there's
something going on up there. Could be drugs, could be guns,
could be anything, but I need you to investigate. If I start poking

around, they'll know I suspect something. But if you go, they'll think you're just another dumbass crazy celebrity with more money than brains, and it won't bother them. Anyway, it's just what you said you needed. Complete rest."

"But why meet here? Why couldn't I meet you at Police HQ?"

Como looked straight in my eyes. "There's a mole in Police HQ. I'm going to smoke 'em out, but in the meantime, I'm not taking any chances, so if we need to communicate we'll do it privately. Use my personal number, or send a message via Barney. Here's a brochure for the commune. And guess what—it's printed on vellum."

I took the brochure, admiring its production values. The illuminations on each page were most exquisite.

"One other thing," said Como, lowering his voice three semi-tones to denote extreme gravity. "Be careful."

I wondered what sort of care he had in mind. It was the kind of thing my Bronx mom used to say, albeit it a more manly voice.

"You mean . . ."

"Two days ago, the body of a monk was found at the foot of the cliff below the sheer wall of the praesidium. The story from the Abbot is that the young man was troubled, and therefore suicide was the most likely verdict. But, you know . . ."

Yes, I knew. The 'did he fall or was he pushed' conundrum was the oldest cliché in the book, or so far anyway, and I wondered how any supposedly serious writer would consider using it. I also wondered how long it would be before I got a text from a reader to say that praesidium was the wrong word and I should have written aedificium. What these readers don't seem to understand is that it would take you a month to finish a book if you had to keep checking everything.

"Don't worry, Como. I'll be careful. If you don't hear from me by the end of a week, look for another body below the praesidium."

We shook hands. I shuffled out from behind the table and left.

It felt like I should be starting a new chapter, but when I looked back, I was still only five hundred words into this one, because I'd ended Chapter One prematurely on account of Como's hurtful quip. That just goes to show the unintended consequences of cheap jokes. I decided to write some extremely wooden dialogue to set a low bar for the rest of the book, so I called the commune on the number listed at the back of the brochure. Conveniently, I got through to the Abbot straight away.

"Is that the Abbot of the commune?"

"Speaking."

"This is mega-selling writer, Marco Ocram. I was looking at your brochure and I wanted to book myself in for a detox fortnight."

"That would be our pleasure, Brother Marco. When would you like to check in?"

"Thirty minutes?"

I punched the address of the commune into the sat-nav and followed her instructions. Speaking of the lady sat-nav reminded me that in my last book I'd got into trouble with Germaine Greer, who said my writing embodied the prejudices of a male-dominated publishing industry. That made me realise I'd fallen into the same trap by setting my new book in a commune run as a medieval monastery, where there would be no women. Perhaps I should make some of the monks cross-dressing lesbians asserting their masculine side—that might appease my feminist sisters.

THE AWFUL TRUTH ABOUT THE SUSHING PRIZE

"Turn down the track to the monastery," said the sat-nav.

I turned obediently down the track, which wound for three miles up a snow-covered valley, the drop to its side becoming increasingly precipitous. I rounded a tight bend, and there was the monastery, perched like an eagle's nest on a rocky outcrop. It was surrounded by a forbidding chain-link fence, which seemed almost to be a continuation of the cliffs themselves. The majestic praesidium grew from the highest point of the cliff, and was roughly—no, make that exactly—square in shape, with tetragonal towers at each of its five corners, and a six-faceted heptagonal conservatory jutting from each of the towers, above which each battlement had thirteen crenellations, from which twenty one flags flew. I wondered if my readers would notice that the monastery was an architectural analogue of the Fibonacci sequence, possibly with a few other numbers thrown in to make it harder to spot, or whether I should spell it out for them.

Before I could decide, my ruminations were interrupted by the sight of a monk in the heavy woollen habit of his order, weaving up through the snow-covered track as if drunk or high on some stimulating substance. As he neared me, I lowered my tinted window. He looked at me in surprise.

"Hey, Marco."

I looked at him in even more surprise.

"Hey, Tom."

I wondered what Tom Cruise was doing under the influence of drugs at the monastery. He absent-mindedly high-fived me, then turned down a side track that led to a muck heap.

Mystified, I drove on.

As I came close to the imposing gates of the monastery, the Cellerar came trudging towards me up the hill, with four brothers in a line behind him. I lowered my tinted window again.

"Greetings, Brother Marco. We heard news of your arrival from the Abbot."

"You are searching for an inebriated Brother Tom, I perceive."

"But how . . .???" The Cellerar was dumbfounded that I knew.

"You will find him down by the muck heap."

"How do you know? Did you see him go there?"

This was the point at which an ordinary person would have said "Yes." I am no ordinary person, however. I decided that it would be useful to remind my brethren that they were dealing with a writer of enormous intellect and observational powers.

"No, but I can assure you you will find him there," I said. The 'you you' was an example of the epizeuxis that characterises my best work. It rarely occurs in such an early chapter, so things were looking good.

"Thank you, Brother Marco," said the amazed and grateful Cellerar. "You will find the Abbot awaits you."

I drove through the gates and into the central courtyard, following the signs for guest parking. A valet monk took my keys and carried my meagre luggage to the reception hall, an imposing room with vast vaulted ceilings that continued the Fibonacci theme, with thirty four down-lighters per vault and fifty five individual LCDs in each down-lighter.

"Brother Marco, welcome."

The distinguished Abbot strode over to meet me, his cowl thrown back to show his fine aquiline features and his silvery mane. He kissed my hand.

"Your cell is ready. Please check in. Once you are settled I would be most grateful for an audience. Perhaps we could meet in the grand refectory after lauds."

"Indeed, Brother Abbot. I am keen to hear the ways of your community."

"So be it."

I was so excited about a joke I had lined up for my meeting with the Abbot that I decided to skip the opportunity to pad-out a couple of thousand words with a detailed description of my cell. Besides, I wasn't sure of all the technical terms for things like the wooden contraption that you knelt-on to pray, or the monk's equivalent of a trouser-press that kept their habits fresh, or the triangular brass and ivory instruments they used to query the alignment of the planets, and the small metal things they used to bleed the radiators. So I donned my hooded robe and fast-forwarded the plot to my meeting with the Abbot.

We squeezed in behind a quiet corner table in the busy grand refectory. For a person who writes the first thing that comes into his head, I was amazed that I had conceived a scene which so closely paralleled my earlier meeting with Como, even down to the hooded garments worn on both occasions. I really was wasting my talent writing this rubbish- one day I'd try something serious.

"Brother Marco, your arrival was indeed timely."

"Yes, well, when I say I'm going to be somewhere in ten minutes, I'm there in ten minutes. Punctuality is the whatsits of kings, don't forget."

"No, forgive me, I was not referring to the timeliness of your arrival in relation to our earlier telephone call, I meant in relation to . . ." the Abbot looked around and dropped his voice three semi-tones, and I don't need to say what that means because I said it in the earlier scene with Como, ". . . a most disturbing incident."

"Indeed," I said, wishing to encourage him to speak further of the incident.

"But before I speak further of the incident," he said, entirely ignoring my encouragement, "perhaps, Brother Marco, you might explain how it was that you knew the Cellerar was seeking Brother Tom, and how you knew Brother Tom was inebriated, and how you knew he would be found by the muck heap. We are aware, of course, from your books, that you have extraordinary powers of detection, but even so, we were astonished by the perspicacity you displayed to the Cellerar."

"It is easy for me to explain, Brother Abbott," I said, hoping that it would be. "I knew that a person of some distinction was being sought, since the Cellerar would otherwise have sent a minion rather than leading the search himself."

"Brilliant!"

"That the person sought was inebriated could be divined straightforwardly from their meandering footprints in the snow."

"Astounding!"

"That the person would be found at the muck heap I was able to predict with confidence, since the footprints led onto the side path which ends there."

The Abbott clapped his hands at my brilliance. "And how did you know that it was Brother Tom whom we sought?"

Ah, well, that was a bit trickier. I tried evasion. "Come, Brother Abbot, you may think me guilty of the sin of boasting were I to reveal that to you."

"Yes, but far greater would be the sin of omission. You must tell me."

Lesser novelists would have been stumped at this point, but not I. I wrote the first thing that came into my head.

"That was the most straightforward of all. The footprints were most distinctive. The snow had been fused by the warmth of the shoe far more at the toe than at the heel. That suggested to me that the shoes were fitted with internal lifts that increased the height of the wearer while effectively insulating the heel. At the same time, the briars that grow at the corner of the path had caught a lock of hair, dyed jet-black, at a height of five feet above the ground. I knew, therefore, you were looking for an important guest with jet-black dyed hair standing around five feet tall in shoes with lifts. To cap it all, the inebriated guest had dropped a Scientology leaflet at the bend in the path, which pointed to one famous person in particular. To confirm it, I checked Brother Tom's twitter stream, and there was the tweet: 'Freaked out on monk's dope. Going for a walk in the snow at monastery near Barton Hills.' So you see, Brother Abbot, it was simplicity itself."

The abbot kissed the ancient Thracian cross that hung from his martyr-teeth rosary-beads, while I continued to dither about spelling abbot with a lower- or upper-case a.

"I thank the Good Lord that he has sent you here at such a time, Brother Marco, as we have a need at present for your remarkable powers of detection."

"Indeed," I said again.

"Indeed," said the Abbot. "If I might say so in complete confidence, two days ago the body of a young novice was found at the foot of the cliff directly below the main windows of the praesidium. The young man had been deeply troubled about the meaning and purpose of life . . ."

I knew how he felt. I was feeling deeply troubled about the meaning and purpose of life myself, as would you if you had to write this tripe.

". . . so we assumed at first that he had tragically decided to end himself notwithstanding the sternest admonishments of scripture about the sanctity of life. However, it subsequently occurred to me to inspect the windows above his fall, and . . ."

I cut him short. "And you found them closed."

The Awful Truth about The Name of the Rose will be available in all good bookshops once Barney has found a company rich enough to pay the extortionate price for the publishing rights.

ACKNOWLEDGEMENTS

After seventy five thousand words of lunacy, it's time for a serious thank-you to those who helped bring the book about.

First chronologically are ten people who left comments suggesting Marco write a book, following his birth in a two-page skit on a well-known website. Sadly I can't contact them to ask if they'd like to be blamed here individually for Marco's subsequent output.

Next the fantastic Jonathan Eyers, who played the Herbert Quarry role in my development as a writer. I engaged Jonathan as a mentor through the literary consultancy, Cornerstones. As an author and an editor at a major publisher, he had expertise in everything I needed to know—writing, how the publishing industry works, how to approach agents and publishers, contracts, covers, and the rest. He set my expectations at a realistic level, and encouraged me to press on.

Having completed countless revisions, I shared the book with my brilliant beta-readers—the people who voluntarily gave all sorts of illuminating feedback on the drafts. Thanks go, in alphabetical order, to Robert Burton, Kathy Feest, Tom Martin, Keith Oxenrider and Geetha Stachoviak for the hours they put into it, for their friendly interest and encouragement, and for their insightful critiques.

THE AWFUL TRUTH ABOUT THE SUSHING PRIZE

To loud and sustained applause, enter Galen, Jenn and the team from Tiny Fox Press. A tweet from Galen had led me to their website, where I saw a joke that might have been written by Marco himself. It was fate. I had to send them the book, and they got Marco's humour (or should that be humor?) right away. Since then they have led me through a whole new world of book production, and helped tame some of Marco's more extreme literary tendencies.

Finally, my special thanks go to my lovely wife. Leona has kept me sane, contributed great ideas, censored inappropriate content, scrutinised proofs, and put up with my obsessive introspection when I'm working on my books. Without her, I couldn't have written this.

ABOUT THE PUBLISHER

Tiny Fox Press LLC
5020 Kingsley Road
North Port, FL 34287

www.tinyfoxpress.com